A
Harlequin
Romance

OTHER

Harlequin Romances

by GLORIA BEVAN

1309—THE HILLS OF MAKETU
1400—THE DISTANT TRAP
1459—BEYOND THE RANGES
1510—MAKE WAY FOR TOMORROW
1576—IT BEGAN IN TE RANGI
1608—VINEYARD IN A VALLEY
1682—THE FROST AND THE FIRE
1730—FLAME IN FIJI
1809—CONNELLY'S CASTLE
1860—HIGH-COUNTRY WIFE

ALWAYS A RAINBOW

by

GLORIA BEVAN

HARLEQUIN BOOKS

TORONTO
WINNIPEG

Harlequin edition published November 1975
SBN 373-01923-8

Original hard cover edition published in 1975
by Mills & Boon Limited.

All the characters in this book have no existence outside the imagination of the Author, and have no relation whatsoever to anyone bearing the same name or names. They are not even distantly inspired by any individual known or unknown to the Author, and all the incidents are pure invention.

Printed in Canada

1923

To Russell, manager of a seven-thousand-acre sheep and cattle station in the far north of New Zealand.

CHAPTER ONE

Shielding her eyes with her hand from the brilliant sunshine streaming in at the open bus window, Angela glanced idly out towards the passing New Zealand countryside. It was all new territory to her as yet and she was enjoying every moment of the journey—the friendly informative comments of the Maori driver, the small settlements that went flashing by at ever increasing intervals and most of all the heat-hazy day that was in such contrast to the grey English winter so recently left behind.

Earlier in the day the vehicle had swung out of Auckland city streets to take a motorway winding north, moving over the graceful arch of the harbour bridge with the sun-dazzled waters far below. Presently she was gazing down slopes where thickly growing flax and punga-fern had recently been cleared to make way for clusters of pastel-tinted houses with their gay red and green roofs. Then gradually as she travelled further north the rolling farmlands stretched away on either side of the winding road. Along the edge of the roadside toa-toas tossed in the breeze, their silky plumes translucent in the late afternoon sunlight. On the summit of cleared hillsides she caught passing glimpses of farm homesteads, red roofs gleaming through a screen of tall shelterbelts of native trees. A heat haze shimmered over the hot bitumen of the highway and the traffic was made up of an occasional farm truck, dust-spattered jeeps, stock transporters and long trailers tightly packed with sheep.

As the bus swung around yet another bend Angela glimpsed ahead a small settlement—a petrol pump, a garage and general store. Presently the vehicle drew up beside an old timber shop with peeling paintwork and faded awnings. The elderly man seated beside Angela, who had dozed throughout the journey, now awoke with a start and getting to his feet began to move towards the exit door. It was at that moment as she glanced back over her shoulder that Angela became aware of a familiar face amongst the crowd of passengers. Imagine seeing Martha again so soon! For throughout the whole country there surely couldn't be any other girl with that certain shade of red hair. Angela's own hair was inclined that way, especially when the sun sparked the long dark copper strands, but Martha's hair was a startling, flaming *red*!

Even though Martha's face was turned towards the window Angela could see that the pallor that had been so noticeable on that first day when both girls had met aboard the *Ocean Monarch* had like her own given way to a light patina of tan. The bus began to gather speed as it moved on and Angela's thoughts wandered.

During the voyage out from England on the luxury liner Martha had appeared to be slightly older than most of the young crowd who gathered together on the dance floor, sunbathed around the pool or idled away the hours up on the boat deck. Angela mused that you couldn't call Martha attractive, her face was too thin, her features too sharp for beauty, and yet there was something about her. Perhaps a well-defined fashion sense was the answer, for Martha wore her clothes with flair and imagination. Or could it be her quick tongue? It was just a pity that the brittle wit was all too often barbed with malice. Could that be the reason why during the voyage the various men friends who had at first been attracted by Martha's amusing brand of chatter had soon lost interest and drifted away in search of other feminine companions for dancing and sunbathing?

Given other circumstances it was unlikely that the two girls would have touched the fringes of friendship, and Martha Stanaway was not a type of girl whom Angela would have chosen as a companion. On the first day aboard the *Ocean Monarch*, however, they found themselves seated together at table and Martha's gay company had helped to dispel Angela's initial sense of bewilderment on her first trip overseas. Before many days had passed, however, she was easing herself out of a friendship she had no desire to develop. Not that the other girl had changed towards her in any way. It was just that there had been so many incidents, trivial in themselves yet indicating a nature that was utterly ruthless in dealings with others. Clearly Martha was one of the "takers" of the world, using her acquaintances mercilessly to her own advantage. Friends were worth cultivating only if they could be of use in some way, otherwise they were quickly abandoned. Probably at the start of the voyage Angela had been helpful to Martha as a stopgap—but afterwards? Angela failed to realise that her own youthful enthusiasm, the direct gaze of the hazel eyes she always considered much too big for her small face, her downright honesty of purpose, drew both men and women to her side and kept them there without conscious effort on her part. To be with Angela was to gain an immediate admission to a lively, fun-loving circle of youthful passengers.

They were a gay and friendly group and Angela liked them all. She would have been content to dance away the evening hours and enjoy the varied amusements of the day with various escorts had not Harvey attached himself to her side early in the voyage. He was a stockily-built young man with neatly brushed dark hair and a serious outlook on life, and his businesslike approach to living contrasted with the light-hearted attitude of the others. If there were times when Angela thought him ponderous for his years, his day-by-day presence a trifle irksome at times, she told herself that he was basically a nice person with a quaint old-fashioned chivalry and a determination to please her in every way possible. If only he didn't put her so much in mind of Graeme! Indeed, it would seem she had made her goodbyes to one adoring male on the Southampton docks only to acquire another on board ship. For the two men so unalike in appearance appeared to share the same attitude towards her. But what odds? Once the *Ocean Monarch* berthed in Auckland it was unlikely that she and Harvey would meet again, even though they were both bound for the same destination in New Zealand. Harvey had told her that he planned to start in business in the new country in the line of food-processing and selling. That too was odd, because Graeme's pet dream had been to manage a business of his own. What was there about her that seemed to attract these careful, conscientious types?

As it turned out, however, it seemed she need not have concerned herself regarding the future, for all at once Harvey appeared to lose all interest in her. She had no idea of the reason for his sudden change of heart, she only realised with a delightful new sense of freedom that he no longer sought her out at every available opportunity. Indeed he was now obviously taking pains to avoid her and if by chance they happened to meet his fresh-complexioned face would grow a shade pinker and he would throw her a forced uneasy grin before hurrying away. It wasn't long before he had taken up with Martha and when they were all part of a group Angela would be aware of Martha's sly, triumphant glance from beneath pale lashes.

One day, alone for once up on the boat deck, Angela lay back in the sunshine, watching the other two stroll along the deck. Maybe it's the red hair that attracts Harvey, she thought in secret amusement. I suppose you could call mine red. Tossing back over her shoulders the long glinting mass of burnished copper, she went on thinking about Harvey. Funny how those serious good-old-Graeme types with business aspirations seem to gravitate in my direction. And Harvey *used* to like to be with me at the start of the trip and Graeme was always declaring he'd love me and no one else for ever and ever, amen. Of course I'm fond of him too . . . in a way.

But not in the right way! A tiny voice deep in her mind suddenly made itself heard. Come on, Angela, why not face up to the truth for once in your life? Isn't it because of Graeme and his cloying affection that you're splashing all your hard-earned savings on this working holiday away out in New Zealand?

Nonsense! I've always longed to travel.

What you mean is that you don't want to settle for married life with Graeme, worthy, saving, serious-eyed Graeme. Admit it now. Didn't you feel deep down that this one year spent right away from everything familiar might serve to settle things in your mind?

Well . . . maybe . . . She could have put those savings towards a home of their own that Graeme was always going on about. She could have, but she hadn't! Instead she had booked her passage on the *Ocean Monarch*, due to arrive at the port of Auckland in the New Zealand summer. When after endless arguments on the subject Graeme had at length realised that her mind was made up, his grey eyes seemed to regard her with silent reproach, but he only said in a strangely quiet tone, "Okay then, if that's what you want! You might get the travel bug out of your system once and for all!" His heavy tone had lightened a little. "When you get back to London you'll be satisfied that you've seen a bit of the world and that'll be it! Then it'll be time for the things that *really* matter like choosing a wedding ring and looking around for a flat not too far from my office, hmm?"

"Maybe," she had answered doubtfully.

The dreadful part of the whole thing was that far from feeling any gratitude towards him for accepting her decision to leave England for a year in New Zealand she was conscious only of resentment and a queer sense of guilt. Why couldn't he just let her go with no tags attached? Wish her goodbye and good luck and let it go at that?

The next morning she had said as much to her friend Janet at the office where they both worked. Janet, however, seemed unimpressed by Graeme's discouraging attitude.

"Could be," she offered mildly, "that he loves you a lot and he's scared to death of losing you."

"If that's the way he feels why can't he trust me?"

"Maybe he does. Maybe it's those husky New Zealand sheep-farming types he doesn't trust."

"Oh, for heaven's sake!" Angela had cried indignantly. "I'm only going on a working holiday out there, not a husband-hunting expedition!"

Are you sure? jeered the small mind-voice. She thrust it aside and banged so heavily on her typewriter keys that she made an error on an important document and had to tear it up and begin all over again.

It hadn't been easy, the savings bit. One isn't exactly in the millionaire class on a typist's wage, but a knack with dressmaking helped to cut expenses and she had a flair for hair-styling that dispensed with hairdressing fees at the salon. It was amazing how much you could do without in the way of luxuries when you set yourself a goal and really put your mind to it! One advantage about being on your own in the world was that it forced you to depend on yourself. Her parents had died in an air disaster when she was a baby and the aunt who had brought her up had some years previously gone to America to share the home of a married daughter there. There was no one to worry about her or to care what she did, except Graeme—if he had his way.

It had taken a long time to get the money together for a return fare to New Zealand plus funds to tide her over for some months in an emergency. Time ... She was twenty-one, pushing twenty-two, and in all those years so very little had happened to her. Of importance that is in the way of romance or love or *anything* that really mattered. You wouldn't believe that you could live in London, in *London*, and have the years just ... slide ... by. There had been school, high school, a period spent at business-training that was followed by work in a city office where she had been employed ever since. A cold hand seemed to clutch her heart. Was this all there was to being young, to living? There must be something ... something ... she groped in her mind ... if only she could find it.

But perhaps the shining miracles didn't happen along just like that. Perhaps you had to go right out and discover them for yourself like the pot of gold at the end of the rainbow. Well, no matter what happened in the future on this trip to the far South Pacific she would have done something with a dull life, met new people, seen other lands. At least she would have caught a glimpse of the rainbow even if she never ever found that pot of gold at the end of it!

Right from the moment when the great liner pulled away from the docks the excitement and sense of change took over and carried her into a new life. A small group, some girls from the typing room and Graeme, waited on the wharf to wave her goodbye. Through the criss-cross of paper streamers wavering between them she could see Graeme looking up towards her, his gaze clinging to her laughing face as she waved back to him. Then the ship began to slide away and the pink streamer she was holding snapped between them. She watched it drift aimlessly away on the tide. Soon the faces far below blurred out of focus, but she went on waving just the same in case the watchers below could distinguish her tangerine dress amongst the milling crowd that lined the decks. When at last the groups on the wharf had become a faceless mass of humanity she turned away and it all began, the novelty and excitement of a do-nothing world where there were no problems other than how best to enjoy oneself amongst the endless choice of amusements that offered. Indeed in the days that followed she felt slightly ashamed at how swiftly she had forgotten everything she had left behind. The girls at the office, the cramped little flat she had occupied for the past four years—even Graeme.

"Angie! I *thought* it was you!" Jerked from her random thoughts, Angela glanced up in surprise to meet Martha's mocking smile. The other girl pushed her dark glasses up on her bright hair and dropped down to take the vacant seat.

"Hi!" Angela swung around to face her. "What have you been doing with yourself since I saw you?" she asked in her sweet husky voice.

"Nothing much," Martha murmured evasively, "this and that."

"Have you been working?"

The other girl shook her cloud of rippling red hair. "Not yet." A secretive smile played around the thin lips. "But I've got terrific prospects of something coming up quite soon—if I play my cards right."

Angela laughed. "Well, good luck! You know," she murmured thoughtfully, "I haven't seen anyone I know from the ship since we left the *Ocean Monarch* in Auckland. It seems an age now, doesn't it? Much more than just a week?"

"Does it ever!" In the silence Angela's thoughts slipped back to the voyage. Already in retrospect the fun-filled days and nights seemed strangely unreal, a little like a gay and exciting party one had attended a long time ago. The thought prompted her to say idly, "I wonder what's become of the others? I've forgotten some of their surnames already, isn't it *dreadful*?—except for Harvey, of course."

"Harvey!" For a moment a startled expression sprang into the pale no-colour eyes. Then Martha jerked the dark glasses down over her eyes, hiding their expression. "This sunlight, it's too bright for me. Funny you should mention Harvey. Actually I'll be seeing him quite soon in Whangarei. He's starting up a factory there. He's just getting it organised and later he plans to build others along the same lines in other parts of the country. Funny to think of his being the boss of it all, isn't it?"

Angela nodded. All at once a picture flashed across the screen of her mind. She had been amongst a crowd of young people gathered around the swimming pool, listening to a discussion regarding the prospects of casual work that would be available in the unfamiliar country. One of the boys had said, "Well, there's one of the gang who won't be losing any sleep over getting a job to tide him over or getting his return fare together. Didn't he let you in on who he was?" For the others had gazed towards the speaker in surprise. "Old Harvey—Harvey Brooks. He happens to be one of *the* Brooks. His old man runs a chain of food-processing works right through England. He's loaded."

Another male voice, slightly envious, had broken in. "Guess he won't be getting work picking hops down in Nelson or gathering kiwi fruit up in Northland. You won't come across old Harvcy next to you when you're picking peaches in the Hawkes Bay orchards either. No, sir! Our Harvey'll be too busy packing those peaches and kiwi fruit into cute little cans."

Martha's voice broke into her musing. "We hit it off together pretty well, Harvey and I." There was a self-satisfied note in the tones. "I can help him a lot when it comes to secretarial work, and luckily I'm experienced. Frankly he tells me he just won't be able to get things organised properly without me."

"Really?" Angela's eyes widened. "I had no idea you two were so friendly. Anyway," she turned her laughing gaze towards Martha, "I wouldn't count too much on the 'can't do without you' bit. On the ship he used to act that way about me. Then all of a sudden he deserted me. Woof! Just like that! No explanation, not even a 'see you around.' He just . . . faded away."

"Did you—mind?"

Angela laughed her breathless throaty laugh. "Heavens, no, why should I? It was just so odd, the sudden drop in temperature, I mean. I wonder—"

"I can help you with that one." Martha's face was averted as she stared out of the window. "It was just—well, we were up on deck one day chatting and he happened to mention some story he'd got hold of about your coming out here to be married to some guy in New Zealand. A sheep-farmer away in the country or something. The story was that you'd left off wearing your engagement ring for the duration of the trip."

Angela gazed back at her in astonishment. "For goodness' sake! What on earth could have put that crazy idea into his head?"

Martha shrugged her shoulders beneath an impeccably cut suit. Once again the small secretive smile played around her mouth. "Oh, you know how it is on board ship. Rumours fly around all the time. You can scarcely believe a thing you hear—" A sudden change of subject. "Tell me, what have you been doing with yourself in the past week? Started on that working holiday of yours yet? Wasn't that what you had in mind?"

"Oh, it is! It still is!" Angela smiled her warm and friendly smile. "Trouble is that I decided to give myself a week's holiday first of all. I mean, to find yourself in a city like Auckland and not be able to have a good look around the place because you're flat out working for a living—No, I just couldn't settle for that! And am I glad I took that week! It was fantastic! The beaches are gorgeous for swimming, lots of sand and surf, not too many people around—and so safe! I could take my choice of big white rollers pounding in on the sand or quiet bays around the harbour. Oh, there were endless things to see and do in Auckland. Ferry trips out to the islands of the gulf, tramps through native bush in hills quite near the city, shopping centres out in the suburbs that are really something! I could have gone on enjoying myself there for ages. But yesterday I woke up in the morning and said to myself, 'Summer's not for ever, my girl! You'd better forget this lotus-eater existence and get out and find some work for yourself before your money runs out.' So here I am!"

"Any particular reason why you're heading north?"

"Not really. Just that a girl at the youth hostel where I was putting up in town told me the scenery up at the Bay of Islands is something out of this world and it seems there are lots of tourist places around where you can pick up something to do—waitressing, motel-work, receptionist jobs at the tourist hotels. Anyway, I'm going to give it a go and if there's nothing offering at the moment I can always move on somewhere else. See something of the country for as long as my funds hold out."

"There's plenty of work offering in the summer evidently for anyone who wants it." Martha's tone was abstracted.

"That's what I gathered."

Martha didn't appear to be listening. All at once she swung around to face Angela. "Look, you can have my job if you like! That is if you've no objection to working on a sheep and cattle station way up at the back of beyond. I wasn't wrapped up in the idea of going there all along, and then this offer of Harvey's came up, so I thought I'd better show up and explain things, seeing I'd offered to help them out." Angela couldn't understand Martha speaking in this jerky and confused manner, Martha who was always so coolly confident. "But it's yours, the job, if you're interested?"

"But I am! Don't you remember my telling you when we were at sea that working on a New Zealand sheep station was one of the things I was looking forward to doing out here?"

"I remember." There was an odd inflection in Martha's tones, but the next moment Angela forgot the fleeting impression.

"Well then, here's your big chance! Why not take advantage of it? I'd planned to stop off at the next town. The man I spoke to over the phone said he'd meet me there at the bus stop. The arrangement was that—well, anyway I thought I'd go with him to his home and explain everything, then pick up another bus going north. I just wanted to tell him . . . tell him . . ." Her voice faltered and she moistened dry lips.

Angela couldn't understand why the other girl appeared to be so embarrassed, almost guilt-ridden, over such a small matter as having changed her mind about a job on an outback station. Or why Martha seemed so anxious that someone else should fill the vacancy. Unless it was because she wished to ease her own conscience in the matter. Funny, one would never imagine Martha giving a second thought to letting anyone down, especially a strange man whom she had never met. It just went to show how mistaken you could be about folk whom you thought you knew. Aloud she murmured slowly, "You mean you promised to take this job and now you feel you're letting the people there down by not turning up as arranged?"

Martha appeared to grasp eagerly at the proffered explanation. "That's it! That's it exactly! You see, it was a promise . . . well, sort of." She glanced towards Angela, taking in the direct gaze of the clear hazel eyes, the long coppery-coloured hair lifting on her shoulders in the breeze blowing through the open window, the vulnerable young face. "You'd suit him fine, I would think."

"What sort of work does he want you to do on the station?" Angela queried. "It'll be helping his wife in the house, I expect." An apprehensive light sprang into her eyes. "Because if it's cooking for the family it's out—definitely! All those healthy country children with colossal appetites! It gives me the horrors just to think of it! I just couldn't face it!"

"Don't worry," said Martha, "it's not cooking, at least I wouldn't think so." She sounded unusually vague. "I only spoke to the man on the station for a minute or so. The one I wanted to contact wasn't available, but this other one said he'd put me in the picture about everything when I got there. When he first began talking to me he mentioned something about wanting someone to help with the shearing—"

"Shearing?" Angela jerked herself upright. "I wouldn't have a clue!"

"I think he mistook me for some other girl," Martha broke in hurriedly. "It was a bad connection and I couldn't hear very well. No, what they'll be wanting up there is a girl to lend a hand with the housework. Who knows," she added with a smile, "it might turn out to be a kind of holiday."

Angela said thoughtfully. "I had planned to stay the night in a motel somewhere up north, get a newspaper in the morning and see what was offering in the way of casual work."

"Well then," cried Martha triumphantly, "what are you waiting for? What have you got to lose?"

"Nothing really, I guess. Only . . ." Why was she hesitating? It was the type of job she had been seeking and now it was being handed to her on a plate. Yet something, some small voice of caution, held her back. Was it because in her heart she didn't altogether trust Martha? You couldn't live in the close proximity of shipboard life with anyone for six weeks and not learn something of them, and experience had taught her not to trust Martha's motives, or her smooth persuasive tongue. But surely there could be no possible harm in taking the casual work she was being offered. What could be wrong in that?

A thought came out of nowhere. Had it been Martha herself who had been the means of alienating Harvey from her? Because she wanted his company herself? It would seem so. Not that it mattered in the least. In a way it had been a relief to be free of his constant presence, his almost pathetic attempts to give her pleasure at no matter what cost to himself. No, it didn't matter one little bit that Harvey had transferred his affections to Martha. But what if it had?

"I don't know what you're worrying about." Martha's impatient tones broke into her thoughts. Did the indecision in her face show so much? "If you're thinking he may not turn up to meet you you can put that thought right out of your mind.

I'm to be called for at the bus stop at the nearest town to Waikare Station. He'll be waiting there to collect you. No problem."

"It's not that." Angela stared abstractedly out of the window. The road ran between high banks of fern and gorse, sweeping towards a fringe of blue gums traced against the luminous blue of the sky. As the vehicle topped the rise she could see ahead a long wide street lined with old buildings, a parking area with jeeps and Land Rovers, a dilapidated timber hotel. Time was running out. She *must* make up her mind. Why was Martha so anxious that Angela should take her place? Why was it of such importance, this back-country job on a station about which Martha had had second thoughts?

"I know! I'll toss it over to fate!" Fishing in her woven flax kit, she took out a coin purse and found a five-cent piece. "Heads I take the job, tails I don't!"

"Hurry then," there was an odd tense note in Martha's voice, "we're almost there!"

The silver coin flashed in the sunlight, then settled on Angela's outstretched palm. "Head's it is!"

Martha let out her breath in a long sign of relief and the fleeting thought crossed Angela's mind that the other girl seemed in an awful hurry to get rid of her. Perhaps Martha did have a conscience in the matter after all.

"Got your bag with you?" Martha enquired, still in that tense tone.

Angela nodded, then glanced out to the wide street where the bus was pulling in.

"If he's not there yet he won't be long," Martha said quickly, standing aside to allow Angela to pass her in the narrow corridor. "He could have been delayed a little, but he'll be along. He promised. His name's Hillyer, Brian Hillyer—Oh, I almost forgot! Give him this, will you? It's just something he might want." She pressed into Angela's woven flax kit a bulging manila envelope. "And tell him I'm sorry. 'Bye!"

Angela bent to scan the quiet street. There was no one waiting there, that was for sure. Was she being wise in trusting Martha, knowing Martha as she did? Already, however, the Maori driver was standing in the open doorway regarding her enquiringly. "What name, miss?"

"Oh—Twentyman!" She followed him out towards the luggage compartment at the rear of the vehicle. "There it is, the blue canvas one beside the mail bags."

Grinning goodnaturedly, the driver placed the travel bag down on the path beside her. "Have a good holiday!"

"Thank you." The bus was moving slowly towards a stream of country traffic when a cloud of red hair was thrust from a window. "Land Rover!" screamed Martha. "He's coming for you in a Land Rover with deer antlers on the front!"

Angela smiled and nodded to show she had got the message, then stood watching the bus as it traversed the wide street that appeared from this point to run directly into the mountains ahead.

She had been the only passenger to disembark at the small township and feeling all at once self-conscious standing alone in the sunshine, her travel bag at her feet, she moved into the shade of an awning over a store and pretended to interest herself in a display window filled with tractors and farm machinery. She was conscious of feeling very much alone waiting on a strange street for a man she knew only by name. She pulled herself together. It was the type of employment she had dreamed of back in the London flat, wasn't it? So why feel this stupid trepidation, this sense of rushing headlong into the unknown? Thrusting the doubts aside, she scanned the roadway, but could see only dust-coated cars and cattle trucks, a long beer tanker and behind, a man driving a red tractor.

Maybe this Brian Hillyer man wasn't coming to meet her after all. Perhaps he had found another girl to take on the duties at his sheep station, whatever they might be. Odd to think she wasn't even aware of what she was supposed to do there. But everyone had told her that New Zealand farmers' wives were often desperately in need of household help, especially in an emergency such as illness, the arrival of a new baby in the family or a mother's sudden call away from home that left young children in need of care. If only her thoughts wouldn't continually stray to some type of cooking job. What if it transpired when she got there that her duties involved exactly that? If that was the job she hoped that "he" would never arrive to collect her. Nonsense! She called on her common sense, reminding herself that there were endless other duties required on sheep stations—there must be!

A quarter of an hour later she was still standing at the bus stop, an anxious-eyed girl with auburn hair and a deceptive air of fragility, her sprigged cotton blouse clinging around her slim figure in the breeze and long skirt blowing around her ankles. But how long did a girl wait? And who was this man, anyway, who kept her standing on a windswept street corner to suit his own convenience?

As if in answer to her thoughts at that moment a battered Land

Rover drew to a stop beside her and her gaze went to the deer antlers branching from the bonnet. A tall deeply suntanned man got out of the vehicle and came striding towards her.

It was the type of face one couldn't easily forget, lean and dark with soft black hair falling over a bronzed forehead. The next moment she became aware of his cool appraisal. "I was told to look out for a girl with red hair. Are you—"

"That's me—or near enough!" Her young face flooded with relief and she sent him her wide and friendly smile. "Gosh, I began to wonder if you were ever coming to collect me! I feel as if I've been standing on this street corner for ever."

"I've come now."

She found herself meeting the chilliest blue eyes she had ever encountered. He wasn't even offering her an apology! He was young and broad-shouldered with a lithe grace, and the thought spun through her mind that at any other time she might have considered him attractive in a tough, sun-weathered sort of way, but now all she was aware of was his icy stare. Clearly there was no welcome for her here, not even the slightest hint of friendliness, just that glowering look. What had she ever done to him, for heaven's sake, to merit that forbidding expression? Anyone would imagine that *he* was the one who had been kept waiting for ages! In a nervous gesture she caught up a long strand of hair and twined it around her fingers. I don't know that I'm all that anxious to go with you Mr. Brian Hillyer, not now. If you're to be my employer—no, thanks!

Thrusting the whirling doubts aside, she said hesitantly, "You *are* Brian Hillyer?"

"Not me!" The flint-like tones cut across her soft husky accents. "I'm his brother Mark."

"Oh!" Now she was certain of the hard antagonistic note in his voice. Well, at least she had contacted the right family. She had an absurd sensation of fumbling around in a darkened unknown room, but willing herself to disregard his forbidding expression she said, "But your brother is expecting me today? You see, the arrangement was that I was to be picked up here and taken to—" wildly she searched her mind for the name, but the Maori syllables eluded her, "the station." She hesitated. "He does still . . . want me?"

He was silent for a moment, regarding her with an odd look she couldn't interpret. "You'll have to sort that out with him yourself when you get there!" He swung open the passenger door, then picking up her travel bag tossed it into the back of the vehicle amongst coils of fencing wire, a sack of dog nuts and drums of drench. Angela got the distinct impression that it would have given him the greatest satisfaction to toss her in after the bag with the same savage gesture.

She hung back uncertainly. "Just a moment. I'm not sure if I—"

"*Get in*!" he rasped.

Two schoolgirls had paused, giggling, to take in the little scene and Angela with an impatient, "Oh, all right!" climbed inside and seated herself on the high seat. As he came around the side of the Land Rover and dropped down to the driver's seat she flung him an indignant glance. "Do you always order folk around like this?"

He didn't even turn his head but swinging the vehicle in a circle headed for the darkening hills ahead. "Only when it's something that happens to matter a lot."

"I don't see how it can matter all that much," she protested. "It was just a promise. I'm keeping it that's all. Look, there's something I have to explain."

He threw her a brief enquiring glance and her smile died away in the face of his bleak hard stare.

"Save all that for Brian," he broke in harshly. "He's the one you have to tell, explain things to, if you can."

Angrily Angela subsided in her seat. Never had she come across a man of such utter rudeness. Yet something told her that he was a person who was naturally well-mannered, and incredible though it seemed, she suspected it was her own appearance that had triggered off his state of barely controlled fury. But he was a stranger to her, she had never seen him before. Could his animosity be something to do with Martha? Had something happened of which she was ignorant and she had simply stumbled into the middle of it? But Martha had given her to understand that they were strangers, she and Brian Hillyer.

It was all very odd and definitely disquieting. More than ever she regretted having given way to the impulse that had landed her in this situation, on the way to an unknown destination with a stranger whom she couldn't fathom at all. A man who in other circumstances—she stole a sideways glance at the strong masculine profile, the soft dark hair, the firm sensitive lines of the mouth—she might have thought definitely attractive. Again she had the impression that he wasn't as a rule like this, so off-putting and terse. If he refused to hear her explanation of how she happened to be taking the place of the girl to whom her brother had offered the job, that was all right with her. It didn't matter anyway. She wouldn't be staying at the station, not with this grim-faced man, no sir! She'd see this Brian man, explain what had happened about the position, then ask to be brought back to town where she would catch a bus and move on. She glanced towards the set face of the man at her side. She couldn't imagine he'd have any objections to bringing her back, it was having her with him that seemed to be making him so incensed.

Thrusting the disturbing thoughts aside, she peered out of the window. They had swung off the main highway and turned into a road winding between gentle green slopes evocative of the English countryside. Timbered farmhouses and mellow red outbuildings gleamed from shelter belts of tall pines, and weathered tea-tree loading ramps were built at the roadside.

Soon, however, the smooth bitumen of the road petered away into rough metal. The pleasant cultivated farmlands were left behind and ahead were only the endless sheep-dotted hills. A hawk rose from the dust of the track and soared into the blue.

To Angela the winding grey road seemed to go on for ever as they took the steep slopes, dropped down the hairpin bends on the other side, only to rise once again with always the pockets of native bush running up the valleys. They were climbing ever higher, and glancing down she could see sheep and black steers grazing in cleared paddocks far below. A purple haze lay over the cloud-shadowed slopes and around them echoed cascading notes of silvery bird-song. Angela would have liked to have known the name of the songster, but a glance at the grim profile at her side dissuaded her from enquiring. It was all new and colourful and exciting—or would have been had she had any other companion but this particular one. As it was she couldn't wait to reach his home, wherever it was and arrange her return to civilisation just as soon as she possibly could.

Soon they were running downhill, taking a track through thickly growing native bush where giant forest trees towered far above and the air was fresh and fragrant with the damp smell of moss and undergrowth. Then once more they were out in the open, sweeping along a track where tall cabbage trees tossed green streamers in the breeze and dust-coated flax and punga ferns brushed the vehicle as they passed by. All at once Angela became aware of another smell, the pungent odour of burning timber. Forgetting the Trappist monk vow-of-silence attitude of her companion, she cried, "Look—up there on the hills, a bush fire! Is it all right?"

He nodded. "They're burning off manukau," he explained

briefly. "It's under control."

Angela's soft lips tightened. Piqued and annoyed by his deliberate lack of response, she shrank back in her seat as far away from him as possible. If he insisted on playing the strong silent male, if he wouldn't even accord her the common courtesy due to a stranger, let him! She stared resentfully out of the window.

As if in sympathy with her mood at that moment the sun passed behind a heavy bank of cloud, a grey pall spread over the sky and heavy raindrops spattered in the dust of the track. The bush on the hillsides that in the sunshine had seemed green and sparkling was all at once heavy and sombre, a dark curtain enclosing them in a twilight world of swirling mist.

He switched on the headlamps and the beams threw into relief the rough metal of the road ahead. Beside them half concealed in the trees a timber building loomed up out of the gloom. Once again forgetting her own vow of silence, Angela said in her soft eager tones, "That place we just passed. Who lives there away up here in the bush?"

"No one. It's a hut where trampers can put up when they're up this way. Hunters use it too." His eyes were fixed on the fragment of roadway ahead.

Angela's attention, however, had been caught by something else she couldn't understand. The metal bands running around telegraph posts. She couldn't imagine any reason for them, she mused, turning her head over her shoulder to look again. Mark Hillyer must have read the question in her eyes. "Keeps the possums from climbing up to the wires."

The rain was becoming heavier now, streaming down over the windows and blotting out everything except the vaporous outlines of range after range ahead. She realised with a stab of apprehension that the narrow winding track was slippery with mud. Great mounds of earth were piled at intervals along the route where roadworkers had apparently been making recent repairs. Angela told herself that there was no danger whatever. She reminded herself that the mud-grip tyres of the Land Rover could cope with even these greasy slopes on twisting roads where each corner was a hazard with its sharp hairpin bend.

All at once he appeared to recollect her presence. "Not nervous, are you?"

"Of course not," she lied bravely.

"You wouldn't say these roads were much like smooth English highways, would you?"

"No."

"But then," he pursued, "you wouldn't have expected them to be?"

"No."

At that moment there loomed up through the gloom of the narrow pathway the shape of a bulldozer. Its appearance was so unexpected that Angela drew in her breath sharply. They were travelling at speed, there was no time to stop and there surely wasn't room to pass. If only the Land Rover hadn't been on the outside of the track with a sheer drop at the side! She was unaware that she was clutching Mark Hillyer's sinewy brown arm in a convulsive grip. She only knew they were scraping past the earth-moving machine. At the same time she caught the sound of rocks and rubble tumbling hundreds of feet through fern and tea-tree to the gully far below.

Swiftly, guiltily her hand dropped from his arm.

"I thought you weren't nervous!" It wasn't so much the words as his maddening triumphant tone that was making her feel so infuriated.

"Anyone would feel nervous in a spot like that," she retorted with spirit.

"Just one of those things you have to get used to if you think of settling in this part of the world. Shall we say a preview? Something to help you to make up your mind?"

Neither the chill inflection of his tone nor the words made any sense to her. If he was referring to her accepting the job on the station she had already made up her mind. No one but a dumb cluck like herself would have let herself in for a drive to an unknown destination with this ill-natured stranger in the first place.

Incredibly they were still climbing up among the peaks. Was there no end to the misty wetness of the bush, the fern-encrusted banks? For a long time now there had been no sound but the clickety-click of the windscreen wipers and the occasional thud of a loose rock flung upwards against the undercarriage. The silence was getting on her nerves, in fact it was becoming downright unendurable! Suddenly she decided that she would crack that stony calm of his, and she knew just how she'd do it too! Glancing towards him, she said, "Look, I'm sorry, but I've changed my mind. So please, if you don't mind, I'd like to go back to town."

No answer. But for the frown creasing his bronzed forehead she might have imagined he hadn't caught her soft tones above the drumming of rain on the roof. She raised her voice. "I said I've changed my mind about the job. I mean, it's just wasting your time taking me any further, isn't it? I'll go back—"

"You won't you know!" He was staring directly ahead, his eyes fixed on the fragment of wet pathway vanishing into wet bush. "I'm taking you with me to Waikare today."

"Won't!" she cried. "But of course you can take me back to town!" His darkened face wasn't conducive to any hope. She tried for lightness. "What is this? A kidnap or something?"

"Don't worry, you won't come to any harm with us."

"But I don't want to go there! I've changed my mind!"

"Too bad, because you'll be there," he consulted a silver watch strapped to a tanned wrist, "in just about thirty minutes, I'd say."

Angela subsided in her seat. He didn't look crazy. One read of such things happening, but not to ordinary girls like herself. One thing was for sure, there was no sense in arguing with him, not with that dark expression in his face. She would simply have to push away the terrifying thoughts and hope that matters weren't as frightening as they seemed.

His voice seemed to echo her vague apprehensions. Did she imagine the note of sardonic amusement in his deep tones? "There's no need to look like that. Nothing's going to happen to you, you know. I'll take you back as soon as you're ready," his tone deepened, "but you did want to give your explanation to Brian, remember?"

Oddly in spite of herself the fears died away, leaving only the resentment. What was the matter with him? Well, she would soon see.

The next moment she was flung roughly forward as the Land Rover jerked to an unexpected stop, and watching the reason for the sudden braking she didn't know whether to laugh or cry as a large bird with iridescent blue-green plumage strolled nonchalantly on long red legs across the rough metal of the roadway, followed by four small editions of the mother bird.

"Pukekos," Mark Hillyer remarked briefly, and put a hand to the gear lever. As they plunged on over long shadows of tree ferns lying across the pathway he added, "They come from the swamp down there." Angela followed the jerk of his dark head towards a raupo-choked stream in the hollow of the hills.

So he could be tender and thoughtful with forest birds, she thought, but not with a strange girl. There was just no understanding him, and thank heaven once she reached her destination, she wouldn't need to worry about him. The odd part of the situation was that she felt no real fear about the journey. Tight-lipped and antagonistic though he was, one thing got through to her, and that was that he was interested in her for reasons connected with his brother. Why, she couldn't even begin to imagine. She realised he had condescended to toss her a sideways glance. "You'll be all right," he said again.

She was too annoyed to answer. Edging herself as far away from him as possible, she rubbed a clear space and looked out of the window. Not that there was anything to see outside but the misted shapes of wet bush. Up and up, bend after bend. He said out of the silence, "You can take off first thing tomorrow . . . if you want to."

For answer she flung him an exasperated glance. *If she wanted to!*

"I thought," he said smugly, "that you'd see it my way in the end."

Angela didn't even trouble to argue further with him. What was the use?

But it doesn't matter how beastly he is to me, she comforted herself. Anyone can put up with a difficult person for a short while. After tomorrow, lovely thought, I need never see him again. In an effort to relieve her pent-up feelings she raised her hand to the window and with her finger marked out letters on the misted glass: HATE YOU.

His sideways glance flickered towards her and she knew by the sardonic twitch of his lips that he had noticed the words. She was glad that he had got the message. If this was the way he treated prospective employees it would be a miracle if he ever got any of his staff to stay. Probably they all had to be practically abducted as she had been to even get them to the place. But she would get away from it. She would come back to town tomorrow even if it meant walking all the way on the bush track or begging a lift from those burly knights of the road who it seemed were to come to her rescue by clearing away the slip of earth from the road in the morning.

The rain eased at last, but there was still the roar of the wind in the trees, drops clinging to the beaded windscreen and the sombre curtains of bush closing them in. Ahead a curve of road swept up to meet a slate-grey sky with billowing clouds. It was like a journey in a dream, Angela mused, one that seemed as though it would go on for ever. She couldn't decide which was the more oppressive and nerve-racking, her companion's savage cracks of which half the time she could make no sense, or the long silences that seemed so unnatural.

They were dropping down into a valley and all at once she caught sight of a tiny school, a few scattered houses, then they swept once again up a slope.

A rough signpost nailed to a tree loomed up at the fork of the roads. Waikare Station. So at last, she thought with relief, they were nearing their destination.

"This is the eastern boundary of Waikare," he volunteered and she glanced around her seeking some sign of habitation. But there were only the cleared hills with their seven-barbed sheep fences running up to meet the sky and on either side of the track, a sea of densely growing tea-tree.

"Only a few miles to go now." Even without looking at him Angela was aware that he was throwing her one of his derisive looks. "Feeling excited?"

"Not really."

"I didn't think you would be."

Now what in the world did he mean by that? What could he possibly know of her feelings? She turned puzzled hazel eyes towards him. "How do you mean?"

"Can't you guess? It takes guts, a special brand of girl to come straight out from a city like London and be enthusiastic over taking on living on a sheep station in the heart of the New Zealand hill country."

Stung by the note of censure in his voice, she came back swiftly, "And you don't think I qualify?"

Again that bitter inflection she couldn't understand. "We'll see later, shall we?"

Once again she reflected that she had never met a man who was so thoroughly deliberately disagreeable. *Or one so good-looking*, whispered a tiny traitorous voice in her mind, but she thrust it aside. Had she known he was to treat her in this off-hand fashion she would never have come here.

They sped up a rise and as they reached the summit she gazed down towards the foot of the incline where at the side of a small timber bridge, the tangled wreckage of a late-model car lay on the grass. She leaned forward, "My goodness, that must have been a bad smash! It couldn't have happened long ago either, by the look of it."

"Last Saturday, actually." The inflection of his low voice was more intimidating than ever, but she decided to ignore his discouraging tone.

"The driver of the car, was he killed?"

"No."

"He was lucky."

He made no answer and she did not pursue the subject. She would have liked to have known whether the injured driver had been a local man, but in her companion's present dark mood she very much doubted if he would tell her. Clearly he had no intention of telling her *anything*! So instead she watched the seabirds wheeling and soaring overhead. Probably, she mused, they came from the blue-grey sea she could glimpse between a gap in the hills.

"This is the start of the drive to the homestead," he told her as they swept over a rise and came in sight of a sprawling white timber house, green-roofed, in the shelter of tall trees. To Angela the carefully tended homestead and grounds below appeared a peaceful haven in an empty wilderness and for a moment she forgot her forbidding companion. "Is that it?" she cried with interest.

He nodded carelessly. "That's Waikare."

They turned beside a big shed at the roadside and rattled over a cattle-stop. This time he anticipated the question that rose to her lips. "The shed is handy for deliveries. It takes the milk supply for the week, all the stores."

"I can imagine it must be awfully useful." They were taking a curving driveway lined with dust-coated flax and tattered toa-toa, white-starred tea-tree, all blowing in the wind. Presently they passed a cluster of modern timber bungalows. Probably, Angela mused, they belonged to married men working on the station. They swept by shearing sheds and timber stockyards. Then a second cattle-stop rattled beneath the wheels and they continued on the long curve of the winding driveway. When the Land Rover came to a stop at a wide timber gate Angela glanced enquiringly towards the driver. "Shall I—?"

He nodded unsmilingly. "It's the custom around here that the passenger pays for the honour and glory of being in the front seat by opening the gates."

Angela leaped down to the sheep-nibbled grass, chasing away two fat woolly Perendale sheep who had made for themselves a comfortable hollow in the dust beside the gatepost. She waited until the vehicle had passed through the opening, then closed the gate. By the time she had gone through the procedure for the fourth time she was becoming accustomed to jumping up and down, though it was difficult to be sufficiently quick to get rid of the sheep and close the gate before a few determined stragglers could make their escape. As she climbed back into the Land Rover she told herself that at least he couldn't now regard her as completely useless. Not that his opinion of her mattered, of course.

As they swept around another curve of the driveway they came in sight of barns and implement sheds, the wet roofs gleaming in the pale sunshine, then they were approaching the homestead. Angela couldn't seem to tear her gaze from the white timber house where flowering shrubs and long flower borders broke the wide expanse of sweeping green lawns. The property was long established—you could tell by the massive Moreton Bay fig trees growing by the house. A sun porch running the length of the dwelling was filled with long benches of cascading plants. Surely there must be a woman who tended them with loving care. Her gaze moved to a swimming pool near the house, a blue rectangle whose surface was thickly strewn with pink hibiscus blossoms fallen from the bushes growing on the bank above.

She had little time to dwell on the scene, however, for they were skirting a line of garages, passing a tractor and a farm motor bike. The next minute, to a wild barking set up by a line of sheepdogs confined in their kennels, they drew up at the steps at the back of the dwelling.

Mark Hillyer turned to face her. "Welcome to Waikare." Angela thought she had never in all her life known anything quite as chilling as the blue of his eyes—unless it was the ice tinkling in his tone.

CHAPTER TWO

Leaving the Land Rover standing in the driveway, he led the way through a porch cluttered with men's outdoor clothing, tattered sunhats and stockwhips, and they moved into a long passage with rooms opening off from either side. There seemed to be no one about, though Angela could hear a radiogram playing softly from somewhere in the house.

At length he paused outside a closed door. "He's in there. You can go in."

"In there?" She was baffled by his cold hard look. "Is your brother too busy, or something, to come out to see me?"

"Why don't you go right in there and find out for yourself? You came here to see him, didn't you?"

"Yes, of course, but—"

"Well then . . ."

There was nothing for it but to do as he suggested. Suggested? It was more in the nature of an order! Nevertheless . . . She turned the handle of the door and found herself in a sunny bedroom. A fresh breeze stirred the crisp floral curtains at the window. On the bed lay a young man with a pale strained face. His tightly-curling brown hair was almost concealed by a bandage fastened around his head. His vague troubled gaze moved towards her. "Martha . . . thought it was Martha . . ." The words slurred away into silence.

"*Hold his hand,*" commanded the inexorable voice from the open doorway.

Angela moved to the bed and clasped the man's hand, calloused with physical toil. Already, however, the sick man's eyelids had fallen over his eyes and the hand in her's was limp. Either he has fallen asleep or he had lapsed into unconsciousness, she couldn't tell which. Very gently she withdrew her fingers and tiptoed away from the bed.

"He's under sedation," Mark Hillyer told her. "In a few days he should be well on the mend."

Angela's thoughts were still with the boyish face. "He looks terribly ill. He didn't know . . . he called me Martha."

His quick glance raked her face. "What's so funny about that? You are, aren't you?"

"No, no, I'm not—"

"You're saying you're not Martha Stanaway? He was staring

at her incredulously. "Why didn't you tell me this before?"

They were speaking in lowered tones because of the man just through the wall. Now as he led the way along the passage Angela cried desperately, "It's your own fault! I tried and tried to tell you, but you wouldn't listen! You brushed me off every time!"

She became aware that suspicion merged with the resentment in his eyes. "You'd better come in here and we'll try and sort this out." He threw open another door and she preceded him into a small room evidently used as an office. Sweeping aside a pile of account forms lying on a chair, he pushed it forward with a sandalled foot. "Sit down." Then perching his long length on a corner of the desk he picked up a pipe. "Mind if I smoke?"

"No, of course not."

He rammed tobacco into the bowl, struck a match, then blew out the flame. "Well, go on, I'm listening. If you're not Martha Stanaway then who the devil are you?"

She met his gaze unflinchingly with clear hazel eyes. "I'm Angela. Angela Twentyman, Martha's friend."

At his startled glance she knew that at last she had cracked that cool composure of his. "Go on, Miss Twentyman."

"Well, you see, we came out from England together on the same ship and we got to know each other. I hadn't seen Martha since we left the *Ocean Monarch* in Auckland a week ago—" It was his stare that was doing things to her, making her strangely unsure of herself. "And then," she rushed on much too fast, "coming north on the bus today she told me she was planning to come to see your brother Brian. She said she had arranged a meeting with him at Waikare Station—"

"True enough." His tone was ironic.

"And seeing I was on the lookout for something to do on a sheep farm (she must have been out of her cotton-pickin' mind) we talked it over and decided that I'd come instead." At his intimidating expression she faltered, "if I liked."

"Just like that!" he exploded. "You'd come instead!"

To her chagrin she could feel the tell-tale colour creeping up her cheeks. "Yes, in a way. You see—"

"I get it," he cut in savagely. "No doubt you both had a hell of a lot of fun over arranging a practical joke like this!"

Angela didn't know how to answer the unprovoked attack. "Not really. I couldn't decide whether I wanted to come up here or not, so in the end I said I'd toss a coin and settle it that way—" Her bright smile died away beneath that implacable blue stare.

"I see. Very simple . . . toss a coin."

All at once she realised that she had made it sound exactly as he thought, a joke that had somehow misfired. The maddening part of it all was that it hadn't been a joke at all. But he would never believe that. On another level she wondered why it was that this stranger's opinion of her should matter to her.

"It was only a job," she offered in her soft husky tones. Why couldn't he understand? He seemed determined to doubt the truth of her explanation, to believe her guilty of something of which she was entirely ignorant.

He swept on unheedingly. "It wouldn't have occurred to either of you to give a thought to *his* feelings, let him have a say in things? After all, if he was good enough to pay the passage out to New Zealand he was entitled to some choice in what happened afterwards, wouldn't you say?"

Angela's thoughts were whirling. "Are you saying that your brother paid Martha's fare out to New Zealand?"

"That's right. It was a one-way ticket because the arrangement was that they'd be married almost right away. He borrowed a thousand dollars from me to finance the trip, clothes, wedding gear, travel tickets, spending money. Would you consider yourself worth a thousand dollars, Miss—what did you say your name was?"

"Twentyman," she whispered. "Truly, Martha didn't say a word to me about all this."

He shot her a sardonic look. "So you tell me. I'd better put you in the picture, then, fill you in on the missing bits. Just in case you don't know all the facts about your *friend*," he gave the word a mocking emphasis, "and my kid brother."

She shook her head. "Martha never mentioned him to me until today."

"She didn't let on to you that they'd been pen-friends for two years?"

"No!" With a sudden lift of her spirits Angela realised that he seemed prepared to believe at least part of her story. But not, unfortunately, the part that mattered.

"Oh, Brian's always had a thing about pen-friends. He's got scads of them in countries all over the world, has had since he was a kid in high school. He's one of those odd bods who can write reams to some girl he's never met in his life, someone who lives on the other side of the globe, but put him face to face with a pretty girl right here and he clams up like an oyster. Not that Brian writes to girls as a rule. He acquired your friend

Martha through corresponding with her brother, but somehow or other she began writing back to Brian instead. That would have been okay, but the idiot got all carried away about her.

"The first I knew of it was a few months ago when he borrowed the money from me to bring her out to New Zealand. Seems they were all set for the wedding day once she arrived at Waikare. Brian's a guy who doesn't let on much of what he's feeling. He never got around to showing me the girl's picture even, the only information he ever passed on was that she had red hair. I gathered, though, that he'd made up his mind to marry the girl. I did my best to talk some sense into him—pointed out that he was doing a crazy thing in rushing into marriage blindfold with a girl he scarcely knew, but I might just as well have been talking to myself. Nothing I could say would make him see reason. He kept on saying it would work out."

Mark Hillyer's lips tightened. "By the time the ship was due to berth in Auckland there was no holding him. He was to bring his Martha back to the station that day and then I'd see how well the idea would work out. He sold the old truck he had and got himself a brand new Chrysler car, a pricey job. Then off he went, all carried away with excitement and love of his fair lady." His face hardened. "Three days later they brought him home in an ambulance from hospital."

He turned away, moving to a cabinet where decanters and glasses stood. "What'll you have?"

"Nothing for me, thanks. What—happened?"

He studied the whisky in his glass, his voice grim. "Oh, he made the wharves all right, after the new Chrysler had let him down with a breakdown on the way and put him an hour late. When he got to the ship Martha had gone, no one knew where. There was no message left for him over the loudspeaker, no letter in her cabin, nothing.

"He took it hard. Like I said, he's a quiet reserved sort of guy, keeps things pretty much to himself. I gather he waited around the wharf most of the day hoping she'd turn up, thinking there must have been some slip-up over arrangements. A couple of times he rang back home, but there'd been no message left for him here either. When it looked hopeless hanging around any longer he drowned his disappointment in one of the pubs in the city. It must have been pretty late when he finally took off for home. He nearly made it too. A roadman came across the car in the morning. Well, you saw what was left of it. Brian was thrown out and lying beside the wrecked car. At first the man thought he was a goner, but he was breathing all right. So he phoned for an ambulance and I got the news from hospital.

"Could have been worse considering the Chrysler's a total write-off. Head injuries are the main trouble. They kept him in hospital for a couple of days, then sent him home. The doc says all he needs now is rest and quiet for a few days, no shocks, no worries. He's under sedation now, of course, sleeps most of the time. But the doc assures me he'll be a different man in a week's time and before long he'll be as good as new, except for the odd headache. So there you have it, Miss Twentyman!"

"I can't believe it," Angela murmured dazedly. "Martha didn't ever mention having a fiancé out here. She never wore an engagement ring—"

"But she did have a boy-friend on the ship?"

Angela hesitated. He had taken her by surprise, darn him, and she had no ready answer. Martha's mocking tones echoed in her mind. "The prospects are terrific!" No doubt the prospects she had in mind were far more exciting than a lonely life in the outback as the wife of a young sheep farmer she had never met. How right she had been in suspecting Martha's motives! And imagine her having the nerve to invent that story to tell Harvey concerning herself! How easy it must have been too. Martha wouldn't even have to invent it, seeing it was all true except that the facts applied to Martha herself. She wrenched her mind back to the deep quiet tones.

"I'm right, aren't I?"

"You could be," Angela admitted slowly, "but there was nothing definite. It could have been just a shipboard romance for all I know—"

"But you think not?" If only he wouldn't probe her with those icy blue eyes.

"I just don't know."

"You're a rotten liar, you know."

"Well, it's true!" she flung back at him. "I don't know a thing about Martha's affairs. She didn't say a word to me about being engaged to your brother."

He shot her a suspicious glance. "And yet you were friends, you tell me?"

"Not *real* friends, you understand. We used to get around with the same crowd on board ship, that was all."

His disbelieving stare did nothing to ease her mounting sense of confusion. "I can never make you understand!" she cried desperately. "Don't you see, all I knew about coming up here was that it was a job. A work thing you get paid for."

"Almost you convince me, Miss Twentyman." But she knew

he was only being sarcastic. "And what," he enquired drily, "was the particular job you had in mind when you got here? Or didn't you enquire?"

"Of course I did, but she didn't tell me."

"*Didn't tell you*? And you agreed to come all this way on the offchance, without having a clue of what your duties were to be?"

"It was all done in such a hurry," she protested defensively. "Martha only told me about it as we were nearing the township where you picked me up, but she did mention something about —" another trap loomed ahead but having begun she would have perforce to continue, "helping the wife with the housework . . . or something."

The thick black brows rose in a mocking V. "Interesting, the wife bit, especially as that was to be her role, according to Brian's reckoning."

His cool tone stung her into saying wildly. "I remember now! She did say something about helping the shearers—"

"*The shearers*?" The moment the words were out she knew she had said the wrong thing. This time, judging by Mark Hillyer's expression of stunned incredulity, she had really done it! So Martha had lied about that too.

She realised he was eyeing her consideringly and somehow she distrusted the mocking twist of his lips. "You know something, Miss Twentyman? You've just given me an idea—"

But her thoughts were elsewhere. "Tell me, did Martha know your brother had been hurt in an accident on his way back from meeting the ship?"

"She knew." The deep tones were inflexible. "I let her into all that when she rang me yesterday."

"I see." So that was why Martha had planned to break her journey north and make a brief visit to the station. Apparently she did have some slight conscience in the matter. Trouble was that being Martha she had quieted her own misgivings by persuading another girl to take her place. It was just too bad that the "other girl" happened to be herself! And even worse that she found herself forced into explanations over something she knew nothing about with this grim-faced man. He was hateful, hateful! If Mark Hillyer were a typical New Zealand sheep farmer, employment on a station was the last job in the world she wanted. She gathered her thoughts together and all at once remembered the package in her care which up till this moment she had been too taken aback to think about. Drawing it from the woven flax kit on her arm, she held it out towards him. How odd, her fingers were shaking. Ridiculous really, for all this had nothing to do with her. At least the enclosures in the package would prove to him how mistaken he had been in his snap judgement of Martha—and herself. If only he wouldn't persist in lumping them both together.

"Martha asked me to give this to Brian, so I'll leave it with you. I expect," her voice quivered in spite of herself, "it's the money your brother sent her."

He took the bulky envelope from her. "I wish I could share your faith in your friend's motives, but I'm afraid I can't, not after what's been happening around here lately. Let's make sure, shall we?" Slitting open the flap with a tanned finger, he took out a bundle of closely-written sheets of notepaper, tied with a blue ribbon. He flipped through the pages briefly, then tossed them aside. "There's something else here too!" The next moment he shook on to the desk a small jeweller's box and flicking open the lid revealed a glittering diamond solitaire ring lying on a bed of black velvet. "Nothing but the best, evidently! So that's why he had to borrow the money from me for the fare!"

Angela stared back at him with lips lightly parted.

"Maybe you'll agree with me now that Brian's lost quite a lot through your friend, one way and another. His car, his savings and a heck of a lot of faith in human nature, I shouldn't wonder. Still trying to vindicate your girl-friend?" He was pushing the love-letters back into the envelope, slipping the jeweller's box in after them.

"She *wasn't* a great friend—"

"So you said before."

"I'm sorry," Angela murmured inadequately. For what could you say to this embittered man who for some reason appeared to take full responsibility for the actions of his kid brother? "I only wish I could do something to help, to make up—"

"You can, you know."

"Me?" She eyed him in amazement. "What could *I* do?"

"Quite a lot in that direction, actually." For a moment he was silent. "It wouldn't occur to you, I suppose, that you happen to owe him something? At the very least some explanation, when he's well enough to hear it, seeing that you're in on this too?"

"But I'm not! I keep telling you—" Close to tears, she floundered on, nervously twisting a strand of hair round and round her fingers. "It wasn't my fault!"

"Oh, I forgot, you tossed for it, didn't you?"

All at once confusion and frustration merged into anger. She was furious that he refused to believe her. "I told you before that I wished I could do something—"

"I'll bet." He was grim again.

"Honestly! I mean it!"

He bent on her that intent blue stare. "Well then, why not stick around for a while until Brian's well enough to take the truth about his missing girl-friend? Why not hand this back to him yourself," he indicated the jeweller's box lying on the desk, "complete with explanations? The way things are at the moment once he gets to thinking things over he'll worry himself out of quick recovery. Not knowing what happened, hoping against hope that Martha'll be along with apologies and sweet talk for not meeting him at the ship. Better for him to have a clean cut, take it straight no matter how much it hurts at the time!"

"Do you really think," Angela cried incredulously, "that I'd stay on here after after . . . ?" Her voice trailed away.

"That's the idea." His tone hardened. "You can spell it out to him and hope he'll believe you."

"Don't *you* believe me?"

All at once the answer had become awfully important. She found she was holding her breath.

He smiled his cool lopsided smile. "My feelings don't come into it. It's Brian we're concerned with. He's taken a pretty bad knock through your girl-friend—"

"Why do you keep calling her *my* girl-friend?"

He ignored the interruption. "He's the one who needs you around at the moment, the one you can help back to health—or didn't you mean what you said just now about being sorry, wanting to help?"

He had trapped her neatly and effectively. What made it worse was that he was aware that she had come here in search of employment. If only he didn't guess as well that in some obscure way she did feel she owed his brother something, even though it was really Martha who had caused all this trouble. It was a second-hand sort of guilt, but it was there, no doubt about that. She was unaware of the transparency of the thoughts passing across her troubled face. She brought her mind back to the vibrant tones.

His voice said, "You *said* you wanted a job on the station." His tone said, Or was that just just another fabrication, something made up to suit the occasion?

At last she got out in a choking voice, "I know I did, but that was before I knew all about your brother and Martha. Now everything's different—"

"No difference so far as you're concerned, that is if what you're saying is the truth."

She hated him and always would! Hated him so intensely that she just had to prove to him that she was far from the girl he took her to be. Another Martha, scheming, callous, self-seeking. *Could* that be her own soft tones agreeing to his preposterous proposal? "Just until your brother gets well enough for me to talk to him, then."

The slight lift to his lips told her that once that happened she would no longer be needed at Waikare. At his cool smile she was driven to retaliate, "And it'll be okay about that shearing job if you do need a girl to give you a hand?" She was conscious of a sneaky hope that no such opening would exist. After all, he hadn't taken her offer seriously before. On the contrary. The next moment hope did a nose-dive. His tone was mock-serious "Believe me, I do, Twenty—you don't mind if I call you that?"

Her soft lips tightened. "I can't very well stop you."

"You couldn't have dropped in at a more opportune time!" She didn't trust the new soft note in his voice. "The shearing gang moved into their quarters yesterday, but it was too wet for them to do any work. Their cook got brassed off waiting around all day. She took off back to town and hasn't been heard of since. Luckily the rain held them up this morning, but they'll be all set to start tomorrow—if they can find a replacement. And that's where you come in! They work a long day up here, six to six, but the money's good, thirteen dollars a day and keep for a six-day week. Meals have to be bang on time, of course—but I'll fill you in on that later. He met her look of wide-eyed horror. "You did say," he reminded her in that maddeningly soft tone, "that you wanted to give the shearers a hand?"

Never one to resist a challenge, especially this particular one, Angela lifted her chin and gritted her teeth. "Okay," she said recklessly, "I'll try." Under her breath she added, "And heaven help the shearers!"

CHAPTER THREE

"That's it, then."

Even had Angela wished to retract her wild promise to take on this job pride would not now permit a change of mind. She comforted herself with the reflection that it was only for one week. One could surely endure anything for a mere seven days! Besides, if other women could cope, so could she! The thought sustained her against an almost overpowering temptation to call the whole thing off and go away just as soon as she could. But it was already too late for regrets. Mark had picked up her travel bag and stood waiting expectantly. "You'd better come up to the house and have a word with Doris. She's a sort of aunt by marriage who keeps the place going for us."

In a dreamlike state of mind where nothing seemed to matter very much any more Angela accompanied him along a passage and into a spacious modern kitchen. The pleasant sunny room was painted in tonings of cinnamon and cream and the walls appeared to be entirely lined with cupboards. A huge freezer ran along the end of the room and sunshine sparked gleams in long stainless steel sink benches.

A tall slender woman who was standing at the electric range swung around at their approach, and though the stranger tried to conceal her attitude with a forced smile Angela was aware, for the second time in a day, of being faced with an expression of antagonism and dislike.

"It's Martha, isn't it? So you came after all?" Cold condemnation rang in her polite tones.

Angela's swift imploring glance went to Mark's impassive face. Let him do the explaining as to how she came to be here. The whole situation was getting beyond her, and besides, she was becoming very tired of being mistaken for someone else, regarded as an intruder, someone who insisted on pushing herself into a home where she was definitely unwelcome.

Mark made short work of introductions. "Wrong! This happens to be Miss Twentyman. Doris, Mrs. Blackman. I met her in town today," he ran on evenly, "seems she was on the look-out for a country job, so I booked her in as shearers' cook starting from tomorrow."

So he wasn't going into explanations regarding the real position. He was saying nothing regarding her connection with

Martha. Perhaps it was wiser to leave it that way. What did it matter? She would be here for such a short while.

With a sense of relief Angela realised that the older woman's expression had changed to one of friendly interest. For her part Angela felt an instant liking for this attractive-looking woman with short curling fair hair turning grey and clear tanned skin innocent of make-up.

She realised Doris was saying with a smile, "Have you taken on that sort of job before, Miss Twentyman? Done much in the way of cooking, I mean?"

Avoiding Mark's penetrating blue stare, which she felt rather than saw, Angela said faintly, "A little," and pushed away a mental picture of hurriedly thrown-together simple meals prepared for girl-friends in the tiny London flat.

Mark said, "Miss Twentyman will be staying up at the house with us."

For some reason Angela couldn't fathom the simple matter-of-fact statement appeared to surprise the housekeeper. "Not down at the shearers' quarters?" she enquired blankly. "Up here?"

"That's right."

Mrs. Blackman appeared to recover herself. "Oh—I see. Well, there's oodles of room here, Miss Twentyman. I'll give you my alarm clock tonight to make sure you don't sleep in in the morning. Come along with me and I'll show you to your room. You'll want to unpack your things. After that we'll have a cup of tea together."

Mark lifted a hand to his forehead in a careless gesture of farewell. "See you later about the job, Miss Twentyman."

Angela responded with her warm smile. "Thank you."

Oh, it was wonderful to be treated as a person in her own right once again rather than some sort of spare part belonging to Martha Stanaway! Even if being herself in her new position as cook for a shearing gang did involve a swift downward slide in the social scale.

There seemed to be a number of rooms opening off the long passageway, but at last her companion took her into a small neat bedroom simply furnished with a dressing table and chest of drawers. Fluffy orange-shaded sheepskin rugs lay on the floorboards and her travel bag lay on a neatly made bed covered with a hand-crocheted wool spread in tawny tonings of tans and golds.

Mrs. Blackman crossed the room to fling open french doors and Angela caught a slimpse of a sunshiny porch. There were the shelves of flowering pot-plants and trailing greenery she had noticed when approaching the homestead. Her gaze travelled beyond to the slopes of sheep-dotted hills.

"You'll find the bathroom at the end of the passage," Mrs. Blackman was saying. "In summer, showers instead of baths are the order of the day. We had a drop of rain yesterday and a bit today, but not enough to make much difference to the water supply. Come along to the kitchen when you're ready, my dear."

My dear ... It was heartwarming to find oneself made so welcome in a strange place. During her brief stay in this new country this was the first occasion on which Angela had been invited to make a stay in a private residence. And away in the country too! Nice ... almost like home. Swiftly she caught herself up. Home! How could she have forgotten whose home this was! And she still had to face him tonight and be given her instructions as to details of the unfamiliar duties she had so rashly taken on. And only really because she just had to prove to *him* that she was capable of holding the job down. It must be her day for rushing into crazy decisions—first the journey to this faraway station in the hills, now letting herself in for a week's work and heaven knows what else besides in the way of back-breaking physical toil.

As she made her way along the passage something Martha had once said to her on the ship came back to mind with hurtful emphasis. "You're so soft, Angela, honestly! If you go on believing everything folk tell you it'll land you in trouble one of these days!" How right she was!

In the bathroom with its huge array of towels Angela washed her hands, then returned to the airy bedroom to touch her mouth with lipstick and run a comb through wind-tangled hair. A little later when she made her way back to the kitchen she found Doris already seated at the long table in the centre of the room. The hot tea served with man-sized scones still warm from the oven refreshed her.

Glancing around the spotless shining kitchen, she murmured, "You must have a lot to do here in the way of housekeeping—and looking after Brian," she added awkwardly. This was the effect her employer's censorious attitude was having on her, she thought wildly. Already he had made her feel embarrassed over the matter of the recent accident, as though she really had had something to do with it.

Doris smiled. "Oh, I'm used to it. I've always lived in the country, I love it. And Brian's no bother at all. I only wish he were, but up till now he just lies there. Oh, he wakes up when I

bring him his meals, then off he goes to sleep again."
"Mr. Hillyer said he'll be better before long."
"Yes, that's what I keep telling myself. As to that Martha—" Unconsciously Angela braced herself for another hate session directed against the girl these people had never met.
Propping her elbows on the table, Doris gazed reflectively over her teacup. "I don't mind telling you I wasn't feeling too pleased a while ago when I saw Mark bringing you into the house. That's why I kept out of the way in the kitchen. When he took off today he told me he had some business in town he had to see about. I knew it must be something pretty important to make him drop everything and go when he's so busy and short-handed here. Then I saw you and your hair looked almost red in the sunshine and I was sure you were Martha. Isn't it funny how wrong you can be when you jump to conclusions? That lovely hair of yours isn't red at all, it's a gorgeous dark copper, and I should have remembered that the shearers are due to start in the morning—if they can find a cook." She eyed Angela enquiringly. "Mark did tell you about Brian's accident? And about Martha not coming?"
Angela nodded, her eyes downcast. "It was bad luck."
"Yes. I'm terribly sorry about the car smash, but as for that Martha, I think it's a good thing that she didn't turn up! In the end," she announced calmly, "it will do Brian a lot of good. He's always been ridiculously shy about girls, and this one that he used to write to away over in England—well, I'm sure he'd built a picture of her in his mind. Not that he ever talked about her, but I've known Brian since he was a little boy and I know how imaginative he is. Over the time they'd been corresponding he'd conjured up a girl from letters and distance, a dream-creature that no real girl would be able to live up to, even if she had turned up here to marry him. Just imagine, he'd actually made plans for an immediate wedding! Without ever having met her! Why, in a week they might have loathed each other. She could have been bad-tempered. She did have bright red hair. That's the only thing Brian ever told us about her."
"Another thing too. What if one of them didn't want to go through with the wedding once they'd seen their pen-friend in the flesh? Think how awkward that would be! Oh, Brian's taken a bad knock, he's been let down, but this way he'll get over it all, in time. Anyway, the way I look at it a girl who doesn't bother contacting him until she's been a week in the country isn't worth worrying about. Wouldn't you agree?"
Angela mumbled, "Maybe." This she knew was the time to

admit her own complicity in the affair, but seeing the boss had seen fit not to mention it . . . Once again she couldn't help thinking how delightful it was to be Miss Twentyman, without any complications, to have no connection whatever with Martha Stanaway. She brought her mind back to Doris.

"Brian needed something like this to make him wake up, realise folk aren't always how you'd like them to be . . . especially girls. Mark doesn't agree with me. He's furious with this Martha Stanaway, blames her for the accident and everything. You've only got to look at him to know the way he feels about her, those cold blue Hillyer eyes of his. You wouldn't think two brothers could be so different, would you? Brian's like his mother, he's a dreamer. He'd much rather have his head in a book than be out on the run. He's a scribbler like she was too. Often when I'm tidying up his room I come across bits of verse written on scraps of paper. Occasionally I throw one of them away by mistake and he gets real mad with me."

Why, Angela wondered, was the housekeeper telling her all this? The effect of isolation, an opportunity of a chat with someone of her own sex, someone new? Aloud she asked, "Does he ever have any of his verses published?"

"Once in a while. Last year he showed me some poems that he'd submitted to a literary publication way over in the States. I never saw anyone so proud as he was on the day the magazine arrived here with two of his verses printed in it. Not that I could make much sense of the poems myself, but I wouldn't let on to him about that, of course. He's one of those folk who are ever so easily discouraged by the slightest hint of criticism. He's had a lot more luck with his articles, though. He calls them "bread-and-butter-stuff", but the newspapers in the city buy all he sends them and actually pay him for them too!"

"Good for him! What does he write about?"

"Oh, country life, sheep-farming gen, what goes on around here through the varying seasons, that sort of thing. Folk in the cities seem to like to read about the outback and what it's like to live on a sheep station up in the hills." She smiled her cheerful smile. "Me, I'd rather be right here on the spot living it, droughts and slips on the road and all!" She broke off as the door was pushed open.

"I knocked and knocked, but there didn't seem to be anyone around—Oh, I didn't know—" The voice stopped short in surprise and Angela glanced up to see a young girl with a freckled friendly face and straight brown hair falling to her shoulders. Her short cotton shift revealed legs tanned to almost the same shade as the leather sandals she wore on her feet.

"Hello, Jill," Doris appeared unsurprised to see the visitor, "this is Miss Twentyman."

Angela smiled. "Angela," she corrected.

To the younger girl Doris explained, "Angela's cooking for the shearers. Mark signed her up today."

"Hello, Angela." Jill's anxious gaze returned to Doris. Clearly she had other matters on her mind. "Brian," she asked with concern, "how is he? Is he any better today, do you think?"

"Much the same as yesterday really, but—"

"Has he been talking to you at all?"

"Once or twice."

The young face fell. "Well, I suppose that's something." Jill slipped the bag from her shoulder down onto the table. "I've brought him some goodies." She took a foil-covered dish from the bag. "He always said he liked the pizza pies I made. And I've brought him some early peaches from the orchard. He must start to take an interest in something soon." The shadowed eyes belied the light words.

"Of course he will. Why don't you go in and see him?"

Two deep dimples appeared in the sun-tanned cheeks. "What do you think I came over here for? See you." With a smile the girl moved away.

A quizzical smile curved Doris's lips. "Now you can see for yourself why I'm not run off my feet looking after Brian. Jill plans to take up nursing, she's just waiting until next month to start training at the hospital in Auckland. Meantime she says that looking after Brian is good practice for her, even though half the time he doesn't even realise she's there. She's been coming over almost every day, usually earlier than this, and she stays with him for ages."

Angela looked after the girl as she hurried away. Her eyes twinkled. "I thought you told me Brian was shy with girls."

"Shy isn't the word! He'd rather run a mile in the opposite direction than face someone new."

"Well, there seems to be one girl around here that he feels happy with."

"You mean Jill?" Doris's voice held a careless note. "You can't count her. She's just a sister to him."

"But I thought—"

"Not a real sister, of course, but as good as. Jill was brought up at the homestead with the two Hillyer boys. Years ago she was left an orphan. Her parents were strangers in the district and there was no one to look after her or care what happened to her. The Hillyers took pity on her, they'd always longed for a daughter anyway and she was only a few years younger than Brian. She and Brian always played together and they got on well together later on when they used to come back from boarding school in the holidays. This summer Jill took a job as land girl on a cattle farm over the hills. She's just filling in the time until February when she's due to start her hospital training in the city. It's a long drive over here and back again, but she doesn't seem to mind. Those two always were the best of friends."

Friends . . . Angela had a feeling that Jill's interest in Brian, her devotion to him even at times when he couldn't be aware of her presence, indicated something a little more than a sisterly sympathy. Or could she be mistaken? Perhaps Jill happened to be that rare person known as a "born nurse", someone anxious to help others back to health without ever counting the cost to themselves.

She brought her thoughts back to the woman seated opposite her at the long table.

"Usually I have a houseful of children staying all through the long summer holidays, but Brian's accident put a stop to that for awhile. The kids will be disappointed, but I expect there'll still be time for them to come later once Brian is feeling better."

"It must have made a difference to everyone?"

"Accidents do, don't they? Mark doesn't say much, but I guess he's feeling pretty disappointed too over that trip he missed out on. A group of young sheep farmers were taking off for a conference overseas, then travelling around various countries—England, America, Japan, studying farming methods and wool marketing. He would have learned a lot and had a holiday as well. He never ever takes any time off, but he was going to make an exception for this. He'd been looking forward to it, I know, and the plane takes off with the rest of the party this morning. He can't leave the place, not with Brian laid up." Doris sighed. "Just one of those things."

A tiny bulb lighted up in Angela's mind. Here was yet another reason for Mark Hillyer's bitter resentment against Martha and the accident that for some ridiculous reason he insisted on holding her partly to blame for. She pushed the thought away and said tentatively, "Could I help you get the dinner ready?"

"No, you couldn't!" Clear grey eyes twinkled back at her. "You'll have enough of preparing meals in the next few days to last you all the rest of the season. No, I have everything prepared. There's a rice custard in the oven and there's cold mutton for tea tonight." Doris rose from the table. "Come along and I'll show you around outside—" She broke off, adding after a moment, "That is, if you'd care to have a look at everything. I expect sheep farms are pretty familiar in your line of work. See one, you see them all."

"Oh no," Angela protested quickly, "I'd love to come with you." How could she confess to this kindly stranger that she had landed from the ship from London only a week previously and her cooking experience for a shearing gang was zero? The small voice deep in her mind supplied its jeering answer. How can you help letting her know the truth?

Putting problems aside, she went along the passage with Doris. On the way they passed an open doorway and glancing into the room Angela could see Jill seated on the bed beside the injured man. His eyes were open now, eyes of a pale shadowy blue. How strange that the colour gave an impression of weakness in one brother yet were so coldly masterful in the other.

With a friendly wave to the other two Doris and Angela went out into the fitful sunshine. As they strolled along a winding path with its long flower borders Angela realised that the gardens were ablaze with a variety of roses in full bloom, their perfume rising on the clear air. She stopped to sniff appreciatively the rain-beaded petals of a red-velvet "Josephine Bruce". 'Mm, makes me think I'm back in England in the summertime."

Doris looked surprised. "You come from England?"

Immediately Angela regretted the slip of the tongue. "Yes, from London, actually."

Doris's eyes were alive with interest. "Did you *really*? My parents came from London. They settled out here when I was a small child, so I don't remember a thing about England. Richmond was their home place, they often used to speak of it. Would you happen to know the district?"

Reassured, Angela smiled. "I should do. I lived there for a year."

"Tell me more. You see, it was a dream of ours, Joe's and mine, to take a trip to England when he retired and sold the farm. We used to plan all the things we'd do over there, see London first, then hire a car and tour through the picturesque little villages." The grey eyes clouded. "But things didn't work out that way. Before he ever got around to retiring he died. And then it was too late."

Angela, always perceptive to another's emotion, said quickly, "But couldn't you—"

Doris shook her head. "No, it wouldn't be the same. You'll just have to tell me all about it."

"It's a promise." They strolled across the wet grass towards the blue waters of a rectangular shaped pool. "That looks inviting," Angela commented, "on a hot day like this."

"We use it a lot." They had reached the edge of the pool with its blue tiles. "Oh dear, I keep forgetting to remind Rusty to cut back those bushes. They just grow and grow." Kneeling at the water's edge, Doris began to scoop up handfuls of great fluffy pink blossoms floating on the surface and evidently fallen from the profusion of flowers dotting the hibiscus shrubs leaning over the water from the bank above.

Angela dropped down on the concrete surround to help her, tossing the flowers up on to the grass.

"The pool's marvellous for the men when they come in after a day's work," Doris told her. "They shower in the house, then come out here for a late swim and a cool-off."

"I can imagine. How many men are there working here?"

"On the staff? Well, there are three shepherds, they're all married men living in the bungalows you passed on the way to the house. Then there's Kevin, he's a lad who's just come to us lately to learn sheep farming. He meals with us and sleeps in the house. And a mechanic, Jack, who takes care of the farm machinery and the cars."

"I see." Angela gazed over the spreading green lawns and neatly tended flower beds. "Who does all the gardening around here?"

"That's over to Rusty. He's getting on in years, but we couldn't manage without him. He's a sort of odd-job man, a 'do-anything man', he calls himself."

"Quite a community!"

Doris laughed. "In a way. See those sheep over there—" Angela followed the gesture of a tanned hand towards a paddock near the house where a group of black sheep nibbled the grass. "Those black ones are bred specially for my benefit. I like to spin the wool from the fleece and I prefer the dark fleece to work with, so Mark keeps a few special sheep just for me. Lucky aren't I? But then that's just the sort of thing he would do. He's always so thoughtful."

Odd, Angela mused, that this woman who knew the boss so well should appear to regard him as quite a different type of man from the arrogant bad-tempered male of her acquaintance. They couldn't both be right, and she was willing to bet that her own recent experience of his "thoughtfulness" must count for something. Thinking about her employer, she found, put her in an angry mood, made her feel cross and unhappy and spoiled the peacefulness of the scene around her.

As if in tune with her thoughts Doris said mildly, "You'll be happy working here with Mark. He's one of the best employers one could have. All the staff say the same."

Angela opened her lips to argue the point, then closed them again. Could they really be speaking of the same man?

"You'll find out for yourself tomorrow," Doris was saying.

Tomorrow ... Angela was tempted to ask the older woman for advice. After all she was in need of every bit of assistance she could get in tackling this unfamiliar job. The next moment, however, she decided against it. If it entailed going into the "Martha affair" all over again—no, she'd get through tomorrow somehow. She would have to!

That evening at the dinner table she was relieved that no one appeared to take any special interest in the new member of the shearing gang. Mark was coldly polite to her and Doris friendly and chatty. But of course the housekeeper was a type of country-woman who would extend kindness and hospitality to anyone under her roof. Kevin, the young cadet, looked too young to have left school. He said little, but concentrated all his attention on attacking what appeared to Angela to be a colossal helping of cold meats and salads. Did shearers too eat huge quantities of food? Angela couldn't get through even half of the food on her own plate.

The meal was almost at an end when Jill appeared and took a seat at the table. "Sorry I'm late, folks, but the most fantastic thing happened! What do you think? *He knew me!*" Happiness and relief flooded the young freckled face as she ran on excitedly. "Guess what?" She helped herself to potato salad. "I'm able to stay on for the rest of the week. I rang through to the farm and they said they can do without me for a while seeing they've got a boy staying for the holidays. You don't mind, do you?" she appealed to Doris. "I could give you a hand, help you to look after Brian. You know? Cook some light meals for him, see that he has everything he wants."

"Mind! I'd be delighted," Doris assured her. "My feet are getting rather tired of padding along that passage. That's great news that he's so much better."

"It'll be good practice for you." Mark sent her his lopsided grin. "Your first patient!"

"And I'm going to see that he gets better—and fast," Jill said with confidence. "Tomorrow he can go out to the sun-porch. I've got some books with me I know he'd like, and I've sent to town for a copy of a new book of verses by a New Zealand poet, one he said he wanted."

Looking at the homely, radiant little face, Angela mused that here was someone else who was glad of Martha's non-appearance at the homestead. She was in love with Brian ... Angela was certain of it. Suddenly she was glad that this nice girl had a chance to fight for her happiness now that her shadowy rival had gone for ever.

It was a late dinner and when they rose from the table a faint lemon afterglow of sunset stained the western horizon. The towering Moreton Bay fig trees near the house were black against the luminous clarity of the sky.

Angela had offered to help clear away the dishes when unexpectedly Mark intervened. "You can't do young Kevin out of a job." He grinned towards the youth. "You come with me, Miss Twentyman. We'll take a stroll over to the woolshed and I'll put you in the picture, show you where to find everything you'll be needing in the morning."

The boss had spoken! There was nothing for it but to murmur a hurried "Sorry, Kevin" to the lad and go with her employer.

They strolled together towards the Land Rover and once again she climbed up into the high seat. Now, however, she was ready for the long curving driveway, the gates that must be opened on the way. What she wasn't prepared for as she climbed back after opening a gate and they neared the shearing shed was his laconic query, "Ever cooked for a crowd before, Twenty?"

Twenty! Angela strove to subdue the rising tide of anger, then in spite of herself her lips twitched. The tiny flat in London, the occasional omelette or grilled chops and onions whipped up when friends arrived unexpectedly. She shook her head. "Not like this."

"I get it." Thank heaven he didn't, not really.

He guided the Land Rover around to the back of the big shed and they went inside. "This is the kitchen where you'll work ... plenty of room, latest equipment. I reckon the shearers work a long hard day and deserve all the help they can get."

Was this what Mrs. Blackman had meant when she had referred to the boss's thoughtfulness?

She gazed around the big room with its huge refrigerator and long table in the centre of the room. Her glance moved to the gleaming white electric range and the colossal pots and pans. How could she ever handle them, let alone fill them with meat and veg? She was silent, trying to hide her dismay.

"The power's switched on all ready for you." He was striding across the room in the direction of a meter board on the wall. "I'd better warn you, the power's likely to go off without notice. If it cuts out get in touch with the house right away. A power shortage is really the only thing you have to worry about."

All she had to worry about! Boss, you've got to be joking!

"We kill a sheep a day for meals for the shearers—" The quantity registered at last in her dazed mind. What had she taken on? She wrenched her mind back to his even tones. "You'll find meat cut up ready for you in the fridge. This lot's for lunch." Swinging open the door of the refrigerator, he revealed an enormous quantity of mutton. "And this" he indicated a great pile of chops, "will do for breakfast, with porridge of course.'

"Porridge?" she echoed weakly.

"Swags of toast—here's the pop-up toaster, with jam, honey, marmalade. You'll find it all here. And most important of the lot, tea!" He opened a cupboard door, revealing two aluminium teapots of such a vast capacity that for a moment Angela wondered if her eyes were playing tricks. Could there really be teapots of such staggering size?

"Well, that disposes of breakfast. It's got to be on the table bang on time at five-thirty. The gang gets paid by the bale and they don't believe in messing about. You can fill in time after that by running up some scones in the oven and making sandwiches, that's the usual, ready for ten o'clock smoko. Morning tea food goes into a box," he hauled a wooden crate down from a shelf, "you can take it into the shed with the teapots. The shearers plug in the electric jug and make the tea there. If you want any help get the presser to give you a hand."

Fortunately, she thought, he had turned away and wasn't aware of her bewildered expression. "After that there's lunch—cold meat's okay for that—you can shove in a roast in the morning if there's not one ready—salads, you'll find all the vegetables in the fridge. Bread and butter, lots of it—"

"And tea," she put in faintly.

"That's it! Smoko at three sharp in the afternoon. Scones and sandwiches are okay again for that." The way he tossed off scones and sandwiches anyone would think they were just nothing, she thought wildly. But that's all they were to him, mere words!

"Then for dinner," didn't a shearing gang ever stop eating? she wondered, "a big pot of stew is the usual, or a hot roast with roasted vegetables. A plum duff always goes down well afterwards. They're hearty eaters, these boys!"

"Hearty!" Angela's sensation of utter inadequacy was growing deeper with every passing minute.

How easy to say "I can't." Easy and no doubt exactly what he had been working towards all along, what he was hoping she would say. Angela squared her shoulders, took a deep breath and decided she would go down fighting.

"After that," he was saying, "they'll be off your hands. They're in bed by seven for that early start in the morning. If you have any spare time you could give the place a sweep out."

Privately Angela thought that the chances of the floor being kept clean were fairly remote.

"Well, that about covers it," he shot her a swift penetrating glance. "Think you can cope?"

Not in a thousand years! Aloud she was aware of her own voice amazingly calm saying, "Of course."

Mark's gaze went to her flimsy floral blouse and trailing skirt. "Got any cooler gear with you? It gets hot in the kitchen when the sun's shining and the shed's like an inferno when all the machines are going at top."

"Yes, I have."

"Okay then, I guess that about wraps it up for tonight. Better get yourself a good night's sleep ready for that early start tomorrow." As he closed the door behind them she became aware that twilight had faded and the soft darkness was all about them. A few faint stars pricked the luminous night sky. It was very still, the only sound a cicada piping his summer song. The next moment as she made to follow him down the short flight of steps she stumbled in her high-platform clogs and would have fallen headlong had not his arms shot out to catch her.

"Take it easy." For a timeless moment she felt herself pressed close to him. At the same time a sensation spun through her, an explosive excitement that sent the stars rocketing wildly around her.

Gently he released her. "You're not used to shearing sheds."

Nor to a man like you, she wanted to say. A man who for some reason she couldn't understand moved her to annoyance, to anger—to love? the jeering voice deep inside her whispered. Never! In silence she got back into the Land Rover.

They were drawing up at the steps of the house when lights played in an arc over the driveway and the next moment a long late-model green car came to a stop beside the Land Rover.

"Hi, Mark, it's me!" A girl with a cloud of blonde hair blowing around her shoulders leaned from the driver's seat. "I thought I'd come over—" as she caught sight of Angela the gay tones altered abruptly. "I didn't know—"

Mark climbed out of the vehicle and motioned for Angela to follow. "Susan, Angela. Miss Twentyman," he explained with cool courtesy, "is cooking for the shearers tomorrow."

"Oh, I see." After a long appraising glance contemptuously Susan dismissed her. Angela formed an impression that so far as the other girl was concerned she was no more than a part of the scenery. "I thought it must be something like that." The lovely tanned face turned to Mark. "I wanted to have a word with you about the barbecue arrangements. It's still on?"

He nodded. "Come along inside anyway." Susan linked her arm in his and they moved away. Like old-time lovers, Angela thought, following the other two towards the lighted house. All at once she felt very much alone.

When they reached the lounge room Doris came hurrying towards Angela, thrusting towards her a small gilt bedroom alarm clock. "I expect you'll want this for the morning. Good-night dear, and see you tomorrow."

It was ridiculous, Angela thought hotly, everyone expecting her to retire to bed at this hour. In her room she seated herself on the bed and mutinously kicked off her shoes, those wretched clogs that had forced her to fall into Mark's arms in the soft betraying darkness of the summer night. Because there seemed nothing else to do she got ready for sleep. It seemed hours later when, tossing restlessly beneath the single sheet that was the only covering needed on this hot night, she became aware of the splash of water, a girl's laughter, a man's deep tones.

Pulling the sheet over her ears in an attempt to stifle the sounds, she thought crossly that for the Susans of this world life meant laughter beside a cool blue pool beneath the stars. For herself there was only the cold unwinking brassy eye of the alarm clock. *It wasn't fair!*

CHAPTER FOUR

In the pre-dawn hush of early morning the alarm bell shrilled in her ear and for a moment Angela couldn't remember where she was. Then it all came back in a rush. In a panic she sprang out of bed and began pulling on a blue denim shirt and jeans. Hurrying to the bathroom, she splashed cold water over her face and ran a comb through her hair. Better tie it back behind her ears, seeing this was a work-day. She slipped her feet into the rubber thongs that seemed to be standard summer wear in this part of the world and ran down the passage.

Outside she was greeted by a chorus of birdsong echoing from the tall shelterbelt of trees behind the house. The next moment she heard the toot of a motor horn and a truck moved towards her on the driveway. Kevin's fresh young face appeared in the window opening. "Ready, Miss Twentyman? Mark says I have to take you down to the shearing shed." As she reached him he murmured shyly, "You know something? You don't *look* like a cook!"

Something about the boyish face touched her. Was it the soft childish lips? Or merely that since coming to Waikare she had found friendly faces, especially those of the masculine variety, to be a rare commodity?

She climbed up and seated herself beside him. "I'll tell you a secret. I've never done anything like this before in my life!"

He whistled under his breath. "Wowee! Are you ever going to be busy! You'll be lucky if you get the breakfast dishes done before it's time to put on the lunch. I don't want to put you off, but—"

"Don't worry," it must surely be the fresh and sparkling air that was giving her courage. "I'll get through," and she rather spoiled the effect by adding uncertainly, "somehow." After a moment she asked, "How many men are there in the shearing gang?"

"Well, there's the presser and two fleecoes. Five shearers and four rouseabouts."

"Heavens!" Angela was making a mental calculation. "That means a dozen all told."

As they came in sight of the shed streaks of flame and apricot stained the eastern sky. Kevin dropped her at the back door and she hurried inside. The kitchen was empty but the clock, her enemy for the next six days, stood ticking on a bench. Angela studied the line of switches on the electric range. Which ones would control the top elements? She wished she had asked Mark about this last night T' ere was one sure way to find out, so she turned them all on at once, then pulled a big pan from a cupboard beneath the bench and put in some dripping.

Porridge . . . porridge. She discovered a huge bag of rolled oats and began searching for printed directions, but there were none to be seen. Frantically she attempted to work out quantities in her mind. Say one cup of meal to each four men, and there were twelve men. It was no use, her brain simply refused to function efficiently today. She tipped a quantity of oatmeal into boiling water and hoped for the best.

How many chops would the gang eat for breakfast? She settled for three per man. Surely, though, that would mean a second frying pan. Was there a second pan? At last the chops sizzled merrily on the range, the porridge bubbling alongside. Thank heaven for the convenience of cut bread from the deep freeze—she could scarcely go wrong with that! She found butter, jam and honey and was placing cutlery on the table when she became aware of an ominous smell of burning. Oh *no*! She ran towards the range, but it was too late. No use worrying, the porridge would have to do, for there was no time to start over again.

She was making tea when the gang crowded in at the door. Boiling water splashed down on her hand, but she ignored the sudden smarting pain as a huge Maori man with the smiling relaxed manner of his race paused beside her. "Morning, miss. Breakfast ready yet?"

Angela raised a flushed face. "Ready and waiting!"

They took their places around the table, burly men with skins sunburned almost to the colour of mahogany and powerful muscles rippling beneath their black sweat-shirts.

By some miracle the chops were cooked in time. Indeed they had a lot of singed black edges. But the gang goodnaturedly got down to the business of eating and made no complaints, not even as they consumed the lumpy burned porridge.

Angela was pouring tea into thick china cups when a pleasant voice beside her said, "I'll pour if you like," and she looked up to meet soft brown eyes. A bearded young man took the heavy teapot from her grasp. "Better put some burn cream on your hand," he advised, "it's up there in the first aid box above your head."

"Thanks, I will." Swiftly smearing on the cream, she hurried towards the toaster. It seemed that no matter how many pieces of toast jumped up there was never enough for everyone.

"There's another toaster in the cupboard!" Her helper whipped the toaster into view and she threw him a grateful smile.

Presently the gang of shearers went out, smiling and cheerful, just as though they had enjoyed an enjoyable sustaining breakfast instead of lumpy porridge and burned chops. Angela could have wept with disappointment, only there was no time for anything but getting on with the job. Detergent frothing in hot water, greasy dishes slipped into the sink.

All at once she remembered the scones that must be ready for ten o'clock smoko. Scones . . . hadn't there been a recipe book in one of the drawers? She got it out and began measuring out quantities of flour into a great basin. Thank heaven the switches she had turned had already heated the oven. Never had she handled such a mass of dough, but at last she rolled it out and put the cut-up pieces on oven trays. As she slid the trays into the oven her arm brushed the hot surface. Another burn, deeper than the earlier one, seared her arm, but she ignored it. The important thing was that she had made the scones. Could it be the large quantity of mixture, she wondered a little later, that made the scones so utterly flat? Heavens, she'd forgotten to add baking powder! Would the gang be too hungry to notice? She knew that any attempt to make a second batch would in her present state of haste and confusion result only in her doing something even more stupid. So she concentrated instead on the preparation of sandwiches, filling bread slices with thick pieces of meat, pink salmon, crisp lettuce.

It was incredible how time could fly by so swiftly, for when she glanced towards the clock she found it was time to prepare food to take to the shed for morning smoko. Swiftly she began to transfer piles of sandwiches and buttered scones to the box, adding tea, sugar, milk, mugs. At length she staggered down the steps and took the path that led past the penned sheep held in readiness for shearing.

As she neared the wide-open doors a man's head appeared at a window opening and she heard a sudden shout, something that sounded like "DUCKS ON THE POND!" To Angela it made no sense, but she had no time to ponder the matter now.

Dust was blowing in from the roadway as she stepped inside, making her way carefully over the black and white dog sprawled across the entrance. Heat met her in a wave as she entered the scene of ceaseless activity. The air was full of the smell of fleeces as the shearers, stripped to the waist, with perspiration running down their tanned necks, bent low over the sheep from which they were shearing the thick creamy wool. Her swift glance around the big high-raftered room took in a worker who was tossing fleeces into the press, another man was leaping up and down ramming wool into place before putting the press on. The Maori rouseabout who had spoken to her this morning at breakfast was busy with a long broom sweeping up the endless litter of wool pieces on the oil-slippery floor. At that moment there was a cry of "sheepo!" and another sheep was brought in from the outside pen.

Glancing around her in search of the young man with the black beard who had been so helpful this morning, Angela saw that he was engaged in sewing up the filled bales and marking each one with the name Waikare in black stencil. From his neat appearance and the manner of his speech she would have taken him for a city man, yet here he was working to the clock every bit as hard as the rest of the gang.

Impressions chased one another through her mind, the noise of the machines, the oppressive heat, the fleeces piled in towering heaps on the floor. Then suddenly the machines were switched off and in the silence the bearded young man hurried forward and took the heavy box from her. Someone else plugged in the electric jug. Men wiped sweating shoulders with towels hanging on the door, then dropped down to take a seat on the filled bales. With the speed of long practice the tea was made and brewed and the gang thirstily gulped down the hot strong liquid.

Angela was kept busy pouring endless cups of tea, for it seemed that these men had an endless capacity for liquid. No wonder, working at speed in the heat of the shed. She realised the dark young man with the steadfast eyes had paused beside her. "How's the burn?"

"Burn?" She had forgotten such a trivial matter. "Oh, it's all right, I guess."

"It doesn't look all right." His gaze was on the red weal running up the soft skin of her arm.

"Oh, that? That's another one from the stove."

"Better put a dressing on it."

"I will when I get time."

Time . . . The men were stubbing out cigarettes and moving back towards the stands and press. The next moment the machines were switched on and a cry of "Sheepo!" went up to the man whose job it was to bring in the sheep from the pen.

Angela picked up the box that was now so much lighter than when she arrived in the shed and threading her way between the workers already busy at their tasks, made her way to the kitchen. It wasn't until she was back in the kitchen that she realised she hadn't yet finished washing the breakfast dishes, and lunch time loomed ahead. Lunch that was to consist of salad and cold meat. Cold meat! And she hadn't yet put it on to roast!

Frantically she gazed at the clock. The oven was already hot, thanks to her scone-making. Swiftly she found a baking dish, placed the massive joint in it and soon a sizzling sound from the oven told her that all was not yet lost after all. Salads . . . Long before she had finished cutting up the piles of lettuces and tomatoes her hands were stiff from the effort of holding a knife. Of all the painfully slow tasks, and when every moment was precious. It would help a lot if her fingers weren't so unsteady.

In the end she only just got the salads prepared in time before the gang arrived. The roast was barely cold, but with lashings of bread and butter at least it was a meal. Luckily the shearers made no criticism. Perhaps they were waiting in the hope that her cooking would improve with practice.

As the last man hurried out of the doorway Angela poured a cup of cold tea for herself and stared at the remains of the roast congealed in the fat and the mountain of greasy dishes. Somehow she would have to wash them before dinner time but how was she to find time for cooking and washing up? Wearily she pushed the damp hair back from her face. With only one thought in her mind—stew . . . more mutton . . . she began slicing up the vast quantities of meat, throwing in vegetables. No time to cut anything finely, they could think themselves lucky to get it. At that moment the knife slipped, cutting across a finger. It was only a small cut, but blood spurted out and she paused to wrap a strip of plaster around it.

Now she was progressing even slower. The big pots of stew were on the stove at last and she began washing piles of dishes. It seemed to take an age. Her clothes were sticking to her. She wouldn't wear jeans again in the shed, but something brief and cool. As the last dish was put away she glanced at the clock. Afternoon smoko was in thirty minutes. It just couldn't be possible . . . where had the time gone? All at once it was all too much. She couldn't go on. The red weal on her arm was beginning to throb, but it was too late now to treat it, too late for anything. Tears coursed down her hot cheeks and she dashed them away with the back of her hand.

"How are you making out down here?" enquired a hatefully

amused voice. She looked up to see Mark Hillyer standing in the doorway, an exquisitely groomed Susan at his side. The oppressive heat of the day didn't appear to make either of them look a total wreck, but then, Angela thought viciously, they hadn't been forced to spend hour after hour in this hot kitchen.

"All right." Horrified, she saw a tear splash down on to the chopping board. Right at that moment she would have given a year of her life for a handkerchief. Instead she could only sniff forlornly and wipe her eyes with her sleeve. "It's the onions . . . I've been cutting them for the stew."

Susan had moved to a wall mirror, a perfectly manicured hand raised to smooth pageboy-styled hair. "You'd think," she murmured carelessly, "that she'd be used to onions by this time. You know, you're lucky," she observed to Angela in her slightly patronising tone, "to have a place like this to work in. You should see some of the kitchens I've been in where the shearer's cook has to work. No ventilation, stoves that burn everything in sight, old wooden sink benches. Not like this."

They can have it, Angela murmured rebelliously under her breath.

Mark, after a sharp glance in her direction, went to inspect the contents of the big freezer. "Got all you need for dinner tonight?"

"Y-yes," she gulped.

"Look," he came to stand beside her, "that's a nasty burn on your arm. Better do something about it."

"I meant to."

He was reaching up to a shelf and taking down the first aid box. "Just a dressing to keep it clean." The blister had broken, leaving a raw area. He was probably thinking of his shearers and hygiene rather than her, but she let him put the dressing over the burn and had to admit that it felt a lot easier.

They only stayed a few minutes longer. Mark said, "Mustn't hold up the cook."

Alone once again Angela put a hand to her flushed forehead. Sandwiches, scones—the words beat an endless refrain in her distraught mind. By some lucky accident of calculation of the flour, sufficient scones remained, but sandwiches were another matter, unfortunately. Furiously spreading butter on to slices of bread, she thought how satisfying it would be to walk out of this stiflingly hot shed and never come back. But she must see it through for today at least. One thing, after the visit of the other two she no longer had any desire to weep, she was just plain angry!

"Hey, miss, you needing a hand around here?" A short tubby man with a shock of spiky white hair, merry blue eyes and weatherbeaten cheeks stood in the open doorway. His slacks might be tied around the waist with a piece of rope and his shirt seen better days, but to Angela at that moment he was the day's miracle and the Angel Gabriel rolled into one.

"Oh yes, *yes*!" she breathed.

The stranger gave a deep chuckle.

"Thought you might. Saw you coming in with the boss yesterday. Looks like a new chum to me, I says to myself. That girl's no shearers' cook as a rule, no sir! Know what I'm talking about, you see, girl. These days I'm the gardener and do-anything man around the place, but years ago I used to do the round of the stations cooking for shearing gangs on the big stations all over the country. No fancy grub, mind you, just plain good food, but never heard no complaints on that score!"

"They didn't complain about mine," Angela said ruefully, "but I bet they thought a lot!"

"Not them! Those blokes are too hungry to be fussy. But it sure does keep you going, having to have everything ready bang-on." He was at the range, lifting lids of pots and peering into the simmering stew. "Smells pretty good. Tell you what, you get on with the afternoon smoko stuff and I'll see about the duff."

The duff! Heavens, she hadn't even given it a thought.

"But doesn't a steamed pudding take ages to cook?"

He grinned, looking more cheerful and heartwarming than ever Angela thought. "She'll be right. Whip it up in no time at all! Where's the flour bin? This it? Good, away we go!" He had rolled up his shirtsleeves and was taking a large basin from a cupboard. "We'll give 'em jam roly-poly, that'll keep them happy. Just leave it to me, girl!"

"Oh, thank you! If you only knew what it means to me today—"

"Go on with you! I'd do more than that for a pretty girl like you."

"This is enough for me, Mr—"

"Rusty it is. On account of the colour of my hair used to be. Doesn't fit so well now." He chuckled. "Got some baking powder around here?"

Angela thought that she had never been so pleased to see anyone as this Father Christmas-like little man with the beetling white eyebrows and twinkling eyes, who was experienced in the arduous and demanding duties she had so rashly taken on. He provided too a moral support. Now that she no longer had to face the responsibility of it all she felt a lift of her spirits. Her hands ceased to tremble and the sandwiches were made faster because of it. By the time she had packed the box of food, Rusty had his roly-poly bubbling merrily in a big black dixie on the stove.

"Give me that, girl!" He took the box from her and thankfully she watched him hurry away. He might be elderly, but he was spry and alert.

While he was gone she began peeling potatoes ... and potatoes ... and potatoes. She was still at the task when he returned and gently took the peeler from her. "Down tools for a while. Pour yourself a cuppa—do you good."

Angela sank down on a stool, surprised at the utter weariness that washed over her. "Rusty, will you be here for dinner tonight?"

"Sure I will. Glad to help. Tomorrow too and the next day. Two heads are better than one, they say, and that goes for hands too!"

Presently they did the dishes together. He washed and she dried. "I remember one time when I was cooking at a station down south and the flour ran out ..." The friendly voice seemed to penetrate the waves of tiredness.

Miraculously dinner was on the table when the men, freshly showered, filed in at the door and seated themselves. They all seemed to know Rusty and chaffed him unmercifully throughout the meal. He took it all in good part and gave as good as he got. The stew Angela had made couldn't have been too bad, for it was consumed down to the last slice of onion and Rusty's roly-poly went down with gusto in spite of the many derogatory remarks made regarding his cooking prowess.

When at last the men left the room the young man with the beard lingered. There was a note of compassion in his voice as he took in Angela's wan appearance. "You're looking very fagged, Miss Twentyman. Why don't you sit down and take it easy while Rusty and I cope with the dish-washing?"

"No, it's good of you to offer, but I'm all right." She remembered the long twelve-hour working day ahead of him too tomorrow and summoned a wavering smile. "If I get really desperate I'll call on you for help."

"That's a promise!" He threw her a smile as he went out. A smile and something else, the glance of warm interest that every woman recognises. It was a pity, Angela mused, that to-night she was too tired to care.

During the following days of endless toil and frantic effort to catch up with flying minutes, she lost count of everything but the task of the moment and food, food, food. After the first nightmare day of heat and weariness she discarded jeans for a short cotton shift, sleeveless and cut low at the neck. Even then there were times, especially in the afternoons, when the heat in the kitchen became all but unbearable. Life had narrowed down to mountains of potatoes to be peeled, stacks of mutton-smeared plates and those everlasting sandwiches!

Had it not been for Rusty's timely help she couldn't have managed for even one more day. His cheerful comforting presence quietened her nervous apprehension when her gaze flew fearfully to the clock. Somehow without fuss or bother the small elderly man contrived to conjure up colossal "plum duffs" and stews and roasts, leaving Angela to bake the huge batches of scones and fill endless sandwiches. At the end of the day when the shearing gang had retired to their quarters she and Rusty would attack the dishes. After that she was too tired to think of anything but a shower and resting her aching limbs until it became time for the frantic rush to begin all over again.

Vaguely she was aware of the young man the others called John, and his friendly smile. She had a feeling he would have liked to help her, but for him too time was all too short. Nevertheless there were times during the hectic days when glancing up from her task at the sink bench she would find him regarding her, a look of sympathy lighting the dark eyes. Once he whispered to her under cover of the general conversation going on around them, "Tell me, what are your plans? Are you going on somewhere else with the gang too?"

She put him off with a light, "I don't know yet." But inwardly she shuddered. Never again would she be a shearer's cook. Let the gang find someone else to do their cooking for them—or starve!

As the days passed stress and weariness had their way with her so that she didn't think quite so much—well, not *all* the time, about Mark Hillyer, who was the cause of all this. If he hadn't challenged her, practically forcing her into the job . . . Her mind seemed to have crystallized into a single fixed idea. Stick it out. You can do it if you try! It won't be for long, for there were now only three days left, then two. Then at last the final morning broke.

As was his usual custom Rusty was waiting for her in the truck and they went to the shed together. To Angela his weather-reddened face looked even more cheerful than usual. "Well, girl, you'll get your pay tonight. Hardest work you ever put in, I'll be bound!"

She flashed her gay warm smile. "I couldn't have done it at all but for you!"

As they took the curving driveway between dew-wet lawns her thoughts wandered. Tonight she could claim her wages from the boss, prove to him that in spite of his unconcealed doubts in the matter of employing her to work with the shearing gang she had proved herself equal to the challenge. She couldn't wait to meet him again. All at once she felt herself coming to life. With suddenly heightened perception she was aware of a lightening in the sky, a breathless hush as though everything in the world waited for something that was about to happen, something unexpected and altogether wonderful. Or was that merely her own sense of relief at the end of a tough assignment? Odd to realise that this morning for the first time she would enter the shed without the usual sick feeling at the pit of her stomach, the sensation of forcing herself to cope with all but unsurmountable difficulties. A deepening flush of pink in the sky gave promise of a flawless summer day. No doubt Mark Hillyer would be enjoying it with his lovely blonde girl-friend who seemed to spend so much of her time visiting Waikare. Once or twice on returning to the homestead at the end of a hectic day, Angela had caught a glimpse of the two riding back along the track together. Probably later they enjoyed a dip in the pool, but Angela, once her head touched the pillow, fell into an exhausted sleep until morning and the laughter and voices that echoed from the blue-tiled pool no longer disturbed her.

Jill she ran into at odd times in the house. On each occasion Angela had enquired as to Brian's progress and always the answer was the same. "I think he's better, but he's not saying much yet. If only he didn't keep having those headaches . . ." All at once Angela remembered her promise to Mark that she would stay on here until Brian was sufficiently recovered for her to pass on to him Martha's message. What if she had to remain here after the weekend? She would just have to cross that particular bridge when she came to it. Somehow, oddly enough, she didn't seem to mind the thought of a delay.

At dinner that night the gang were happy and relaxed. Laughter and teasing remarks flew around the table. "Say, Miss

Twentyman," the Maori member of the gang eyed her shyly, "you coming with us to White Mountain station on Monday?"

"Sorry." Angela shook her head. "I thought Mark would have told you. For me this was just a fill-in."

"A oncer, eh?" The liquid dark eyes appeared genuinely regretful.

"Afraid so."

At that moment a chorus of men's deep voices rang out and beneath the table heavy boots stamped in unison. "We want Twentyman! We want Twentyman!"

Angela put both hands over her ears, laughing, and in the end the gang took their leave, each man taking her hand in a powerful grip and wishing her luck in her next job. Rusty they chaffed goodnaturedly about his employment as assistant cook, with emphasis on his nickname.

John was the last to leave. Lingering in the doorway, he retained her hand in his firm clasp. "Wish I could have seen something of you, but there's never been any time to ourselves, worse luck! Look, I'm staying on here for the weekend. Like to come out with me tomorrow night? We could take in a dance—"

She pulled a face. "Dance? After this week I feel I'll never be able to move again!"

"You'll feel differently tomorrow, you'll see!"

"Wherever could there be a dance around this district?"

"It's over at Te Awau, only a few miles away as the crow flies or the Land Rover goes. Say you'll come?" He was very persuasive, the brown eyes pleading, "*Please*, Angela?"

"Oh, all right, then."

His face lighted up. "Tremendous! I'll come around to the house tomorrow night and pick you up about eight." He hesitated. "There's just one thing—I'd better warn you that I haven't any transport, but if you don't mind roughing it, packing in with the rest of the gang in the truck?"

"I don't mind!" A country dance would be an experience—that was, if she recovered sufficient energy to enjoy it.

"See you tomorrow, then."

As he left her she became aware that Rusty was eyeing her, a smile crinkling his leathery face. "That's the spirit! Do you good to get out a bit, get some fresh air. Nice lad, John, you'll be all right with him."

Angela wondered why Rusty appeared to think she needed someone to look after her. The answer came unbidden. After that cooking effort of hers, no wonder!

She dropped down on to a stool. "Seems funny, John working with the shearing gang. Somehow he seems different, more like a city man. He speaks differently, a little, and he's not nearly so tanned as the others."

"Oh, it happens that way sometimes, and he's got his reasons. He's a city bloke right enough or used to be. Now he's given that away and bought a block of land up in the hills. It's a property that's never been broken in, just a sea of scrub and tea-tree. He'll need all the cash he can get together to get it cleared. That's why he's spending the summer shearing. He badly needs the money—and the experience!"

"Now I get it." For the last time Angela ran a wet mop over the linoleum on the floor.

"Heard what you told the gang about leaving," Rusty observed shrewdly. "Had enough, eh?"

"It's not exactly my thing, if you know what I mean?"

Rusty chuckled. "You did a fine job for all that. Didn't hear any complaints about the food, did you?"

Angela ran the mop beneath the table and obligingly Rusty shifted his short legs. "That was because of you, and don't pretend it wasn't! If you hadn't come along that first day I'd have—well, I just don't know what would have happened. I'd have got the sack, I guess. That reminds me, you must take half the pay. You've really earned every cent of it."

"I'll do no such thing!"

She paused, eyeing him enquiringly. "Why ever not?"

"Cause I'm being paid for it already, that's why. The boss sees to that."

The boss? A dreadful suspicion was growing in her mind. She said slowly, "Then you didn't just wander in on your own account to help me. He told you to?"

Rusty had got to his feet and was busy closing cupboard doors, turning off the refrigerator. "Part of the job. Don't thank me, thank the boss. He doesn't miss much, does Mark. Probably thought things were getting a bit beyond you. Didn't say so mind you. He just sort of suggested in a quiet way that if I wasn't too busy maybe I could lend a hand down at the shed. Not that I'm complaining. I'd have done it like a shot if I'd thought of it, but no, it was him. If you want to thank anyone you'll have to thank Mark."

"All the same . . ." But it was all too clear. The feeling of elation, of triumph and success in coping with a difficult situation, came tumbling down and once again she found herself indebted to him. Fate seemed to hand him all the advantages.

It was *his* brother who had been let down through Martha's change of heart, his shearing gang that would have been in difficulties with her inept cooking had he not come to the rescue. And Rusty actually thought she should thank *him*!

After a week of the most exhausting work Angela had ever done in her life it was sheer bliss to lie back in bed and watch a sunburst of flame lighting up the window before turning over and returning to sleep.

The next thing of which Angela was aware was a tap at the door, then a small feminine figure in a short cotton brunch coat came into the room.

"Morning!" She glanced up to see Jill's smiling freckled face. "Feel like some tea?"

"Tea? What luxury!" Angela propped herself on an elbow while the other girl perched at the end of the bed, swinging a tanned leg.

"Tell me," said Angela as she sipped her tea, "how's Brian getting along? I've scarcely seen anyone in the house to speak to all week. Is there any real improvement yet?"

"Well," Jill's light brown lashes swept down to hide her eyes, "he's a little better. Yesterday he talked to me quite a lot and he got up for a short while. I peeped in to see him just now, but he's still asleep." She sighed. "I do wish," she murmured wistfully, "that he'd hurry up and get really well. I've just got to get back to work soon. The boy they had staying is leaving and I can't leave them shorthanded." She rose and went to the window. "The men have gone out to work on number four block. Have you been over there yet?"

"No." All at once Angela felt an illogical shaft of disappointment. She had seen so little of this back country station and soon she would be leaving here for ever. She couldn't understand herself feeling so regretful, considering all she had endured during the past week. Aloud she said ruefully, "The only place I know well is the cookhouse and the shearing shed."

She was aware that Jill was eyeing her curiously. "Now the shearing's over, if you're not staying with the gang I suppose you won't be going on to the next station with them?"

"No." Clearly some explanation was due, but what could she say? "Actually I might be here for a day or so longer. Mark said something about it," she said evasively.

Caught in a web of deceit, she found herself wishing that Mark Hillyer had told his aunt and this nice young girl the real reason for her being here. Seeing he had said nothing, however, she could scarcely admit to the truth.

"Mark said you're fresh out from England." Jill's tanned fingers twisted a corner of the crocheted bedcover. "Did you come out by ship?"

"I did, actually." Breathlessly Angela awaited the question she was dreading.

It came. "I don't suppose you happened to run across a girl named—"

"Crikey, look what I've done!" Angela stared down at the tea spreading over the spread.

"Quick, here's a towel!" In the flurry of the moment the awkward moment passed, but Angela made a mental vow that she would tell both Jill and Doris the true facts just as soon as she had that talk with Brian. She found as the day went on, however, that it would not be possible for a time to bring everything out into the open.

When breakfast was over she made her way to Brian's room, but found Jill already there, the man's sweater she was knitting falling over her knees. She put a finger to her lips indicating the sleeping man and Angela tiptoed away. In the bathroom she washed her hair, then seated herself on the steps in the sunshine and began to comb out the long wet strands.

Presently the housekeeper dropped down beside her. "I forgot all about it at breakfast, Angela. I've got a message for you from Mark. He says I'm not to let you hurry away. Seems he wants you to see something of the country before you leave. He says to tell you to stick around and tomorrow he'll be free to take you for a drive in the Land Rover."

So this was to be the excuse offered to the rest of the family for her staying on at the end of the shearing. Show the English girl around the place . . . good public relations. Aloud she murmured, "Kind of you to have me."

"Nonsense, my dear! We love having folk to stay, especially someone young and pretty like you!"

She really means it, Angela thought, and felt a warm glow around her heart.

"It's funny how everyone's plans keep changing," Doris was saying, "ever since Brian came home hurt."

There was a wistful note in Doris's voice that prompted Angela to say, "How do you mean?"

"Well, one thing was Mark's study trip overseas that I told you about, exchanging ideas with the experts in other countries on wool grading, sheep farming, you know? Even if Brian had been a lot more recovered than he is he still wouldn't have been fit enough to take over the management of the station while Mark was away, especially as—" She broke off and in answer to Angela's enquiring look went on after a moment, "It's just that Brian isn't really interested in the job here and never has been. Oh, he's been brought up on the station, he knows the work and he's stronger than he looks. He and Mark have a fairly satisfactory arrangement on the place really. Mark looks after the stock, all the sheep and black steers you see around on the paddocks, and Brian takes care of the agricultural side of things, sees to the boundary fences and keeps the bridges in order. But without Mark to depend on he'd be lost in an emergency and he's not much of a hand at handling staff."

Doris smiled. "I suppose it's because he's entirely different from his brother. Maybe the trouble is that Mark has always taken the full responsibility for Waikare and Brian's got into the habit of depending on him. Of course he's much younger. Mind you," she ran on, "it could have something to do with the boys' parents being killed in a car smash when the children were quite young. Brian was only five years old at the time and Jill—they'd taken her into the family by then—was a tot of three. Oh, the children were looked after well enough, relatives came to the rescue and saw to that. Every time I came over here on a visit to the homestead I used to notice how Mark seemed to have taken over the special care of his brother. Guess it's just got to be a habit."

Angela nodded. She was thinking that she had already come up against Mark Hillyer's protective attitude towards his kid brother, to her cost. On another level her thoughts were busy with the woman seated beside her on the step in the sunshine. Angela asked, "Was that the only difference Brian's accident made to other folks' plans around here? I mean, Mark having to cancel his overseas study trip?"

Doris's smile was wry. "Wasn't that enough?" Her lips drooped and Angela caught the shadow in the grey eyes. She said gently, "Not you too?"

"How did you guess?" Doris turned towards her. "I'm trying not to think about it too much, but it's my daughter," she ran on in a burst of confidence. "She's all I've got and she lives down in Christchurch in the South Island. She and her husband Jim are expecting a new baby, it's due any day now. I'm just *longing* to see it! I had everything arranged to go down to Christchurch just before the baby came and stay for a month. It would have given Eve a chance to do nothing but look after the wee girl. She's got three boys already, all steps and stairs, but this time it'll be a girl. It's just *got* to be!"

Angela laughed. "How do you mean 'got to be'?"

"It's myself I'm thinking about mostly," Doris confessed, "all this pink knitting I've done each time a new baby is expected down there. Jackets, leginette sets, bonnets with silk ribbons, candy pink cot covers embroidered in tiny rosebuds . . . I've a drawer in my bedroom simply crammed with them, all waiting to be used."

"And you still think-pink and keep hoping?" Angela enquired incredulously.

"Of course. Isn't there something to do with a law of averages?" Doris enquired vaguely.

"I wouldn't bet on it!"

"Well, anyway, I've just finished sewing the buttons on a dream of a peach-coloured angel-frock with panties to match. I meant to take it with me when I went south. Now," she said on a long sigh, "I guess it will just have to be posted instead."

"You're not making just one little blue set? Just in case?" Angela pursued.

"Well," Doris admitted reluctantly, "I did run up a little white jacket and a pair of blue-and-white booties, but," with renewed optimism, "I'm sure I won't need them this time. Actually," she went on in a worried tone, "it's Eve I'm thinking about more than myself, though I'm awfully disappointed over not going to see her. She and Jim run a tourist motel. She's such a busy person, especially right at the height of the tourist season, and always so cheerful and bright. I just wish . . ." her voice trailed disconsolately away.

Impulsively Angela sent her a warm smile, said happily, "Doris, don't post that pink baby set. You might be able to take it down to the South Island after all. I happen to be out of a job, you need someone to fill in for a few weeks. So why can't I stay on for a while and let you get away?"

An expression of excitement lighted Doris's eyes. "Brian doesn't really need me especially. All he wants is someone in the house to cook meals, look in on him occasionally when Jill goes back to the farm tomorrow."

"That is," Angela reminded her, "if the rest of the staff can put up with my cooking. Just plain food and no frills, shearing-gang style. So long as the men don't mind?"

The menfolk, and one man in particular! Mark Hillyer with his sardonic smile and "the cold blue Hillyer eyes". What was she saying? But it was already too late for regrets, for Doris was eyeing her in delighted amazement. "Would you, Angela, would you *really*? I can't think why I didn't think of that solution to the problem myself."

Angela said hesitantly, "The boss—he won't mind?"

"Mark?" It was clear to Angela that Doris's thoughts were already far away in Christchurch. "Heavens, no, why should he? He was real worried about my having to cancel that plane booking last week."

"Enough to put up with me for another month, do you think?"

"Of course! He'll be delighted! You'll see when I tell him the news!"

Somehow Angela entertained some reservations on that score. She wondered if Doris would feel so confident regarding the boss's reaction to the plan were she to be aware of Mark Hillyer's private opinion of "Martha's friend". She brought her mind back to Doris's animated tones. "I'll tell Mark about this idea the moment he comes in—or would you rather talk to him yourself?"

Angela shook back the shining curtain of burnished copper that fell around her shoulders. Her eyes had a wicked glint. "I'll tell him. He can scarcely refuse, it's such a wonderful chance to let his aunt get away. He'll have to put up with me and my cooking! He won't be pleased, but he'll have to make the best of it!" She could scarcely wait to get her revenge for all she'd been forced to endure at his hands during the last few days.

"You came out from England just a short while ago?" Doris was saying.

Angela nodded.

"All the more reason for you to stay on here and see something of Waikare before you go." Angela breathed a sigh of relief that the question she was dreading hadn't been asked. If only she hadn't complicated her life with Martha's affairs!

In the afternoon Jill was still with Brian. Angela washed out some of her garments and hung them on the line where the wind from the hills billowed them out. A little later in the comfortably furnished lounge room with its deep leather chairs and great stone fireplaces, Doris showed her the spinning wheel standing in a corner of the room, the black fleeces she had spoken of heaped beside it.

"You do a lot of spinning?" Angela asked.

"Oh, yes, it's a hobby of mine. Last year at a show in Whangarei the team I was in won the competition. It was a contest to see who could be the first to finish knitting a garment right from the sheep's wool. I was hoping to compete in the show this year, only—"

"You couldn't make it?"

Doris shook her head regretfully. "Not with Brian just back from hospital that day. It was just unlucky for me that the show happened to be on in that particular week."

Blame Martha, Angela mused despairingly. Somehow it seemed that everything of an unpleasant nature that had happened here recently always came back to Martha. She pushed the disquieting thoughts aside and said brightly, "Oh, by the way, I've had an invitation to go out tomorrow night. John's asked me to a dance that's being put on somewhere or other. The others in the gang are going too."

Doris looked a little taken aback. "They've only got their old bomb," she said with a worried air, "and it's always breaking down in the most inconvenient places on the road. Oh they always manage to get it mobile again in the end, but with them you can never be certain what time you'll arrive at your destination or get home again."

Angela smiled her warm friendly smile. "I'll take a chance on it! One thing, it will be an experience going with the gang."

Doris looked doubtful. "I suppose," she murmured uncertainly, "you could put it that way."

CHAPTER FIVE

During dinner that evening Angela made little contribution to the general conversation. She was content to listen as voices echoed around her. Jill speaking wistfully of Brian. "If only it wasn't for those headaches of his he'd be up and about as usual by now." Kevin the young farm hand, querying Mark regarding his work on the station, gazing towards him with a trusting expression as though, Angela thought, the boss knew the answer to absolutely everything. Mrs. Blackman chatting about the departure of the shearing gang in the morning and the possibility of the big golden peaches that were ripening in the orchard being ready for bottling before long.

Once during the meal the telephone shrilled through the room and Mark, excusing himself, went to answer the call. In the sudden stillness his monosyllabic replies were plainly audible. "Yes, okay. See you tonight, then. Bye, Sue." Angela gathered from the one-sided conversation that his blonde girl-friend was asking Mark to take her somewhere this evening. He scarcely seemed enthusiastic over the arrangement and she found herself wondering if perhaps the feeling between them was all on the girl's side.

In her room a little later as she got ready for the evening's entertainment she was glad that she had brought her entire wardrobe, such as it was, with her. Not that she need dress up particularly for the country gathering, nevertheless . . . She chose the flaring emerald green skirt and pulled over her head a black short-sleeved sweater, then clasped around her neck the long silver chain with its silver medallion. She had pinned her hair back from her face and soft and clean and gleaming the mass of auburn flowed over her shoulders. John had been right when he had told her that it needed only one good night's sleep to make even a shearers' cook feel as good as new!

Angela bent to turn the switch of her tiny transistor and dance music flooded the room. She moved to the beat, her green skirt swirling around her ankles, then suddenly she paused, struck by a thought. What if the boss too happened to be at the dance tonight? He'd feel duty bound to ask her for a dance! For some reason she couldn't understand the thought sent her mind flying into wild turmoil. But she could always refuse him. What a wonderful opportunity it would be to get a little of her own back for all she had gone through in the hot shed during the past few days. His sardonic "You did offer?" pricked at her mind, but she thrust the remembrance aside. How he must have enjoyed watching her frantic efforts to see the job through at all costs. Fair enough, he'd be thinking, she asked for it—forcing herself in here, lying to me.

She could feel herself growing angry all over again. No, definitely she wouldn't dance with him, not even if he were to get down on bended knees and plead with her. The mental picture the thought evoked was so utterly ridiculous that she switched off both the dance music and the wild fantasies in her mind. A glance at her wristwatch told her she was a little early, but no matter. She sauntered along the passage and made her way out to the shadowed porch.

Outside the air was crystal-clear, perfumed with the great white blossoms that starred the long tendrils of mandevillia clinging to the end wall. Leaning on the railing watching a fat orange moon as it made a dramatic entrance over the dark ranges, at first she didn't notice the glow of a cigarette in the shadows. Then a man moving along the path directly below paused. Even though she couldn't glimpse his expression she just knew the disconcerting way in which Mark Hillyer would be regarding her. She was directly beneath the overhead bulb and the light burnished the dark auburn of her hair and struck shafts of silver in the medallion swinging on its long chain from her throat.

"Waiting for someone?"

"Yes, I am, actually. John—" Why did she feel she had to explain herself? Her social outings had nothing to do with him. Nevertheless . . . "The presser in the shearing gang, you know? He asked me to go along to the dance with him tonight." His silence was making her feel oddly confused. She heard herself adding stupidly, "He said I'd know when he comes. Seems the old bomb makes such a racket you can hear it miles away!"

"You're not going in that truck." He made the statement quite matter-of-factly as though there weren't the slightest doubt in the matter.

"Why ever not?" she asked quickly. "What's wrong with it?"

"Everything, just about. John should never have asked you to go along in that. I credited him with a bit more sense."

"It's not his fault," she argued. "He hasn't any transport of his own. Anyway, I promised! I said I'd go!"

"That's all right, then. I'll take you. You'll be a whole lot safer with me in the Land Rover."

Well! Angela didn't know how to answer him. He seemed to have a knack of rendering her speechless every now and again. All she could summon up was a faint, "Is it far from here?"

"Far enough. A place like Te Awau," he pointed out grimly, "mightn't seem more than a step or so in a decent car or truck, but in that old jalopy of the shearers . . . Besides—" He broke off, regarding her with a look she couldn't interpret.

"Besides?"

The moon emerging at that moment from a bank of cloud let her in on his lopsided grin. It wasn't what you could call a carefree smile. It was more in the nature of sardonic amusement at her expense—as usual. "Just that I happen to be going to Te Awau myself tonight. Be my guest. You and your boy-friend can come along with me."

Nervously she twisted a long coppery strand around her finger. "He's not my boy-friend. And anyway, he might not want to."

"He'll come." He was so hatefully sure of himself. "Make no mistake, if he wants to get you there he'll have to! Don't expect anything grand," he was speaking as though the matter of transport were already decided. "It's just a country hop—a banjo and a couple of guitars for music, Mum and Dad and all the kids there as well. But if you really want to go—"

"I told John I'd go with him," Angela repeated mulishly.

"Right, I'll get out the Land Rover." As Mark moved out of a pool of shadow she realised that he had changed into lightweight slacks, a white polo-necked sweater, dark reefer jacket.

All at once she remembered the telephone conversation of earlier in the evening. He had arranged to meet Susan at the dance. *Meet* her there—how strange. He certainly seemed most casual in his courtship of the blonde girl. Perhaps, though, Susan lived in the vicinity of the district where the dance was to be held. It still seemed an odd arrangement up here in the hills where vast distances were usual and no one appeared to think twice of a forty-mile drive over rugged country roads.

At that moment, a loud rumbling and clanking noise heralded the arrival of a battered old open truck. As Angela glanced towards the cheerful crowd squeezed in at the back of the vehicle she couldn't help but be grateful towards her employer for rescuing her from an uncomfortable journey. To her surprise John too appeared relieved that Angela had been offered more reliable transport. A little later to loud remarks, chaffing and laughter, the ancient truck with a last loud explosion took off in the direction of the main road.

Doris and Jill wandered out to the porch to see them off. It seemed to Angela that Jill's eyes held a wistful expression. Was she regretting that she and Brian too were not climbing into the Land Rover to dance the night away as no doubt they would have, had it not been for Martha?

Soon Angela found herself seated once more beside her unwilling escort, tucking her long skirt around her while John took a seat in the rear of the vehicle. At least on this occasion John would be on hand to open and close the gates on the property. They gained the main highway and sped up a road winding over dark hills. Around the first bend they came in sight of a truck labouring up the rise and to derisive hoots and calls, swept past the old vehicle.

The two men made desultory conversation about the week's shearing and Angela lapsed into silence. The terms they used conveyed little to her, for it seemed as though these back-country sheep farmers spoke a language of their own. The thought prompted her to say suddenly, "There's something I want to know about the shearing. I asked the gang about it," she added in her soft husky tones, "but they wouldn't tell me."

"No harm in asking." Mark's voice was laconic, his eyes fixed on the road ahead as he guided the vehicle around a sharp tree-lined bend.

"All right, then. It was that first morning when I brought the tea up to the men at smoko time and I heard one of them call out something. It sounded to me like 'ducks on the pond', but it couldn't have been," she glanced uncertainly towards the man at her side, "could it?"

Mark broke into laughter and John joined in with him. Puzzled, Angela glanced from one to the other. One thing, she told herself, she'd made Mark laugh out loud, and that was certainly a triumph seeing that up till now he had treated her with either cool politeness or grim-lipped contempt. "You two might let me in on the joke," she complained. "What's so funny?"

Recovering himself at last Mark said, "What the gang were doing was passing on a message. Something to the effect of 'Hey, boys, woman cook's on the doorstep. Better watch your language'."

"Is that all?" Angela couldn't help laughing too. "You mean, fair warning?"

"Something like that."

Her spirits rose and for a moment she imagined that Mark had decided to revise his initial opinion of her and treat her just as he would any other visitor to the homestead. But a quick sideways glance towards his set profile as he gazed ahead told her all too clearly that he had been sharing a joke with John and that was all. To the boss she was and always would be someone not to be trusted.

The moon climbed high above cloud and the miles fell away behind them. Now there was nothing in the world except the blurred shapes of high hills all around, no sound but the whirring of tyres on rough metal and the plaintive "more-pork" of a native owl somewhere in the dark bush.

They came on the woolshed suddenly, a long lighted building standing in a clearing by the roadside. To Angela it appeared little different from the one in which she had recently spent so many arduous hours. Trucks, cars and Land Rovers were parked at odd angles on the grass and as Mark swung the vehicle alongside a gleaming late-model car a girl who was seated at the wheel tooted a horn. The next moment Susan's smiling face was thrust from the open window.

"Thanks." Angela turned to Mark, but with a brief nod he had turned away. When she glanced back a few moments later he and Susan were standing beside the car. The girl was talking animatedly to him, her face raised to his, her hand laid on his arm.

Angela thought irritatedly, Why must she cling to him so tenaciously? Habit, possessiveness, *fear of a rival?*

"Come on," John was saying, helping her to pick her way in her fragile black sandals over ground deeply rutted from the trampling of cattle in the winter rains.

As they moved into the shed her swift glance took in the high rafters intertwined with coloured streamers and gay crepe paper flowers. Great punga ferns plucked from the bush sprayed their fronds from corners of the room and the long line of the walls was broken by logs and trailing greenery.

Her gaze moved towards a makeshift stage made of piled haybales where two Maori youths strummed guitars and a third plucked the strings of a banjo. There were people everywhere, she mused, as John piloted her through groups and family parties. Girls and men moved on the crowded dance floor slippery from the oil of the fleeces, and children skated around the edges or mingled with the dancers, their small faces puckered and tense in concentration. It looked as though everyone were having a lot of fun, she told John as they joined the maze of figures keeping time with the pulsing lilt. Moving to the infectious throbbing of the guitars, she thought how strange it seemed to hear Maori players in a far-away farming district in New Zealand beating out pop recordings that had recently topped the hit parade charts in London. But of course radio and television brought music to the other hemispheres only a short time after the tunes had gained popularity in London, New York and other great cities of the world.

Among the crowd on the dance floor she recognised two of the shepherds from Waikare with their young wives. Occasionally in a gap in the crowd she caught glimpses of the other members of the shearing gang, scarcely recognisable now they had discarded their black sweatshirts and tough slacks for gay coloured shirts and lightweight longs. Their friendly grins told her they bore no illwill over hectic efforts to get them fed on time, so she couldn't have done so badly after all, thanks to Rusty's help. Or should she thank the boss, even though no doubt he had ordered Rusty's assistance for reasons of his own? For how could a shearing gang proceed without their cook?

Since their arrival at the woolshed she hadn't seen Mark. Was he still outside the hall with Susan? At that moment she caught sight of them both on the dance floor. There was no doubt that Mark was a faultless dancer. He would be, she thought uncharitably. He was the type of man who would do well everything that he attempted—even when it came to hating her! And why on earth must she keep thinking of him all evening, peering through thc scintillating throng in scarch of him, wondering if he would ask her to dance? The shearers' cook? Martha's friend? She must be dreaming.

For a long time John was her partner, then the music changed to an old-time tempo. Angela had taken lessons in ballroom dancing, but John told her regretfully that he had never mastered it. She was swept away into the Paul Jones by a burly young farmer with a red face and a shy expression. Intent on his footwork, he did not utter a word, then all at once the beat of the music changed and he released her to join in with the moving chain circling the big room. As she whirled from partner to partner she looked always for Mark, wondering if she would find herself swept into his arms at any moment and what it would be like to dance with someone who despised you. She need not have concerned herself, however, in the matter, for as the various partners claimed her for the dance and released her at the change of tempo she realised that he was not amongst them. Perhaps he hadn't ever learned old-time dancing and being the boss would never attempt it were he not proficient, flawless. There she went, dwelling on him again!

Presently the infectious rhythm of a modern number rang out

and Angela watched Mark and Susan move on to the floor. The girl's glittering gold dress seemed moulded to her lithe body, her ash-blonde hair floated in a cloud behind her as she swayed to the melody. A golden girl, was that the way he thought of Susan? One thing was for sure, it wasn't exactly the way in which he thought of Angela. "I was told to look out for a girl with red hair". Oh well, everyone couldn't be fortunate enough to be born one of the Susans of the world with every single thing they could wish for right at their fingertips, including Mark Hillyer.

The music crashed to a crescendo and long trestle tables were carried in at the wide open doors, tables laden with such a varied assortment of home-made goodies that Angela regarded the heaped up plates of food in amazement. So this was the Pavlova, the traditional New Zealand dessert she had heard so much about, this delicate snowy mound piled with whipped dairy cream and decorated with strawberries and pineapple slices or circles of some pale silvery-green fruit that was new to her. There were meats and pizzas, curries heaped in beds of rice, delectable seafood, savouries in small pastry cases, oysters and scallops. The selection seemed endless.

Afterwards the tables laden with cups and saucers and empty plates were carried away, the Maori musicians resumed their places on the makeshift stage and the dreamy strains of the waltz "Some Day, My Love" stole through the big room. One of the players younger than the others got to his feet, his soft Maori accents taking up the haunting melody.

A voice said softly, "Dance?" and Angela turned to find Mark at her side. How could he have approached without her noticing? And how mistaken she had been in imagining that he might not be familiar with this style of dancing. This wasn't just dancing, it was heaven, it was something wildly exciting yet deeply satisfying. She was scarcely aware of other couples whirling around them. Once a face met her glance, eyes stormy, lips tightly compressed, and Angela returned to earth with a bump. Susan stood alone on the fringe of dancers watching her. Probably the other girl had never bothered to master the intricacies of the waltz and was annoyed with anyone who had. The next moment Angela had forgotten her.

"I didn't think you'd know the waltz—"

She laughed softly. "I thought the same about you!"

Did she imagine it, or had his arm tightened around her waist? This wasn't just a waltz, it was movement and music and magic all mixed up with a Maori lad's heart-catching tones. It all added up to a wild and potent happiness. She had never known she could feel like this!

When the soft strains drew to a close it was a moment before she could bring herself back to earth sufficiently to master her runaway emotions. Mark released her and flushed and bright-eyed, she gazed up at him. "That was super!"

"Glad you enjoyed it." Nothing could have been more formal, more off-putting than his tone. In silence she went with him from the dance floor.

She became aware that John was making his way through the groups gathered at the edge of the oil-slippery floor. After a short time the music broke out again to the foot-tapping rhythm of "Raindrops are Falling". Somehow, though, for Angela the high excitement of the evening had dulled and she went through the movements of the dance almost unconsciously. Against her will her gaze strayed towards Mark. He was standing with a group of bronzed young farmers near the entrance, apparently deep in conversation. When the number ended he made his way towards her and John.

"Had enough? Feel like taking off now?"

She saw a shadow of disappointment pass over John's steadfast face, but he had no option but to agree. She realised that Mark's enquiring gaze was turned towards her. "How about you, Twenty?"

"I'm ready to go if you are!" It was true. She might as well admit that since that one dance with him everything had gone flat. He had spoilt her for other partners, no use denying it. She was, however, a little surprised at his not waiting until the end of the function. The dance looked like going on for hours yet, probably until morning. Surely Susan would be disappointed at this cavalier treatment. The thoughts flew wildly through her mind. Perhaps the other girl was accustomed to his deserting her, or could it be they had quarrelled?

Moonlight flooded the hills as they swept along the deserted roads. Angela was already beginning to recognise familiar landmarks along the way, a conical shaped hill, a particularly hazardous bend. John leaned forward making desultory conversation, but for the most part Mark was silent, his gaze fixed on the fragment of curving roadway illuminated in the arc of the headlamps. At last they rattled over a cattle-stop and took the winding driveway leading to the homestead. The shepherds' bungalows and shearers' quarters were in darkness, but in the house a porch light glimmered faintly through the trees.

Mark dropped John off at the shearers' quarters. For a moment he hesitated, looking uncertainly towards Angela. "I wanted to ask you," then, evidently aware of Mark's presence, muttered awkwardly, "See you soon," and closed the heavy door behind him.

As they went on Angela got ready to open the gates in the glow of the headlamps. How quickly she had become accustomed to the duties expected of her in this alien life. At last Mark ran the car into the open garage and went with her up the steps and into the back porch. Still in silence he flung open the back door and pressing a light switch, preceded her into the hall.

Belatedly it came to her that she hadn't yet mentioned to him her idea of relieving Doris in the house for a time. Whatever had become of that plan of revenge of hers? Somehow it didn't seem to matter any more. Tonight she couldn't think about anything clearly, she was too suffocatingly *aware* of him. If only he didn't guess at her feelings!

They reached her room and she paused at the door. "Well, goodnight. And thanks for taking me . . . I mean us . . . to the dance tonight."

"My pleasure—Oh, Twenty, one moment. There's something I wanted to see you about. Come on in here, will you?" As he spoke he strode ahead, moving into the lounge room and switching on the table lamp with its red shade. "Won't keep you long."

Slowly she followed him into the room. What now?

Mark picked up a pipe from the mantel and said carelessly, "That's a long thirsty drive back from Te Awau. How about some coffee?"

Coffee! She might have known that was all he required of her. Unconsciously she sighed. "I'll get it." In the kitchen she plugged in the electric jug and reached up to a shelf for instant coffee and the Irish pottery beakers. Then she went back to ask him, "Black or white?"

He paused in the act of lighting his pipe. "Black for me, thanks."

Angela preferred it that way herself and soon she carried the tray into the lounge room. Music echoed softly from the stereo and she recognised songs from one of the German operas. She seated herself on a leather pouffe, the emerald skirt falling around her ankles. Cupping her hands around the beaker, she glanced across at Mark, lying back relaxed in a shabby wing chair. Something about the expression in his blue eyes was definitely . . . disturbing. With an effort she wrenched her gaze aside. She said in a rush of words, "What did you want to see me about?"

"Oh, that." He appeared content to stay there for hours. "Just that Brian still seems a bit groggy, not really fit for much. So how about your staying on here, waiting a bit longer before you make that confession of yours to him?"

"It's not a confession," she protested, tight-lipped.

"No?" Irony tinged his voice, but she let that pass. There was no sense in letting him rile her all the time. Besides, she had her own news for him in that direction.

"There's something I wanted to ask you about too. I had an idea—"

"An idea?"

"Yes, that is, I mean Mrs. Blackman was telling me how disappointed she is at not being able to get away to look after her daughter in the South Island when the new baby arrives, and I thought that maybe . . ." Heavens, this wasn't coming out at all the way she had planned it. She sounded as though she were pleading with him to let her stay instead of the other way around. She took a deep breath and floundered on. "I could stay here and look after things. Just," she added hurriedly, "until Doris gets back." What if he took this to be a typical "Martha" proposition? A trick to work her way in here and eventually marry the boss, or his younger brother?

He was regarding her in a lazy inattentive way, but she knew he missed nothing. "What did Doris think of the scheme?"

"Mrs. Blackman? Oh, she was so *pleased*! I think she started packing her suitcase the moment I left her."

"Right! In that case you can consider yourself hired, Twenty, as from now. Temporary housekeeper for the duration!"

"Thank you." Once again their glances met and held and she heard herself rushing into speech, anything to break the dangerous moment of silence. "There's something else too . . . thanks for sending Rusty down to the cookhouse to help me in the shed. You know something," she ran on in her soft husky tones, "just at first I thought it was his own idea, that he'd taken pity on my ignorance and decided to come to the rescue."

Mark got to his feet and began to knock the ash from his pipe. "Just a matter of expediency. No meals ready for the shearers means no clip!" His expressionless tone chilled her.

"Yes, I understand all about that now." She gathered up the beakers and placed them on the tray. "You'll let me know about your brother?"

"Don't worry, Twenty, I'll keep in touch. A day or two

should make all the difference."

Once again he was aloof and distant, very much her employer. Well, that suited her too. Definitely she must have imagined that moment on the dance floor when he had seemed to draw her close to him. Glancing towards his set features, she thought that nothing could have been further from his mind.

Still she hesitated. There was a question she must ask, something she must know if she were to continue staying here at the homestead. She said very low, "Why didn't you tell the others?"

"About Martha, you mean?" His voice was steel. "Why should I? It's up to Brian, his business, nothing to do with anyone else. Personally I reckon he's taken a stiff enough knock without adding to it. He always was a sensitive touchy sort of guy. He'd loathe knowing that folks around here were pitying him for the way he's been let down. While things go along as they are anything could have happened to Martha to delay her, stop her keeping that appointment with him. Illness, accident, a thousand different things. But once you come out with your little story he hasn't even got that shred of self-respect to fall back on. He'd feel he was a laughing stock at the station. No, best to leave things the way they are for the moment."

Angela looked unconvinced. "But what," she persisted stubbornly, "if he tells someone else?" It was a possibility that had niggled uneasily at her mind ever since she had suggested to Doris that she could fill in while the housekeeper was absent from the house.

"He won't! He'd be too darned self-conscious about the whole affair to breathe a word about it to anyone."

"He might. He might confide in Jill."

"Jill?" Mark bent on her the searching look she had come to dread. "Why would he do that?"

"Why not? She's in love with him." Angela bit back the words. Let him discover the truth for himself, if it were the truth. Or was that too merely her own imagination?

She turned away and immediately his laconic tones jerked her back to awareness. "Just a word of advice, Twenty, now that you're staying on for a bit. About John—"

She swung around, staring bewilderedly over her shoulder. "I don't need any advice about him."

"You're dead wrong there, Twenty! John's a nice guy, I'll give you that, but chasing all over the country in the shearing gang's jalopy could land you in a heap of trouble. And that includes getting yourself stranded miles from civilisation with no way of getting back. Better stay put while you're here, hmm?"

The hot colour flooded her cheeks, but she was so angry she didn't care. "Don't worry, Mr. Hillyer," she said tensely, "I've no intention of running off with anyone! You'll get your meals served on time every single day I'm here!"

She might just as well not have spoken.

"The name's Mark, remember?" He heaved himself up from the depths of the chair. "Glad we've got that little lot sorted out. 'Night, Twenty!"

"Good *night*!" Had she not had both hands fully occupied with the tray she would have slammed the door behind her—hard!

It was at breakfast time the next morning that an excited Jill proclaimed that at last Brian was acting and talking like his old self again. The small freckled face was radiant with relief. "No more headaches. I don't mind so much having to go back to the farm now that he's so much better!" She turned towards Doris. "You won't need to look after your patient any more! He tells me he's getting up today. Isn't it *super*?"

As Angela's anxious glance flew to the man seated at the head of the table she met his challenging look. His message registered as plainly as spoken words, "Right, Twenty, get on with it!" All at once the toast and marmalade she had been enjoying turned to sawdust in her mouth. She told herself that she would get the unpleasant duty over and done with as soon as possible, and as the others finished their meal she seized her opportunity.

Turning towards Doris, she said, "I'll collect Brian's tray."

Doris sent her a twinkling glance. "Are you sure Jill will let you?"

Jill answered with a beaming smile. "I'll give you five minutes and if you're not back here by then I'm coming right in to investigate. Trouble is, he always did have that weakness for red hair!"

The words fell into a pool of silence and hastily Angela rushed into speech. "I'm on my way, then!" Excusing herself from the table, she hurried along the passage and into her room taking a bulky envelope from a bureau drawer. A few moments later she knocked on a closed door.

"Come in." The man lying back on pillows raised a curly brown head from the magazine he held in his hand. He regarded her with surprise. "Oh, hi! Who are you?"

"That's what I've come to tell you." Angela dropped lightly down at the end of the bed. "I was cooking with the shearing gang last week." If only, she thought on a wave of longing, it were as simple as that!

"Crikey!" The pale rather shortsighted eyes regarded her in amazement. "Mark told me he had a girl jacked up for the job, but you—Oh well, I guess you can put it down to experience. Hope you don't mind my saying this, but if anyone had asked me I'd have said you were fresh out from England. You've got that look about you, that complexion doesn't belong out here."

She tried to infuse a light inflection into her tone. "You could be right at that." For something to say she enquired, "What were you reading when I came in, a farming manual?"

"Come off it!" The wry twisted grin put her in mind of his more forceful brother. "When I feel like reading, and that's most of the time, it's for pleasure, not work—tell me, do you go for poetry?"

Angela nodded, striving to wrench her thoughts from her own immediate problem.

"Me too." Brian didn't seem at all shy with her, she thought in surprise. The answer came unbidden. No doubt he was regarding her in the light of shearers' cook rather than a not unattractive girl, *like his brother*.

She realised he was eyeing her thoughtfully. "Ever get home-sick for England?" he asked.

She laughed.

"I haven't had time yet."

He was thumbing through the slim book he had put down when she appeared in the room. "I was just reading a few lines written by a Kiwi living on the other side of the world. Guess it takes an expatriate to really pull out the stops when it comes to making you feel a real longing for your own country. This was taken from a *New Zealand News* of a few years back." In the turmoil of her mind Angela was scarcely aware of the light tones.

> "The tui sings in the kowhai tree
> On the other side of the world from me,
> Yet if I say so here folk stare
> Not knowing how it is out there."

"How does that grab you?"

She had only half heard the words. "Yes, I can see what you mean."

"Bet you're glad you're done with the shed for a while—or have you?" The pale eyes regarded her with a puzzled look. "What did you say your name was?"

"I didn't!" She took a deep breath and plunged in to the words that must be said. "I'm Angela, Angela Twentyman.

Actually I've only been in the country for a few weeks. I . . . came out on the *Ocean Monarch* with Martha Stanaway. Didn't you two used to correspond with each other?"

"Martha!" At the light that sprang into his eyes her spirits plummeted. How could she dash his hopes like this? Yet somehow she must. In this one instance she had to admit that Mark had been right in advising her to make the news of Martha a clean-cut blow. Even if it were a blow to the heart! Aware that he was regarding her intently, she forced herself to go on. "Martha couldn't come here to see you herself, but she asked me to give you a message. She said" . . . avoiding his eyes . . . "that I was to tell you she was . . . sorry . . . about everything. And I was to give you this." She laid on the bed-cover the thick envelope. As she took in his stricken expression she said in a low tone, "Would you rather be on your own? I mean—"

"It's okay." Brian's voice was thick. Listlessly he shook from the packet a small square box. He snapped the catch, then closed it again. "Well, thanks anyway," he murmured awkwardly, and sliding down on the pillows turned his face to the wall.

"I'm sorry." She seemed to be always saying "I'm sorry" to someone, she thought miserably as she went out of the room.

In the kitchen she found that the men had left and gone out into the sunshine of the yard. Doris was singing softly to herself as she cleared dishes from the table. As they washed up together at the sink Doris launched happily into a description of her daughter and son-in-law, appeared not to notice Angela's preoccupied expression. The question hammered in her brain. What if the shock of her news had affected the injured man, set him back in health? Perhaps she ought to have waited another day, perhaps—

"What did you say to him?" Both women looked up in surprise as Jill hurried into the room, her small round face flushed and eyes bright with anger.

"Say to him?" Angela was playing for time.

"It was something you told him, I know it was! He looks dreadful, white as a sheet, and he was getting along so well! All he would tell me was something about a message!"

Doris threw her an exasperated look. "Oh, Jill, don't be so stupid! How could Angela have upset Brian? She scarcely knows him."

"Doesn't she?" A dawning suspicion was growing in Jill's eyes. She flung around to face Angela. "You were on the *Ocean Monarch* and that was the ship that Martha girl came out from England on, or was supposed to."

Angela had never been the slightest bit clever at hiding her feelings. She could feel the colour hot on her cheeks.

"That's it," Jill cried, "you knew her! You were a friend of hers! *She sent you here, didn't she?*"

"Yes, but—"

"There you are!" Jill's tone was triumphant as she swung around towards Doris. "I told you! All that about getting a job here was just something to pull the wool over our eyes. All you wanted," she threw a furious glance towards Angela, "was an excuse to get in here to make things worse than ever for poor Brian!"

"I didn't! I didn't!" Angela dried a soup bowl for the third time. "It wasn't like that at all! If you'd only let me tell you—" She rushed on before Jill could stop her and misunderstand the position even more. At least Angela would make her *know*. "It's true we were on the ship together and we used to know each other, all the young ones did, but she didn't say a word to me about coming to Waikare to be married to Brian. I hadn't the faintest notion."

Jill's sceptical young face hardened. "But you did come here with a message for Brian?"

"I know, I know but it wasn't like you think. If you'd only *try* to understand." She was getting very weary of proffering this explanation that no one appeared to take seriously, but she forced herself to go on. "I don't care whether you believe me or not, but this is the way it happened. I happened to meet Martha Stanaway again by accident, she was on the same bus as I was coming north and we got to talking. I told her I was on the look-out for a job on a sheep station in the North Island and she put me on to this place. She said she had been offered work here and had changed her mind about coming. She had intended stopping off at Waikare to explain why she wasn't interested in the job. She said that if I liked I could take it on instead."

"What job?" demanded Jill suspiciously.

"I don't know. That's what she told me, and I believed her."

Jill looked half convinced. "But," she said thoughtfully, "you must have said something about her just now to make Brian so dreadfully upset all of a sudden."

"It was a message from Martha," even to her own ears the words sounded phoney, a last-minute excuse to suit the occasion. "She asked me to tell him she was sorry and hand him a package she wanted him to have."

"A package?" Clearly Jill's moment of understanding had vanished. "You mean a parcel of his letters to her, and the ring!

I bet the engagement ring he sent over to her was in the packet too?"

"Actually—"

"I knew it! And don't try to tell me you two didn't hatch the whole scheme up between you. I'm not as green as all that—" She broke off. "Does Mark know about this, this story of yours?"

"Of course."

"I bet he didn't place much faith in a tale like that either."

Angela didn't answer. She turned away before she could betray the trembling of her lips.

"Mark's pretty shrewd," Jill persisted. "He wouldn't be taken in by a story like that any more than I am!"

Doris finished drying the dishes Angela had left on the draining board. "Don't worry, Angela," she said kindly, "*I* believe you! And if Jill had as much experience of human nature as I have she would too. All this fuss about Martha!" She flung the teatowel on a rail. "Even though he might not realise it at this moment it's the best thing that ever happened to young Brian, getting out of that muddle he got himself into with Martha. She must have been an odd sort of girl, wanting to marry someone she'd never met. Probably she would have been horribly unsuitable for him. And anyway, who's to say she hasn't got another man friend by this time, perhaps someone she met on the voyage out from England. Someone she knows and likes, not just a silly pen-and-paper romance. Believe me Jill, he's well rid of her. Any girl who would let him down without a word of explanation all this time could well make him a whole lot more miserable than he is now in the long run. He'll get better—yes, he will, Jill, in spite of Angela's message. The other way he'd be letting himself in for a lifetime of misery." She went on composedly, "I can usually tell just by looking at them if folks are telling me the truth or not, and I'd put my money on Angela any day of the week."

Jill managed at last to get a word in. "Mark—"

"Mark's a Hillyer, and the Hillyers give nothing away. He's entitled to his own opinion. I'm sorry you've got this bee in your bonnet, Jill, because you could have been a big help to Angela while I'm away."

Jill looked aghast. "You're not leaving?"

"Just for a month. I was planning to go and stay with Eve and see the new baby before everything here went haywire, remember? I'd given up the thought of going south, but now Angela's offered to stay on here and look after things, so I'll be able to make the trip after all. Isn't it wonderful?"

"I can't see," Jill muttered sulkily, "why you believe every word she says. You seem to be wrapped up in her."

"That's got nothing to do with it. Either you believe in people or you don't." Angela could have thrown her arms around the crepey neck and hugged Doris. "She's pretty and she's got plenty of pluck. So she did know Martha. Well, what of it?" As a parting shot towards Jill she said significantly, "I should imagine that anyone who really cared for young Brian would be real grateful to Angela for telling him the truth, putting him out of that hell he's been in for weeks, wondering, hoping against hope and all for nothing." She smiled towards Angela. "I'd better let you in on the meal situation. We order food in big quantities, have it delivered down to the big shed at the entrance gates. The deep freeze is crammed full and there's oodles of frozen stuff—fish, meat, vegetables, fruit pies."

Angela was scarcely listening to the cheerful tones. She was aware of the closing of the door and guessed that Jill had gone to Brian's room. All unwittingly she had made an enemy. A pity, because she had liked the younger girl and up until half an hour ago Jill had seemed to like her. She sighed and brought her mind back to Doris's voice.

"There are swags of plastic bags with frozen corn fritters in them that I got ready ages ago. They'll come in handy if you get stuck for something to serve for lunch. Meat pies too, so don't mind making use of anything that's quick and easy, that's what they're for—emergencies like you having to cope with everything all at once."

Angela nodded, her thoughts still with Jill. In this male-slanted household she would have welcomed the friendship of a girl of her age or thereabouts, especially someone she had liked from the start. Now that hope had fled.

Odd that the prospect of coping with three meals a day no longer filled her with alarm. Perhaps because there would be time to plan ahead, to dispose of a failure if need be and start again. Or was it that compared with the problems facing her such mundane matters faded into insignificance? Problems like Jill hating her. Probably, she thought with a sigh, Brian would feel the same way about her once he got around to thinking things out. And Mark . . . somehow his lack of trust in her hurt most of all, she couldn't think why.

At the dinner table that evening Doris could talk of nothing but her forthcoming trip to the South Island. When at the end of the meal she paused Jill said suddenly, "Well, I'm staying on here. That is, if it's okay with you Mark," she added quickly.

"Just until Brian gets on his feet again, I mean."

Mark's voice was careless. "Please yourself. You don't need to ask me. You know you're always welcome here for as long as you like to stay. And if they can do without you on the farm—"

"They'll just have to. I'm not leaving Brian—" the small mouth closed mutinously and Angela could almost hear the unfinished sentence. *"In her clutches!"*

Her gaze went to the man seated at the head of the table. "I guess you won't be needing me, then, if Jill's staying on?"

"No, you don't, Twenty!" Mark reached for his pipe. "You don't slide out of it that easily! Jill might be staying for a month or she might not. Her plans are all up in the air. All depends on how Brian gets along. The rest of us have to depend on you so consider yourself hired, no matter what!"

Angela couldn't understand her sudden sense of relief.

CHAPTER SIX

Later that day as she wandered out of the house and out into the afternoon sunshine Angela couldn't feel entirely unhappy in spite of the unpleasant situation in which she found herself at the station. Odd to think that although she hae been at Waikare for a whole week she had as yet seen little of the property. And views from the house told her that there was a lot to see.

Idly she strolled along the driveway, passing the garages and pausing to admire the roses blooming in the long gardens that bordered the path. A farm motor-cycle propped against a post no doubt was ridden by Kevin. Somehow she would imagine Mark Hillyer to be more at home on horseback rather than lurching over the rugged terrain of the hills on the "mountain goat" of which the young cadet spoke with such pride.

As if in tune with her random thoughts at that moment she caught the soft thud of hoofbeats as a horseman came galloping down a grassy slope. He turned into the winding driveway and a few minutes later Mark drew rein beside her. "All alone today, Twenty?"

She glanced up at him, the sun in her eyes. Something in his ironical inflection sparked a quick response. "If you're thinking of John," she snapped defensively, "I haven't seen him since last night! I don't even know where he is!"

"I can answer that one for you." Dropping lightly to the path, he reached up to the sweating horse, removing the saddle and fluffy sheepskin and slipping off the bridle. "Off you go, old fellow." He flung open a side gate and the big black stallion trotted into the house paddock. "I sent John back to Te Awau this morning with the truck and mechanic."

"Te Awau?" Angela bent to pluck a blade of grass. "Wasn't that where the dance was last night?"

"That's right. Evidently the shearing gang struck trouble on the way back. Someone passed them half-way home, but they haven't arrived back. Seeing they're due to pack up their gear and move on to another station for an early start tomorrow I thought I'd better find out what's happened to them."

"Oh." She thought over what he had said. So he had been right in the matter of the gang's transport difficulties. Thank heaven he had rescued her in the nick of time, otherwise she too would now find herself stranded somewhere in the hills miles from any habitation. Somehow, though, it was difficult to say "thank you". She made a half-hearted attempt. "I guess I should be grateful—"

"Think nothing of it, Twenty!" The blue eyes had a sardonic twinkle. "I can't risk losing the cook, most important thing around the whole place! You'd be surprised!"

"You mightn't say that next week," she told him gloomily.

"Proof of the pudding, Twenty! And think what a Christian act you'd be doing in letting Doris off the chain for that holiday she's been looking forward to so much."

She said in a low constrained tone, "I suppose you think it's the least I can do . . . the way things are?"

"I told you before, Twenty, it's not my concern. It's over to Brian. You haven't seen much of the place yet, I take it? Today's a good day, not much doing on a Sunday." His cool glance raked her slim figure, taking in the pale blue cotton shirt open at the throat, the flared jeans with their wide embroidered legs. "Come as you are, you'll do."

"Thanks very much." Might as well get the unpleasant chore over with? Is that what you're thinking, Mr. Mark Hillyer?

"I'll take you for a run around," he was saying, "give you an idea of the property even if you can't get around to seeing all five thousand acres of it at one go!" He picked up the saddle fleece and bridle and they strolled towards the shed. "Anyway, I guess if you're from England it'll all be new to you, so it won't matter much."

Angela made no answer. She didn't want to discuss England at the moment, for to do so would bring too close the subject of Martha, and she felt she never wanted to hear Martha Stanaway's name ever again. If it hadn't been for her . . .

Presently they moved towards the Land Rover and Mark held open the door of the passenger seat. "Jump in!" She seated herself inside the vehicle and a few moments later they swept around the drive, passing the shepherds' bungalows and he drew to a stop at the first gateway. "Get rid of those Perendales, will you?"

With the toe of her rubber sandal she pushed at a woolly sheep dozing in a dust-bath, shooed another away and finally got the gate open and closed behind the Land Rover. Three gates further on they were out in open country amongst the sun-bleached hills.

"This is the start of the run," Mark told her as they swept up the steep winding grade of a cleared sheep-dotted hillside. Rubble and small stones tumbled down from the narrow track as they went on, then they reached the summit and Angela glanced down at a sea of tea-tree far below. It was very still. From the dust of the narrow track a hawk rose and circled over the homestead grounds. In the distance a shepherd on horseback patrolled a boundary fence and she noticed Mark's keen glance searching the far paddocks.

From here she could see cleared hills with bush running up the valleys, fences climbing to meet a hot blue sky and inlets of sea where small wavelets lapped the sand.

Soon they were taking a winding grey ribbon of road and all at once she came in sight of a sheet of water, the beaten silver of a placid lake in a hollow in the hills. The far side of the water was choked with mangroves, but on the water near the track black swans sailed with majestic grace. Mark pulled to a stop in the shade of overhanging tree-ferns at the water's edge.

"Lovely!" In spite of herself Angela found she was enjoying the drive. "I've never seen black swans before."

"Plenty of them on the lake here. Just before you arrived we had a man up here from the acclimisation society, taking baby swans away to other lakes further south. The odd thing around this part of the country is that the swans take to the sea-water too, maybe because the bay near the homestead's so sheltered."

"Really?" She turned her wide gaze towards him and once again she was conscious of the electric atmosphere as something potent, unseen, leaped between them. A moment later Mark was putting the vehicle into gear and they swept up the narrow track. The breeze that seemed to be always blowing up here in the hills was fresh and spiced with the tang of sea and bush. In spite of herself, in spite of everything, she couldn't help but enjoy all this. It must be the novelty of her surroundings.

All at once she caught sight of a wide swathe of cut grass running up a slope. "The track to the airfield," Mark told her. "I had it bulldozed last winter. The trucks need a decent track to get up to the take-off. That shed at the top of the hill is where the super's stacked. Couldn't get along on the land without the supermen. When I took over here these hills were unproductive, covered in scrub and tea-tree. Now that the topdressing planes come over and scatter the dust over them—well, you can see what I mean. Here comes one of them now, off on a job at a station further north, by the direction he's taking."

Angela watched the tiny plane as it skimmed the peaks, then disappeared in a haze of distance. Such daredevil tactics as flying low amongst these hills must, she reflected, require a lot of nerve.

On and on, under the bluest sky she had ever seen. The wind was becoming stronger now, flick-flacking the green streamers of the cabbage trees, tossing long fronds of tree-ferns, bending the tattered creamy plumes of toa-toas. Everywhere she looked was movement and warmth and colour. She stole a glance towards the man at her side. At that moment he swung around to face her and hurriedly she looked away. They were speeding up a slope towards the summit of yet another green peak and as he braked the Land Rover to a stop she gazed around her at the endless hilltops. "It's very big, Waikare, isn't it?"

"Think so?" She was suddenly very much aware of his nearness. "Broken your news yet?"

"Oh, you mean to your brother? Yes, I have. I went in to see him early this morning." A shadow fell over her face and her voice dropped. "I don't know whether it wouldn't have been wiser to wait, though. He looked terribly upset. He was so pale all of a sudden, and Jill—"

"Blames you for it?"

"Yes, she's pretty annoyed. You know," her habit of blurting out her innermost thoughts asserted itself and she said impulsively, "I'd say she was in love with Brian."

"Would you now?" Amusement was in his laconic tone. "You seem to have romance on the brain, Twenty."

Angela was unaware that she was twisting a long strand of hair nervously around her finger. Why had she spoken so unthinkingly? Why give him further chances to ridicule her?

He said in a milder tone, "Maybe you didn't catch on about Jill's position around here. Didn't Doris put you wise about her being brought up at Waikare as one of the family? She's like a sister to Brian, me too."

"Don't be too sure," Angela persisted stubbornly. "I still think she cares for him a lot, whether he thinks of her in that way or not. That's why," she asserted in her soft husky tones, "she's so mad with me and jealous of Martha."

"Oh, I guess she's fond enough of him." With a careless wave of a bronzed hand he dismissed her romantic imaginings. "Don't worry about Brian, he'll survive! From now on he'll make great progress, you'll see!"

Angela wished she could share his optimism. If only she could forget Brian's pale, shocked face when she had given him her message this morning. She wrenched her troubled thoughts back to the present.

"I'll take you down to have a look at the beach," Mark was saying, and he swung the Land Rover around on the narrow track. They were bumping over steep undulating ground with pitches so high that as they topped each rise it was impossible to see down to the rutted ground below. They lurched on over the grassy slopes, slowing down to a snail's pace as sheep scattered in mad panic around them. All at once Angela caught sight of white sand, the sunlit waters of the empty sea. Near at hand were boatsheds in a paddock sloping down to the beach and she asked him, "You keep a boat here?"

He nodded. "A sixteen-foot outboard runabout. The twelve-foot dinghy in the other shed belongs to friends of mine. They leave their craft here and come up for a day's fishing whenever they can take off from town."

They were running on to firm white sand of a small bay. Wavelets were creaming in on the shore, receding and washing in again. Along the shoreline Angela could see the imprints of horses' hooves. Ahead of them a cluster of sheep subsided contentedly in hollows in the warm wet sand. All at once Mark pulled to a stop facing the water. "You're in luck today, Twenty," he said softly. "Do you see what I see?"

"How do you mean?" She was far too much aware of his arm thrown carelessly around her shoulders as he pointed towards the sea to take in what he was saying. Over the excitement that quickened her pulses she forced herself to follow his gaze towards a graceful white bird alighting at the water's edge. "That bird—"

"Not just a bird, Twenty. It's something rare and rather beautiful. You might not come across one again in a lifetime."

"What . . . is it?"

"I can see I'll have to take your education in hand, particularly in the matter of New Zealand bird life. That happens to be the white heron—the *kotuku,* the Maoris call it. They used to weave the feathers, when they could get them, into the cloaks worn by their chieftains. The odd thing is that up to a few years ago no one could ever discover the secret nesting place. Then the scientific boys found it at last in one particular tree growing in a wilderness deep in the South Island."

Angela's gaze rested on the snowy egret. It stood so still it might have been carved from marble. "You're not having me on?" She glanced up at him wide-eyed and once again that disturbing shaft of awareness shot through her.

"Honest! The Maoris have a saying about the sacred white heron. They call it *He kotuku rerenga tahi,* the traveller of a single flight."

Impishly she smiled up at him. "Like me?"

He was silent for a moment. "Could be." At something in the stern line of his jaw all the lighthearted happiness of the moment drained away. Too late she realised all too clearly his probable interpretation as to the purpose of her "single flight". Oh, why must she always spoil the brief moments when they were in rapport by saying something stupid?

"Like to take a look around the point?" Once again he was coolly impersonal as he got out of the vehicle and came around to open the door. Together they strolled along the sand, then climbed over the low rocks at the end of the bay. As they rounded the point they came in sight of red and white painted poles, jumps, a brush barrier set up on the long stretch of sandy beach. Angela gazed around her in surprise. "Whoever would have expected to see a pony club away down here?"

Mark nodded carelessly. "This happens to be Susan's number one project. She's a keen show jumper and she started a district pony club earlier this summer. The local kids are terrifically grateful to her. They truck their mounts for miles to get here for meetings at the week-ends. They should be rolling along any time now."

Unthinkingly Angela murmured, "I wonder why Susan didn't have the pony club on her own property?"

"Thing is," he explained, "we've got the stretch of coastline over here and the kids love to gallop their ponies along the beach. Believe me, it's much more fun for them than the hill-sides at home. It suits everyone fine."

Especially Susan. Now what had made her think that? It could well be true that the young riders would prefer riding along the seashore to anywhere else. It could also be true that Susan happened to be very much interested in the owner of Waikare. With a sigh Angela thrust the thought aside. What was happening to her of late? She was becoming like so many other folk on the station, suspecting everyone of ulterior motives. And what had Mark and Susan's relationship to do with her anyway?

"Here comes Sue now," he was saying. "Would you care to stick around for a while and see what goes on? The rest of the club will be along any time now, complete with parents."

She followed his gaze to two Land Rovers towing horse-floats that were approaching down the narrow path. "Thanks, but I'd better get back to the house. Doris is going to talk over a few things with me. It's all new to me, this ordering stores on such a big scale." It was as good an excuse as she could think up on the spur of the moment.

"You'll soon get in the way of it," he returned carelessly. All very well for the boss, he wasn't faced with the task of coping with looking after a household at short notice.

Mark made no move to start the vehicle, waiting while the other Land Rovers pulled up on the firm sand. The next moment Susan sprang from the driver's seat and came strolling towards them. Today she was impeccably attired in tailored riding jacket and jodphurs, her blonde hair drawn severely back from her tanned face. She swung a black riding helmet from her hand. "Hi, Mark!" Her slightly condescending glance moved towards Angela. "Oh, I thought you'd have moved on by now with the rest of the gang."

"No, I—"

"Miss Twentyman's staying on at the house," Mark informed her. "She's offered to fill in while Doris takes off for the south to see her daughter."

Susan opened her lips to speak, then closed them again. She appeared to be having difficulty in finding words. "S-staying with you?"

"That's right," Mark said pleasantly. "Temporary employment for her, a way out for us. Who's complaining?"

It was clear that Susan was anything but pleased at the prospect of Angela staying on at the homestead. Before the other girl could say any more, however, a middle-aged couple strolled from the other vehicle to join them. Angela took in a spare kindly-looking man with the weathered skin of an outdoor worker and a woman with faded blonde hair who appeared to be an older edition of Susan. As introductions were made Angela could see that the middle-aged woman was puzzled as to where Angela fitted into the picture at the homestead. Her daughter's voice, very clear, very cutting, enlightened her. "Angela's been cooking for the shearing gang all week." The arrival of a cavalcade of trucks, cars and floats at that moment made further conversation impossible. As Susan left them to get her mount from the float Mark said to Angela, "I'll take you back to the house, then?"

"Thank you."

They were moving away when Susan called imperiously, "You'll be back, won't you, Mark? I'm depending on you for some advice about the height of the jumps! And bring me some red paint when you come back, will you? There wasn't a skerrick in the shed when I looked just now."

"Can do." He lifted a lean brown hand in farewell. As they climbed over the rocks at the point Angela had a feeling she wouldn't be missed amongst the crowd of children and ponies milling on the sand.

It was after dinner that evening when Angela, standing at the sink, caught sight of lights approaching along the driveway. In the way in which one notices everything in an isolated district she peered through the window. A truck was followed by a second one, a battered old vehicle that even in the fading light appeared vaguely familiar.

Doris came to stand beside her. "That's John and the mechanic bringing the shearers back. Poor John, he must have put in a long wait while Jack got the old wreck going again. What a waste of a day's holiday! Still, they have to have transport, seeing they're booked in at another shed in the morning!"

A short time later Angela answered the door to John's knock. "Angela!" Relief and pleasure kindled his dark eyes. "If I'm not glad to see you! I thought you might have gone away somewhere and I'd never find you again!"

She laughed. "I'm not going, I'm staying right here until Doris gets back from the south."

He sighed on a breath of relief. "Thank heaven for that! That's the best news I've had today!"

"Come in—"

"No, no," he shook his dark head. "Look, I've only a few minutes. A few minutes!" he groaned. "The others are getting their gear together, then we're all taking off for the next contract, two hundred miles north. Couldn't we go some place, a walk, anywhere," his voice softened, "just so we can get to know each other a bit better? Wouldn't it! I meet a girl like you and have to take off almost right away! I've just got to do something about it!"

"What's wrong with out here?" Angela dropped down to a low coolie chair on the shadowed porch.

John perched himself on the railing. "If you prefer. You know something Angie, I don't think you even know my name—"

"John?"

"John Travers." His voice had a rueful note. "I'm just the presser to you, isn't that right?"

Angela hesitated. She scarcely liked pointing out that she had scarcely thought of him one way or another.

"No different from any of the rest of the gang to you, eh?"

"Well, there is something different about you, but I can't tell you what it is."

"What would you say if I told you I'm a high school teacher

by profession? Maths is my line. That I've just turned down a cushy job in town because I'm mad keen on living on the land—so keen I've sunk all my savings from heaven knows how long in a block fifty miles from here." He sent her an anxious look. "Guess you'd think that was a crazy decision, taking on hard slog for years and years when you could be having it easy?"

"Oh no, I don't think that at all—if it's what you want."

"It's what I want, more than anything. That's one reason why I'm working with the gang this summer. The money's good and I need a lot more capital than I've got to buy farm machinery, put up sheds, clear and fence—it all takes money. Besides, the experience will come in handy for me. If only," he said very low, "this shearing stint didn't take me away from here, keep me on the move for a month or so yet."

"But you said you need the money and the experience?"

She couldn't fathom his long silence, unless . . . But he scarcely knew her, or she him. Hurriedly she said, "Well, I think it's just fantastic, your having a stab at what you really want." She smiled. "Even if it is a hut to sleep in and some sheep up here in the wilderness."

He turned to face the darkening hills, staring out over the cleared sheep-dotted slopes. Lights from the homestead windows streamed out over smooth green lawns and from the long borders below wafted the scent of roses. "This isn't a wilderness, Angie. This station is every sheep farmer's dream. It's one of the oldest homesteads in the north, and the most productive. Those big Moreton Bay fig trees," his sombre gaze went to the massive trees black against the clarity of the sky, "they've been here ever since Mark's grandfather got the land from the Maoris for a few blankets and axes, plus a musket or two. One day I'm hoping my place will be something like this." He slanted her a wry grin. "A man can dream, can't he?"

"I don't see why you shouldn't make a go of it," she encouraged. The flush of the setting sun merged into pink and lilac, shading up to a clear translucent blue. She was thinking that Mark would be still down on the beach with Susan and the ponies. He wouldn't be back to the house before dark, Doris had told her, but there was no need to wait dinner. He would have cold meat and salad when he came in.

"Angie!" She wrenched her thoughts aside, realising that all at once John was beside her, clasping her hand in a warm pressure. "You don't know how different it would be if I knew I had someone to work for, someone who cared—" He broke off as lights beamed over the curving driveway and to the accompaniment of loud tooting a truck braked below. "If only I didn't have to go," he groaned. Suddenly in the shadows of the porch he was holding her close, whispering against her hair, "Don't think you're getting rid of me though. I'll be back just as soon as I can. 'Bye, Angie!" His bearded chin brushed her face and she felt the quick pressure of his lips on hers. The truck driver was still holding his hand on the horn—was that the reason why she hadn't heard Mark's approach as he came up the steps on his way into the house? In the gloom she knew he couldn't help but catch sight of the entwined figures and he'd think—what would he think? She wrenched herself free. "They're waiting for you down there."

"Don't I know it!" His tone was urgent. "You'll be here for a while yet, Angie?"

"About a month."

"I'll manage something. See you!" The next minute he was running down the steps and hurrying along the path towards the waiting truck. She watched him climb inside, then the vehicle turned and soon the winking red tail light vanished around a curve of the path. If only Mark hadn't come up the steps at that particular moment. What was he thinking? That she allowed any man to kiss her on the briefest of acquaintance? She tried to tell herself that it didn't matter what he thought of her, that it couldn't be much blacker than the opinion he already held of "Martha's friend". Nevertheless, she turned aside on a sigh.

As she moved along the passage she was aware of Doris's excited tones as she answered a ring on the telephone. "I'll have to find out. Will you hold the line, please? Mark—"

He came strolling towards her and Angela caught the wistful note in Doris's tones. "It's the Auckland airport on the phone. You know how I told you they were too busy with school holiday traffic to let me have a booking until early next week?—well, something's happened! They have a cancellation for one on the night flight. Mark, do you think—"

Angela found herself listening for the deep quiet tones. "No problem. Tell them to reserve you that seat!" He glanced down at the watch on his tanned wrist. "That is if you can fling some gear into a suitcase and be ready in ten minutes flat!"

"Oh, I can! My things are all packed ready and I've only got to change my dress!" Flushed and radiant, Doris turned back to the telephone to confirm the booking, then flung a hurried glance over her shoulder to Angela. "There's some washing out on the line that I need! Be a dear and bring it in for me, will you?"

Angela fled out of the door and into the darkness of the dew-wet lawns. She was only just in time she thought as drops of rain splashed down in the grass. At that moment a peal of thunder rolled over the hills and a shaft of lightning threw into relief the giant Moreton Bay fig trees. Even before she could gain the shelter of the porch her hair was damp and a second flash illuminated a dark and menacing sky. Hurrying up the steps, she all but collided with Mark on his way out to the garage. He paused to throw a casual glance over his shoulder.

"You may as well come along too, Twenty, if you're not doing anything else. You'll be company for Doris on the run through."

"Me?" She stared up at him in surprise. "Thanks all the same, but I—"

"Why not?" His glance went to the inky-blue sky, heavy with the threat of impending rain. "Looks like we're in for a wet trip, a real summer storm by the look of that sky. We only get one or two in a season and when we do they're really something —violent thunderstorms and lightning. This one has all the signs of being a real electrical storm before the night's out—" He threw her his lopsided grin and she caught a hint of challenge in his tones. "Feel like trusting yourself to me on a rugged trip back from the airport?"

The words of protest somehow died on her lips as something else took over, the dangerous "something" that undermined all her defences. She said, "I'll get my jacket."

"Don't trouble to dress up," he called as she turned away. "We'll drop Doris at the airport, then push off for home. She's used to the trip. As far as she's concerned it's an annual event. That's why she was so down in the mouth about having to miss out this year."

Angela paused, a teasing note in her voice. "You mean, a baby every year?"

"Just about, plus other eventualities. Not that Doris needs an excuse for getting down south every summer. If she hasn't got one she manufactures something."

Angela laughed and hurried inside. All at once for no reason at all she was feeling ridiculously light-hearted. In her room she hummed a bar of melody as she ran a comb through her hair, touched her mouth with lipstick and snatched up her wind-breaker.

Fast as she was, Doris had been even quicker, for when Angela entered the lounge room the older woman was already waiting there, an unfamiliar figure in a crisp blue crimplene suit, on her feet neat dark shoes in place of rubber thongs.

Her fair hair was covered by a chiffon scarf and she carried a light raincoat over her arm. "Oh, hello, Angela! You're coming too? That's marvellous! Now I must check to make sure I've got everything. Money, glasses, gifts for the boys, pink knitted outfit for the new baby. I don't think I've forgotten anything."

"Right!" Mark came into the room and picked up her suitcase. "We're on our way! I asked Angela to come along just too for the ride."

"I'm so pleased," Doris said happily. "On the way she can tell me some more about London."

"But I've told you just about everything I can think of," Angela protested. For Doris, nostalgic for a city she had left so long ago, plied Angela endlessly on the subject and never tired of hearing of changes in various districts or of entertainments offering in the theatres.

"Nonsense, I'll never ever hear enough of London!" As they moved towards the door she said, "Now I don't want either of you staying at the airport to see me off. Planes are often late getting away and you won't be home until morning as it is."

"What in the world—?" Jill, strolling into the room at that moment, eyed Doris in amazement. "No one told me you were taking off from here tonight."

"She didn't know herself," Mark explained, "until we got a ring from the airport a few minutes ago offering her a cancellation on the night plane for Christchurch."

"Goodness!" Jill paused as a roll of thunder reverberated overhead, startlingly close to the house. "I don't envy you the trip back over the hills tonight, Mark."

"Not to worry."

"He's taking me along too," Angela put in gaily, "just for the ride. But I'll be back on the job in the morning!"

Jill made no answer. Her tightly set lips and angry expression made it quite plain that if Angela never returned to Waikare it would be too soon for her.

As they moved out into the moist darkness Mark hurried on ahead to open the door of the Land Rover and Doris said on a sigh, "It's too bad about Jill. I feel dreadful leaving you with this poisonous atmosphere to contend with as well as everything else! She's quite a nice kid too as a rule. If only she wasn't so *stubborn*! Once she gets an idea into her head nothing on earth will shift it!"

"It doesn't matter." Yet somehow it did matter. It wouldn't be so hurtful, Angela told herself bleakly, if she were really guilty of the machinations of which so many folk here appeared to suspect her. "Oh well," she tried to make her tone cheerful, "I expect it will be only for a few days. Brian seems almost better now." But in her heart she knew that the last thing Jill wanted was to leave the man she loved to the questionable ministrations of a girl who had been a friend of Martha's.

As they swept out of the main gates of the homestead rain was falling steadily, splashing down into the dust of the driveway. At intervals flashes of lightning lighted up a sombre sky and in the hills long rolls of thunder seemed alarmingly close.

Doris had asked Angela to sit in the rear of the vehicle with her and as the Land Rover plunged on through the darkness the older woman chattered continuously. Didn't Angela think that Kelly was a most attractive name for the new baby, providing of course it turned out to be the long-awaited girl, and this time, judging by the law of averages, it must be! Angela nodded. She was scarcely listening, her eyes fixed on the windswept road ahead.

At length they turned into the main northern highway with its smooth bitumen surface and vastly improved grades. As they sped over the quiet roads towards the city the scattered lights of farmhouses twinkled on lonely hilltops and presently they joined in the stream of traffic churning up a steep grade. "Is all the north just a series of high hills?" Angela asked Doris.

"Just about, but it's worth it all! Wait until you've seen a bit more of the district further north. Whangarei's a gorgeous town, so gay and colourful with flowers everywhere and the most fabulous swimming beaches all within driving distance of the city. There's a boat harbour too and a bush-covered mountain almost in the centre of the town. Further on is the Bay of Islands—"

"Isn't that the historical part of the country where all the tourists go?"

"That's it, but it's got to be seen to be believed! Bush-covered islands, deep-sea fishing, white sandy beaches—" Doris broke off, leaning forward in her seat. "Mark, why don't you take Angela up there for a look around while she's at Waikare?"

Angela felt hot with embarrassment. The boss taking her around the north on a sightseeing expedition, just for the fun of it! "Oh no," she protested quickly.

"I'll—"

"I've got that in mind!" The cool masculine tones cut across her husky voice. "Meantime," Mark went on as lightning zig-zagged its way across a dark sky, "we'll be lucky if we make it back to the station. If this downpour doesn't let up soon there'll be slips all over the road."

"Just what I've been thinking." Doris's tone held a thread of concern. "Remember the storm we had about this time last summer, Mark, when the power and telephone lines were down for two days and no one could get across the river? Do you think you and Angela should put up somewhere in town and drive back in the daylight?"

Angela found she was holding her breath. Imagine being forced to spend the night at some strange motel in the company of a man who disliked and distrusted her! Worse, who seemed bent on taking revenge on her for a fancied slight to his younger brother. That really would be the end!

"We'll make it," Mark said, and Doris relaxed against the seat.

"I guess if anyone can get through to the station in a storm you can, Mark!"

Angela made a mental note to keep her fingers crossed.

Time passed swiftly and to Angela it seemed only a short time before they were moving along suburban streets with their shaded windows, pausing at traffic lights where coloured smears wavered in sheets of water on the roadway. They followed the airport road for some miles and turning a curve came suddenly on a blaze of lights. Ahead was a modern terminal building. The tall column of the control tower winked its navigation lights and overhead a plane droned as it circled the airport before landing.

Doris gathered up her hand luggage. "It's goodbye, then. I feel mean leaving you with everything."

"You needn't," Angela disclaimed with a smile. "After a week of coping with shearers in the shed, normal appetites will be just nothing. The men will have to put up with my plain fare, though."

"That's all they want—and you know I didn't mean that anyway! You'll manage fine with the housekeeping, I know, but it's Jill, she's going to be difficult. It's not going to be much fun for you while I'm away."

"Don't worry, she'll be far too taken up with getting Brian back to work to waste time on me."

"I know, but all the same—"

"Now don't *worry*! Just have a good time and enjoy yourself! Drop me a line if you have time—and give my love to Kelly when she arrives!"

"I will! I will! Now you're not to come out in the rain, dear.

I'm used to this trip south, so no one needs to wait to see the plane take off. That goes for you too, Mark."

"If you say so." He was guiding the vehicle among lines of cars standing in the spacious parking area.

"I'll wire you when I'm coming back," Doris said. "Goodbye, Angela, and thanks for everything!"

CHAPTER SEVEN

Mark picked up Doris's suitcase and Angela watched the other two as they crossed the rainswept roadway towards the lighted terminal building, the man's tall figure shielding Doris from the full force of the gale. Tonight Angela knew it would take more than blustery winds and driving rain to dampen Doris's high spirits, for wasn't she travelling towards all the warmth and welcome of happy family life with the added excitement of the expected arrival of a new small person to love? Unconsciously Angela sighed. Not like herself, for now that she had said good-bye to the one person at Waikare who believed in Angela's integrity of purpose, she was returning only to dislike and suspicion. Why on earth, once she had learned the truth about Martha, had she agreed to stay on? She must be a devil for punishment, she told herself ruefully, to continue to put up with Jill's contemptuous glances and Mark's two-edged remarks. What *was* there about the place that held her in spite of everything, made it worthwhile enduring so much downright unpleasantness? There was no answer to the query. She only knew that in some sad mixed-up way she enjoyed being at Waikare. She wouldn't be anywhere else for anything, not even tonight in the long trip back to the station in the teeth of the storm . . . with Mark.

He was back at the parking area in a few minutes, and climbing back into the vehicle. "Doris is okay. She's just met up with a friend who happens to be travelling on the same plane to Christchurch. She's in a tizzy about us getting through on the road tonight and said not to wait to see her plane take off. So come on, Twenty!" He got out to open the passenger door and a gust of wind struck her with sudden force. "If you sit in the back by yourself folks will think we don't get on!"

Don't get on, Angela thought hollowly. He must be joking! But she slipped into the front seat, he slammed the door, then went around to the driver's seat, brushing the wet thatch of dark hair back from his eyes.

Soon they were moving away. The mechanical arms of the barrier lifted to let the vehicle through and they swung into the brightly lighted thoroughfare with its stream of moving buses, taxis and private cars.

As they left the terminal buildings behind and took the quiet road towards the city he said: "Doris will be on top of the world once she gets to Christchurch and sees that daughter of hers." He swung her a sideways glance. "How about you, Twenty? You never let on much about yourself. Got a family of your own back home in the old country?"

"No."

"Just you?"

She twinkled up at him. "Just me. My parents died so long ago I don't even remember them."

His tone softened. "Tough on you."

"Not really. A nice aunt took pity on me and brought me up. She's not in England any longer, though. Her daughter went to live in the States and two years ago my aunt joined her there."

"So there's no one back in London who's missing you a lot?" His gaze was fixed on the rain-swept road ahead and the question hung in the air between them. What was he getting at? she wondered. "Oh, boy-friends, you mean?"

"It's not unusual—a girl like you." His brief glance took in the eager young face and softly parted lips.

"Actually," she admitted slowly, "there was someone, or I thought there was—"

Mark caught her up quickly. "Was?"

"You know," she admitted with a slight feeling of guilt, "I'd all but fogotten about Graeme since coming to the station. Isn't it terrible?" she added half to herself. "It must be that hectic week in the shearing shed that put everything else right out of my mind."

"Or someone you met there?"

In the dim glow of the dashboard she glimpsed the sardonic twist of his lips. So it was John to whom he was referring. She might have known he wouldn't have forgotten John's warm goodbye on the shadowed porch. All at once she remembered that this was the boss, inflexible and unrelenting, with whom she was having this cosy little chat. What had her private life to do with him? "Does it matter?" she asked sharply.

He made no reply, or perhaps in the roar of the wind she hadn't caught the low murmur of his voice. For the wind was rising rapidly to gale force, wildly tossing the tops of tall trees bordering the dark paddocks stretching away on either side of the highway and sending leaves and broken branches skittering across their path.

Mark was putting a hand to a knob on the dashboard. "Feel like some music?"

"If you like."

The next moment the beat of a dance melody pulsed around

them, but almost immediately the music was drowned out in a crash of thunder overhead. "It's no use." He turned the switch and they relapsed into silence. Not a dreary kind of silence, though, Angela's thoughts ran. It was almost . . . exciting . . . as though the electricity that crackled through the air tonight had charged the atmosphere within the enclosed vehicle so that she was terribly, achingly *aware* of Mark and everything about him. The damp dark hair, the strong masculine face, even the tanned hand resting on the steering wheel. She wrenched her glance aside, fearful that he might somehow sense the way she was feeling about him. Mark Hillyer, of all men! A man she scarcely knew, a man who didn't even like her . . . on the contrary! She must be crazy!

They had left the city behind them and were taking the bends and curves of the northern highway when the storm broke in all its fury, an electrical storm that sent lightning zig-zagging almost continuously over roadside paddocks, throwing into sharp relief tossing trees and the sheep huddled for shelter beneath. Angela's thoughts went to the road snaking over the high hills to the station. She recalled the many slips that had threatened to block the road on the day of her arrival at Waikare. In a heavy torrential downpour such as this there must be more than a likelihood of falls of earth from the raw cuttings on the hillsides. The disquieting thought made her say anxiously, "Won't it be risky going over the hills in a storm like this?"

"The roads up there are always a risk, whatever the weather." He sent her his lopsided smile with its hint of amusement. "Scared, Twenty? I told you you need to be tough to live out here in the never-never."

"Not scared," she protested quickly, "it's just that I—"

"Don't trust me to get you safely back tonight all in one piece? Is that it?"

"Something like that." She was tempted to point out to him that the question of her spending her life on an outback New Zealand sheep station scarcely arose, but something about the stern set face at her side dissuaded her. The subject was fraught with emotional pitfalls, like the way he insisted on dragging John into the conversation, and somehow tonight she wasn't in the mood for argument.

At length they swung off the smooth wet bitumen of the main highway to turn into rough metal roads. Earth washing down from the banks above lent the pathway a surface of slippery mud. Swish, swish, branches of overhanging tree-ferns scraped the roof as they plunged on through the dark, wind-tossed night. Once again the silence seemed fraught with some emotion she couldn't pinpoint, and for something to say Angela murmured, "You've always lived at Waikare?"

He slewed the vehicle around a bend, sending a shower of mud and rubble over the wheels. "That's right. It belonged to my dad and his father before him. I spent a few years at boarding school in town, put in a stint at agricultural college and after that there was a period of training on another station. There was a manager on the place until I could take over—and believe me, I couldn't get back soon enough! Brian," his voice softened, "he was different. As a kid he was a delicate little brat, always in and out of hospital for one thing or another. The outdoor life here has been the making of him. He's grown out of all that now."

Angela's thoughts went back to what Doris had told her of the Hillyer family history. The two brothers growing up without a father, did that explain the elder one's protective, authoritative attitude towards the younger? In the small community of the remote sheep station Mark apparently held himself responsible for the welfare of his younger brother. Some perversity sparked her to say, "He might be just as well in town. I mean, did he really want to be a sheep farmer all his life? Was coming back to the station his own choice?"

"Fair question, Twenty! But what lad at school-leaving age has a clue as to what he wants to take up when he gets out in the world? Not too many, I'd imagine! Besides, he was always a scary, timid kid, he needed someone to make up his mind for him."

So the decision had been forced on Brian. "And you've never found out from him since," she persisted, "whether he's really happy or not about his life here?"

"Hey!" He swung her a swift amused glance. "What are you getting at?" His tone sharpened. "He hasn't been confiding his troubles to you by any chance, has he?"

"No, of course not!" Belatedly she remembered her own rather questionable position at the homestead. "I guess it's really none of my business, but—"

"But?"

Angela gathered her courage together. In spite of the intimidating note in his voice he couldn't eat her. "Seems to me," she said in her soft tones, "that he's the type of fellow who'd be more at home living in town than in the country. A big city where he could have easy access to good libraries, attend literary clubs and meet people with similar interests. That sort of thing."

"Similar interests? You don't mean those verses of his that he's always scribbling away at? Oh, I grant you they've got something, occasionally he hits a nerve with something he says, but if you're thinking of persuading him to try to live on his earnings in that direction you're way off-beam. He tried that idea out once before and it didn't work. He took off for six months to Wellington and tried to support himself on his writing efforts. He's a stubborn cuss, but even he had to admit after a few weeks that he was beaten. I guess that's another thing that didn't do anything towards bolstering up his sagging confidence in himself. He's one of those unlucky guys somehow, what with that—and your friend Martha!"

Martha. Her spirits plummeted and the warm intimacy of the rain-swept night was dashed. So he was still thinking of Martha Stanaway and no doubt linking her name with that of the other girl. Of all the arrogant, egotistical men! Arranging other people's lives, treating Brian as though he were still the kid brother of nine or ten years of age. And yet could there be some sense in his arguments? Possibly Brian did need a stronger nature to guide him, an older brother to depend on. But was such direction really helping Brian to make a life of his own, discover his own potential for personal fulfilment?

Her unseeing gaze was fixed on rivulets of rain running down the streaming windscreen and her soft lips drooped. Mark has made up his mind about me in just the same way as he's summed up his young brother. In his book I'll never be anything else but "Martha's friend". Right from the start he's written me off as a cold-hearted husband-hunter, and a liar and cheat into the bargain! Unconsciously she sighed. It's a pity, because there's something about him. Call it masculine magnetism, call it anything you like. I only know that tonight it's difficult to fight against it. Yet somehow I must.

He's tough and brown and hard, yet he really does have a care for those around him. There's no doubt he thinks the world of Brian, even though it seems to me he's rather overdone the caring in that direction. Because he knows that Doris has set her heart on getting to Christchurch in time for the new baby's arrival he's taken this long drive to the airport tonight. And look at the patient way he takes the trouble to explain all the details of station work to Kevin when the lad asks about them. Oh, you have to hand it to Mark—he's a good employer. Anyone can see that to the shepherds and hands at the station he stands ten feet tall! Susan likes him too, likes him a lot. How much does he like her? I wonder. I wish I knew the answer to that one. Funny, it's only me he treats with a sort of mocking amusement as though I were a female farm-cadet or something.

What would it be like to be loved, treated as a woman, by a man of Mark's calibre? The thought came out of nowhere and she thrust it aside. That way danger lay.

She had no idea how far they were from the station when above the sound of the motor she heard the crashing of falling trees and rumble of earth as it slipped down the slope beside them. Her quick anxious glance went to Mark and she saw that he too was alerted to the ominous sounds. She said on a sharp breath, "Aren't you going to stop and see what's happened back there?"

"No use stopping, Twenty," he was peering ahead through the misted glass. "Go for your life before you cop it yourself, that's what you have to do in a gale like this! And keep your fingers crossed that the road's clear ahead. This is a bad area, known for slips at any old time. It happens all the time—" He braked with a suddenness that shot her forward in her seat. Righting herself, she peered through the windscreen, her eyes widening in apprehension. The rain had eased and a pale moon emerging from scarves of cloud in a watery sky shone down on the river. River! It had been a mere trickle of water over rocks when they had crossed the bridge earlier this evening. Now flood waters were flowing over the banks and a rushing torrent was sweeping along, taking with it earth and trees, kauri logs and broken branches. The next moment she realised something else. The approach to the bridge had been washed away and now a deep hole foaming with water yawned only a few feet ahead of the Land Rover. "I don't believe it," she whispered. "We could be cut off . . . couldn't we?"

He slewed around to face her. "Not could be, Twenty, we darned well are!"

To her surprise he appeared more annoyed than startled by the torrent of water that barred their route to the homestead. "Incredible, isn't it," he was saying, "how the river can rise in a few hours like that! These flash floods are the devil. We often cop them in the summer, usually after a drought season. The water rises in no time at all on the dry river bank and can go down just as suddenly."

"But what can we do? We can't go back this way." Angela raised hazel eyes wide with apprehension. "Is there another bridge further up the river? One that's wide enough to take the Land Rover?"

"Good thinking, Twenty, but it won't work. Not a chance!

This is the only Land Rover bridge, or was up till an hour or so ago. No, I guess we'll just have to settle for the old hut the road-workers left behind them. Luckily it's no distance away, at the start of that stand of native bush. That old shack by the road-side."

She rubbed a cleared space on the misted window, but could discern nothing but treetops wildly tossing against a gunmetal sky. "A hut?" she echoed faintly.

"That's right." He was reaching to the back of the vehicle in search of raincoat and rug. "Handy for anyone caught out in bad weather to put up for the night. Trampers use it mostly, a few surveyors, hunters. Even the odd touring party caught out in a storm on a summer camping trip. See it?"

"Not really, but I'll take your word for it." She spoke lightly, but underneath her heart was beating much too fast. The thoughts spun in a turmoil in her mind. Did he really mean they were to be forced to spend the night in a one-roomed shack by the roadside? But what else could they do? He had spoken so casually as though it were the most ordinary thing in the world for them to put up there together. Perhaps it was in the circumstances. Clearly in his outback existence such sudden eventualities as washouts and landslides were all in the day's work, an occupational hazard of station life. Obviously this wasn't the first occasion on which the bridge approaches had been washed away and travellers forced to take shelter in the nearby hut. Ridiculous of her to be so prissy and self-conscious over an emergency that was none of his doing.

Well, if he could be unconcerned over a night spent in the wilds so could she! It wasn't as if there were the slightest—well, *feeling*—between them. She was here on sufferance, he'd made that quite plain from the beginning. As for herself, he was her employer, that was all. So why was her heart beating fast in this stupid fashion? Angela shied away from the answer to that particular line of thought. Blame the storm and act unconcerned, that was the way to handle her own personal emergency. Aloud she said, "You're sure there's no other way back to the station?"

His grin was sardonic. "You still don't get it, do you, Twenty? We're damned lucky to have some shelter for the night!" He threw a glance outside where the rain had eased to a light drizzle. "Come on, we'll make a dash for it!" He switched off the head-lamps and the next minute he was out of the vehicle and splashing over the muddy road towards her side of the Land Rover.

Now that the noise of the engine was stilled she could hear water splashing against the broken bridge supports. The roar of the flood waters and the moaning of wind in the trees underlined the fact that tonight was no night to be out in the open. But she would be in the hut, with Mark. She couldn't decide which alternative was the more disturbing.

As he flung open the door the gale tore at her, loosening the windbreaker from around her shoulders and flinging her hair over her face. She fumbled in the darkness in search of the step, missed it and was about to leap down into a pool of water below when in a swift movement Mark picked her up bodily and almost without her volition she found her arms tightening around his neck.

Kicking the door shut behind them, he strode along the wet pathway. Now that her eyes were becoming accustomed to the gloom she could faintly discern a winding track, and the pale blur of a small dwelling in the shelter of bush at the roadside. Rain was falling softly, beading their faces and hair, but she was scarcely aware of it for the tumult of her feelings. She told herself that this—this closeness—signified nothing to him, that to the master of Waikare she meant no more than a sheep he was rescuing from the storm and taking to shelter . . . unfortunately. For something stronger than reason was taking over, an insidious sweetness that made her cling tighter to him, wish the short distance would never come to an end so that she could stay right here in his arms for ever! Already, however, a tiny shack with a tin chimney jutting from an iron roof loomed ahead. Soon he paused to push open the unlocked door with the toe of his shoe. Gently he set her down inside and she was aware of a dry timber floor beneath her feet.

"Welcome home, Twenty!" If only, she thought wildly, he didn't mean by that what she suspected he did! Mark Hillyer carrying her tenderly over the threshold of their temporary home! She was conscious of a hysterical urge towards laughter and tears all mixed up together. Unthinkingly she put the thought into words, "Of all people in the world!"

He tossed the dripping jacket aside and put a light to a candle standing on a rough bench. He straightened, tossing the damp hair back from his forehead and above the tiny flame his eyes seemed to darken. But his tone was the familiar one of faint amusement. "Does that mean you don't care for being carried over the threshold, Twenty?" Softly he added, "Gives you ideas, maybe?"

So he hadn't missed the ridiculous significance of the situation. "No, it doesn't!" All the tremulous happiness of the last few minutes drained away and she was left with the bitter reminder that she was just Twenty, the English girl out to catch a husband in a new country. All at once she felt she'd give anything to change that ready-made opinion of his. She'd even broach the subject again. Tonight would be a good opportunity and maybe with a bit of luck this time he might take her seriously. Suddenly it was desperately important that he should believe her. Slipping the damp windbreaker from her shoulders, she said lightly, "All I know is that I'm grateful for dry feet." She glanced down at his sodden shoes. "Not like yours!"

"Oh, I'm used to it," he said carelessly. His glance took in her damp hair, the coppery-coloured strands curling around her forehead, the rain-spattered slacks. "A fire will chase the damp away. All we need is a match and we're away!" As he spoke he knelt to set a match to the sticks and newspaper already laid in a rough fireplace by a previous sojourner, probably the same man who had left the dried tea-tree logs stacked alongside the open fireplace.

The flames soared upwards, making reflections on the rough log walls and Angela's gaze went to a single bunk bed covered with a plaid woollen rug. "I see we have all the comforts of home!" Even to her own ears her laughter held a forced ring.

He was still kneeling by the blaze feeding it with kindling wood. "Come on, Twenty, may as well get warm." She hesitated. The glint in his eyes did nothing to ease her mounting sense of confusion. "I don't bite, you know!"

Angela dropped down at his side, holding her hands to the blaze. "I think the rain's stopping at last." How banal the words sounded. Mark must be aware of the disquiet she was trying hard to conceal. If that were true, however, he gave no sign but continued to regard her in the cool considering fashion she ought to be accustomed to by now, only she wasn't!

"Guess you didn't have an idea of what you were letting yourself in for when you came up to Waikare?"

Just what she wondered did he mean by that? "No," she agreed faintly.

"No regrets?" He was stocking the flames, his face turned aside.

"Not so far." Heavens, what if he took that to mean that she was referring to being cut off by the broken bridge, forced to spend the night with him in the hut? "I mean," she babbled wildly on, "that cooking job with the shearing gang was tough going, but I guess it was all experience."

She was leaning back, her eyes fixed on the leaping flames and hands clasped around her bent knees.

"Experience for what, Twenty?" he enquired softly, "life as a sheep farmer's wife on a back-country station?"

Startled and indignant, she flung around to face him. "Why do you say that?"

"Just because you get so het-up on the subject—and because of John—"

"Oh, him." Her voice was careless.

"Oh, him, just like that?" His tone was threaded with urgency and all at once it seemed to her that his eyes, "the cold blue Hillyer eyes", were alive with a strange brilliance.

"Well," with an effort she wrenched her glance from his deep compelling gaze, "I don't know him all that well."

But you let him kiss you. Do you let any man kiss you? Was that the direction in which his thoughts were running? It would be in line with his opinion of her as a girl with marriage on her mind. The thought was unbearable and made her say stiffly, "What have you got against John?"

"Not a thing! He's a great guy. He'll make a success of that land project of his later on, he's got what it takes to make a go of things. A good husband too, I wouldn't wonder—"

"But not for me? Anyway," she said very low, "I don't see that all this matters to you."

"Oh, but it does, Twenty, it does! Any decent employer has a duty towards the men and women on his staff, wouldn't you say? Temporary workers included, of course," he added hastily as he saw the protest forming on her lips. "Wouldn't you agree?"

"I . . . suppose so."

He was stacking heavy tea-tree logs on the open fire and the crackling of the dried timber mingled with the moaning of the wind outside. In the silence Angela was aware of a strange emotion that was stealing over her. a breathless happiness, transient as the flickering firelight. How attractive he looked with the flames throwing shadows over the lean face. And those blue eyes. Odd, they didn't appear cold tonight. It must be the effect of the firelight. Mark's voice was different too, as low and caressing that if she hadn't known better she would almost imagine . . . Lazily he reached a hand towards her hair, curling the end of a long coppery-red strand around his finger. "Looking after you, I mean."

At something in his gaze she dropped her own. She had the most absurd impulse to reach up and touch the bronzed masculine face. She simply must take herself in hand, get the better of this electricity, fire-magic or whatever it was that was stealing away her senses. All at once she made up her mind. She would ask him straight out to listen to her. She'd *make* him believe that everything she had told him was the truth! Only this time she would appeal to him, she wouldn't allow herself to get mad and spoil everything the way she had before. She drew a deep breath. "Mark, there's something—"

But he had risen to his feet, mouth set and voice oddly gruff. "Time all little girls were in bed! That fire should keep going for an hour or so yet!" His glance moved to the nearby bunk. "It's rough, but it's better than nothing!" He turned away, said in a strangely hoarse tone, "'Night, Twenty!"

She stared up at him in surprise. "But where will you—"

"Don't worry about me, I'll doss down in the Land Rover. It won't be the first time!" He was at the door, "See you in the morning!" The gale tossed the words back at her, then he flung the door shut and Angela was alone.

She stared into the leaping flames. How strange he was! She would never understand him. For a brief time tonight they had seemed to have a rapport between them. A sudden thought struck her. What it he too had been aware of that electric awareness that had seemed to leap between them? Could that be the reason he had gone so abruptly? Or was she imagining things? In this alien world everything was a puzzle, she mused bewilderedly. Except one thing. The truth hit her like a physical blow. *She only knew she loved him.* Loved the boss, that cold enigmatical employer of hers. All this time she had imagined she hated him, yet somewhere along the line she had allowed herself to fall in love with him. Deeply, irrevocably, hopelessly in love.

A longing so intense took over that it was only with an effort she prevented herself from running after him into the darkness, calling, "Come back! Come back! There are so many things between us, things that need explaining, that *must* be explained before you can ever think of me as—" She brought her thoughts up sharply. What made her imagine he would ever change his opinion of her? To him she was just Twenty, the silly, slightly amusing English girl who had planned a wedding to a stranger that hadn't come off. All at once a pang of anguish shot through her. How could she have been so blind as not to take in his meaning before? He'd made it plain enough, heaven knows! John, the "good guy", too good apparently to be allowed to get into the clutches of self-seeking young Twenty to whom one young Kiwi sheep farmer was as good prospective husband-material as another not now available.

Bemused by the intimacy of the firelit room, she had even forgotten all about Susan, with whom Mark's feelings were already romantically involved. She had forgotten everything but his nearness. A yearning that was almost physical possessed her.

The flames had long ago died to glowing embers, but still Angela lay awake in the narrow bunk, conscious of the lumpy mattress and the regrets that wouldn't go away. If only she had come to Waikare on her own initiative, without Martha's name to spoil everything! If only she'd been able to explain the truth to Mark. Worst of all came the thought that she must live with it through the days to come. If only she hadn't been stupid enough to allow herself to fall in love with him!

A fit of shivering shook her in spite of the oppressive warmth of the closed hut. Now she knew why she hadn't really minded the exhausting work in the cookhouse, why she had offered with such alacrity to stay on at the station keeping house in Doris's absence. It was all plain, too plain, and where did it leave her? It left her in a worse situation than ever. She was in love with a man who couldn't care less about her. And the shame-making part of it all was that in spite of everything that had happened to her here she still didn't regret having taken up Martha's offer to come to Waikare. What she must do now was prevent Mark from ever guessing her feelings towards him. For the knowledge that she loved him would afford him the most amusement of all her pranks. She could imagine the capital he'd make out of that piece of interesting information! Tears squeezed behind her eyelids and slid down her cheeks. Why do you have to win *all* the time, Mark Hillyer?

She fell asleep at last, and when she awoke sunshine was slanting through the small high window of the hut. She opened the door and peered outside, conscious of a chorus of birdsong from the native bush all around. Pools of water lay in the muddy pathway shaded by overhanging trees, but the river that last night had been a raging torrent had dropped to a lower level. In the daylight Angela could clearly see the broken timbers and sagging supports of the narrow timber bridge. How unpredictable was the weather in this part of the world! Now the air was incredibly clear and fresh, patches of blue sky showed between white clouds scudding by in a light breeze. Although leaves and branches all around her were beaded with crystal drops there was no doubt that the storm was over.

As she stood gazing around her Mark came strolling up the pathway towards her, and taking in his drawn, heavy-eyed appearance she felt a stab of compunction. He couldn't have had much sleep last night, huddled in the Land Rover. If he had asked her to share the hut with him—but he hadn't.

His tone however was cheerful enough. "Morning, Twenty!" The words were accompanied by the usual sardonic smile. "Sleep well?"

"Yes, thanks." So they were back to the customary light approach. She wished he wouldn't always talk to her in that tone of careless indulgence as though she were some strange creature who had somehow wandered into his orbit. She did have a name, although he would never acknowledge the fact.

"The river's down," he was saying. "Uncanny, isn't it, the way it can rise ten feet in a few hours, then drain away again? We should be able to wade through to the other side if we pick the right spot. Care to give it a go?"

She nodded, looking past him to the vehicle standing near the washed-out approach to the bridge. "You're leaving the Land Rover here?"

"Can't do anything else but, Twenty! Not to worry, though. There'll be someone zooming over from the house looking out for us before we get far on the other side of the river. They'll guess what happened. Torrential rain like we had last night usually does a heck of a lot of damage on the road to the homestead. We're bound to meet up before long with someone coming to the rescue!" Stepping inside the hut, he gazed towards the fireplace. "We'll have to leave that as it is, the embers are still hot, but I'll send one of the boys over tomorrow to replace the log pile. You never know who'll be coming along next looking for a night's shelter." He glanced towards her flared denim jeans. "You'll need to roll those up and go barefoot for this expedition!"

"That's easy!" Already she had bent to turn up the jeans above sun-tanned knees. "Is that better?"

"You'll do! Here, put this on or the trees will drip right down your neck!" He was standing behind her and she felt him draw her windbreaker gently around her shoulders. For a moment he was motionless, his hands at her throat, and she thought he must surely hear the thud-thud of her stupid heart. Then he turned away, said in a quietly contained tone, "Come on, let's go!" He clasped her hand. "Better hang on tight to me, it's easy to take a header in the mud."

Hand in hand they went down the path, splashing through

pools of water and moving beneath dripping tree branches. As they emerged into the open Angela realised the full force of the flash flood of the previous night, for water filled a great gaping hole leading to the timber bridge. The river was a swollen sluggish stream, choked with logs and fallen trees. She watched debris and fence-posts go floating by.

"There's a better point to cross over further, upstream," Mark told her. "It's wide and shallow and we should be able to wade over without any trouble. That's the spot where they'll be expecting us to cross."

He seemed to have forgotten to release her hand as they followed the winding river. Presently they reached a bend where water spread between wide banks and together they waded through the shallows. Now she was glad of his strong supporting handclasp, for beneath her feet were loose boulders that slipped away as she set foot on them, tree-logs that looked solidly wedged between rocks, then floated away on the current. As they made progress the water became deeper until they were wading waist-deep, pushing their way through clumps of fallen earth, uprooted trees and dislodged fence-posts. But she was with Mark, her hand in his firm grasp. They were splashing into the shallows on the opposite bank of the river when a truck came into sight driven by Alex, one of the shepherds. As they clambered up through the bushes on the bank, Alex guided the vehicle to a stop on the grass above and a cheerful face with untidy brown hair and challenging blue eyes appeared in the opening of the cab. "Just timed it right! I thought I'd be pretty sure of a welcome!" he grinned as Angela and Mark climbed up beside him. "Lucky that Doris took herself off before the storm caught up with you. She'd be having a fit if she'd known you were out in it. You know what she's like when it comes to storms."

Squeezed into the seat between Mark and the driver, once again Angela was swept by that suffocating sense of awareness of Mark. Was that one of the tricks that falling deeply in love played on you? Making you feel powerless against a man's masculine magnetism? Fortunately he was unaware of the inner turmoil his nearness aroused in her. At the moment he was discussing with his shepherd matters of more concern to him, such as had many of the sheep fallen casualties to the rain last night? And the brood mares in the hill paddock, how had they fared in the electrical storm?

They'd been lucky at Waikare, Alex assured him as he guided the truck over sodden paddocks towards the ribbon of road winding over the hills. Half a dozen ewes lost, but that was all.

The two men went on to discuss farming matters, but Angela was only half listening. She roused herself as Mark said carelessly, "I suppose you've collected a few refugees up at the house, waiting for the river to go down so they can go on their way?"

Alex nodded, swerving to avoid a tree recently struck by lightning that was lying on the narrow pathway. "Man! You should have seen the place last night. Talk about a scene of activity! Three different lots showed up through the night. They couldn't get over the river and turned back looking for shelter. There were people everywhere. Jill was doing her best to cope with getting them all bedded down."

Angela realised now the purpose of the empty bedrooms with their beds made up in readiness. She wondered why she hadn't anticipated the arrival of unexpected guests at the homestead through the night. If three lots of travellers had been stormbound there might be others too who had been trapped by the broken bridge. At least, she comforted herself with dreary logic, the extra work involved in the house would serve to take her mind from other more personal problems. If only her special problem didn't have a vibrant heart-catching voice and a way of looking at you at times that made you feel you mattered a little after all in spite of being just Twenty, whose one extenuating characteristic seemed to be that she'd have a go at anything that came her way!

She brought her mind back to Alex's cheerful tones. "When I left the house the new arrivals were champing at the bit to take off, but I told them if they waited a bit the stream'll be low enough for them to ford it. Tomorrow should do it. The only ones that are taking the delay in their stride are a family party, city characters with two boys on their way back after a holiday up north. The kids have never seen a farm before and they've taken to it like ducks to water. We'll be lucky if we get rid of them when the river goes down. Then there's a business guy heading back to town after a stint of deep-sea fishing up in the Bay of Islands. He's browned off with waiting already. Seems to have the idea that the whole works are going to fall apart at the seams if he doesn't show up at the office in town today. He's in for a surprise! I can't seem to get it into his thick head that the telephone lines are down and there's nothing we can do about it."

Mark nodded. "He'll keep. How about the others? Who else

is waiting around?"

"One other party—two middle-aged women. They're in a tizz too. Seems one of them is due in the city today to give a travel talk at some club. The way they're going on anyone would think it was the end of the world not making it back to town today."

"She should be glad, the one who's giving the talk," Mark commented drily. "She'll be able to add a note of adventure when she does get around to it."

"You just try telling her that," Alex muttered gloomily.

"What's the transport, cars?"

"No, they're lucky there. Only one car, that belongs to the women. There's a truck and a Land Rover as well."

Mark glanced up towards brilliant patches of blue in the sky above. "They'll be right!" Angela was becoming accustomed to hearing the familiar Kiwi phrase that seemed to cover all possible eventualities. "Looks like they'll be able to get through the ford by morning."

"That's what I told them." A shower of mud splashed over the windows from the flooded pathway below and Alex peered ahead. "One thing about the storm, though. Those stranded bods got Brian out of bed! He's been wandering around the house half the night brewing coffee for all hands. Reckon he's feeling a whole lot better being busy and doing something for himself for a change instead of letting Jill fuss over him!"

"Great!" Mark's face had lighted up. "Looks like he'll be okay from now on. The doc said that once he got on the mend he'd go ahead like wildfire. Now there'll be no looking back!" He grinned towards Alex. "What do you bet he'll be putting his name down for some of the rodeo events this season?"

Alex shook his curly brown head. "I'm not having that on! He'd be just crazy enough to give it a go, sore head and all!"

Mark was looking so delighted with the news of Brian's recovery that Angela realised all over again how deep was his concern for his young brother. She followed the thought to its logical conclusion, and how resentful he must be of Martha who had bruised Brian's already shaky confidence in himself. Martha, she reminded herself with a stab of pain, included her, or so Mark thought. With an effort of will she wrenched her bleak thoughts aside. Think of Brian, she told herself. Once again she wondered whether it was really to his advantage—Brian with his self-doubts, his slight physique and diffident manner, to live in such close contact with the strong older brother. Might it not be wiser for Brian to leave Waikare and strike out on his own account, make some sort of life for himself, no matter how ordinary?

All at once she realised they were running down a slippery slope towards the main entrance. Pools of water spread over the grass and above seabirds wheeled and soared. Ahead was the store shed and mailbox. The next moment they were rattling over a cattlestop and sweeping around the curving driveway. Already Angela could see a cluster of vehicles in the yard.

"Mark!" As the Land Rover swung around and braked near the porch Susan came flying down the steps. At the sight of the other girl, frilly organza apron floating from a slim waist and blonde hair carefully in place, Angela was uneasily aware of her own wind-tangled hair and crumpled jeans.

"You're back!" Susan's glance went past Angela. She might not be there, Angela thought hotly, for all the notice Susan was taking of her. A red-hot pang of jealousy shot through her. She had never known she could feel like this about another girl. "I've been so *worried* about you!" Susan was saying.

Alex's blue eyes glinted. "Don't blame you for that, Sue. Angela's the prettiest thing that's happened along in this direction for a long while—"

"Alex, really . . ." Angela threw him a reproachful look, but a voice deep inside her was saying, "Bless you!"

Although Susan pretended to ignore the teasing comment the colour deepened beneath the mask of make-up on her tanned cheeks. She ran to stand beside Mark as he helped Angela down from the high seat. "Anything could have happened to you, out in a storm like that!"

In the shepherd's eyes the wicked glint deepened. "Anything", he agreed.

Again Susan made a pretence of not taking in his meaning. She linked her hand over Mark's bronzed bare arm. "I came over here as soon as I could. I knew there'd be travellers cut off by the storm and wanting to be put up in the house . . . and there was no one else." The petulant tone implied that Angela would have been better employed sticking at her job rather than traipsing around the country with her employer. "There's Jill, of course," Susan added reluctantly "and Brian has been busy too. He's in the kitchen now attacking a colossal pile of breakfast dishes. Oh, Mark," she glanced up into his face, "I thought you were never coming back! And don't tell me I should be used to it by now," she admonished playfully, "because I'll never feel any different. I can't!"

As Alex with a parting grin drove the truck away Angela

hurried on ahead of the other two towards the house. Running up the steps, she narrowly averted a collision with two boys of about ten and twelve years who came hurtling past her uttering loud and fearsome cowboy yells.

Inside, the lounge room seemed filled with strangers, all eyeing her enquiringly. Mark had gone to his room and it was Susan who came to stand at her side. Sue flashed her wide and glittering smile. "Folks, this is Angela. She helps around the house," to Angela the contemptuous tone was infuriating, "when she's here. Your apron's hanging on the nail behind the door in the kitchen, Angela."

Feeling like some sort of atomic-age Cinderella, Angela gave an uncertain smile and escaped to the kitchen. She found Brian standing at the sink. Somehow she hadn't realised before how small and thin he was. He turned at her approach, then glanced away, and as always she was conscious of a sense of constraint between them. "Oh, it's you, Angela."

She tried for cheerfulness. "That's right—at last. I thought we were never going to make it back to the homestead when I saw what had happened to the bridge back there." Inwardly the thoughts churned through her mind. If only I could get through to him that I knew nothing of Martha's plans for marriage, that I was only a messenger. I'd like to say to him right at this minute, "Please you've *got* to believe me! I had nothing to do with what happened between you and Martha". But what would be the use? It's not the time or the place for confidences of that sort, and anyway, appearances are too much against me. He'd never believe I was telling the truth! Probably just seeing me here reminds him of her, makes him feel more than ever rejected, deepens his sense of let-down.

"Guess you're about ready for this." He turned towards a huge aluminium teapot and poured a cup of tea, then pushed it towards her. "Don't take any notice of the mess in here," his shy grin was somehow appealing, "and don't let Sue get you down. She just likes to organise everyone. It's a gift she has. You might have noticed."

"I have a bit." Angela perched on a high stool and sipped her tea. "Golly," she murmured in sudden panic, "I'll have to do something about feeding all these people. Whatever did Doris do when she struck an emergency like this? She must have coped with it all somehow."

"No problem." Brian had resumed his task at the sink bench. "She's got oodles of stuff stashed away in there just for occasions like this!" He waved a hand towards the massive freezer at the end of the room. "You take your choice and get something out in time for it to defreeze before you do the serving. I can recommend the corn fritters."

Angela breathed a sigh of relief. "Now however could I have forgotten all Doris told me about that?" Because you're thinking of nothing but Mark all the time, that's why! She thrust the answer aside.

"Forget it right now," Brian was saying. "Why don't you take a hot shower, get yourself something to eat?"

She pushed aside the empty cup. "You know, I think I will. Take a shower, I mean." She pushed aside the bright hair back from her forehead. "Heaven knows what I look like, but I suppose we were lucky to get back here today even though we did have to leave the Land Rover on the other side of the river."

He nodded, plunging his hands into foaming detergent in the sink. "It happens roughly on an average about three times a year! That's when the roadworkers' old hut comes in handy."

"Does it ever! We certainly found that out! Mark—" Angela stopped short, aware of Susan who was standing in the open doorway and listening intently. Why should she have to explain to anyone, least of all this domineering girl-friend of Mark's? Let her draw whatever conclusions she wished regarding the night spent in the open. Feeling all at once grubby and tired and sick of everything, Angela went slowly towards her own room. Why must Susan be here, taking over everything, acting as though this were her own home? Why not? The answer was all too clear. For wouldn't she be mistress here soon, probably before the year was out? And jealousy, she admonished herself, will get you nowhere. There's just nothing in the world you can do about it.

The day went by in a round of ceaseless activity. In the evening as they gathered in the lounge the stranded travellers were in a more cheerful mood. Mark assured them that they could continue their interrupted journey in the morning and just to make certain no harm came to them he offered to take the Land Rover and accompany them over the ford. He brushed aside their expressions of gratitude. Such happenings, he assured them, were all part of the day's work at Waikare and would continue to be so until such time as the remote area was serviced by better roading and new bridges over the river.

Anyway, he told them with his lopsided grin, he'd done nothing, he wasn't the one who had done all the "looking after" of the unexpected guests. His glance softened as his eyes rested for a moment on Angela's fresh young face.

It was Susan, however, who answered. "Don't give it a thought," she disclaimed laughingly, "we just love having folks to stay up here. And don't be so modest, Mark. You know you like showing visitors around the station. I'm with you all the way! It's wonderful to meet new people with different views and ways of living. Boys too!" Her wide glittering smile included the two lads whose downcast faces revealed that alone among the group they had no wish to return to the city. "We don't get many boys visiting up here, especially ones who fit so well into country life! Isn't that right, Rex? Wayne? You wouldn't mind staying up here, would you?"

Two freckled faces were suddenly alive and interested. "We get holidays in August," the elder of the two cried eagerly. "Isn't that lambing time up here? Maybe we could come up then and give you a hand. You know, learn to ride horses and go around the paddocks to make sure the ewes are okay?"

"That's a fantastic idea!" Susan smiled. "Consider yourself hired as shepherds for two weeks in the lambing season. I'll guarantee to find you two good mounts. What do you say to that, Mark?"

Susan's confident tones twisted Angela's heart. The warm initmacy of the other girl's gaze left no doubt as to her position here. If she were not mistress at Waikare already then it was merely a matter of time. And Mark? Pain shot through Angela as she sought to read his face, but he had turned towards the cocktail cabinet and was mixing drinks. "That's a date, then," he said evenly. "We'll be expecting you boys. Your parents too if they can make it."

In the morning Angela prepared an early breakfast for the travellers, then stood watching from the porch as the unexpected guests carried out bags and suitcases from the house and stowed the luggage in their vehicles. Somewhat to Angela's surprise Susan announced that she too must return home today. She pulled an expressive face. She didn't want to leave, of course, but relatives from overseas were expected to arrive during the day and she was expected back to welcome them. As she watched Mark's face, it didn't seem to Angela that he was devastated by this news, but then he never was one to display his inner feelings. The next moment she realised the reason for his unconcern, for Susan, getting into her car, was calling back gaily, "I'll be back for the barbecue on Saturday night!"

Mark went to stand beside the car. "I'll see you to the ford, just to make sure you get through."

She giggled up at him. "I was hoping you would."

The burning thought came to Angela that this was the reason he hadn't kissed Susan goodbye. Why should he, when they could make their farewells in privacy later on when the other travellers had left them? Oh, why did she think these things? Why did it hurt so much to picture the other two alone together? Susan—was she the reason why Mark had left her so abruptly when they had shared the firelit intimacy on the night of the storm?

Wrenching her thoughts back to the present, she became aware of the protestations of friendship and heartful thanks that were echoing all around her. The business man, whose taut nerves had gradually unwound amid the peaceful surroundings of the station, bade Angela and Mark a courteous farewell. The two women friends extended a warm invitation to all at the homestead to come and stay for a visit at the big old house the two shared in the city. No need to give any notice, they told them, just come! As the line of vehicles moved away the two young boys leaned from the window waving widly and shouting "See you in August!"

Angela's parting wave was perfunctory. Somehow she couldn't prevent her gaze from straying towards Susan. The bright sunshine tangled sunbeams in the blonde hair as she leaned from her car, laughing and calling to Mark who was in the lead of the procession of vehicles.

At her side Brian said, "Well, that's the last we'll see of that lot! Now comes the bit Doris didn't like at the end of these emergency set-ups—washing all the bed linen and getting it ready for the next lot!" The thought ran through Angela's mind that Brian was speaking to her without his customary sense of unease. Perhaps in the excitement of the moment he had temporarily forgotten that she was a friend of the girl who had betrayed him. She thought he looked different this morning. A tinge of healthy colour tinged his face and he appeared stronger. "You'll have to get Jill to give you a hand with it," he said carelessly.

The smile forming on Angela's lips died away as she met the younger girl's angry glance. "Why should I?" Jill muttered resentfully. The soft young lips tightened. "She's getting paid for it!"

"Don't bother!" Angela turned aside and went to attack the pile of linen heaped beside the washing machine. As she flung sheets and pillow cases into the churning suds her thoughts wandered. She wouldn't have imagined that Jill's suspicious, hostile attitude towards her could hurt so much. Just a strange girl, whom she wouldn't ever meet again once she left here, and yet . . . One more thing she had to blame Martha for, one more person to dislike and distrust her.

Keep busy, she admonished herself, and don't let all this worry you. Immediately, however, the thought ran through her mind. If only *one* person here believed in me, *if only that one person were Mark*! Since the night of the storm she had tried not to think of him—tried, but it was no use, for waking or sleeping he stayed in her mind. He had become a part of her life, the only part that mattered. She had been grateful for the crowded house that made it possible to avoid meeting his direct glance. From now on it wouldn't be easy to conceal her thoughts when their eyes met, yet somehow she must do just that. If only there was some magical way one could put a lock on longing, shut out the heartbreak.

CHAPTER EIGHT

To Angela it seemed strange to feel so isolated, for telephone lines were down and there were no newspapers or mail deliveries. Not that she was expecting any letters, but it was possible that Doris might have written from the South Island. Her only other correspondent was Graeme back in London, and she had as yet given him no forwarding address. Was it because deep down she wanted to put him out of her life? Since coming to Waikare she had found herself in another world and there was no going back. It seemed, she mused on a sigh, that it took only one man, one special man, to make you feel that way; for you to long never to be out of sight of him, even though you knew perfectly well you were asking for heartbreak.

Nevertheless she must write to Graeme, and soon. Back in her room she dropped down to the bed and sat for a long time nibbling the end of her ballpoint. Of what could she write? Should she describe the scenery here, try to paint a picture of life on an outback New Zealand sheep station? But she knew he wouldn't be interested. The tag of verse Brian had read to her jingled in her mind with a ring of truth.

"But if I say so here folks stare
Not knowing how it is out there."

No, the only subject of interest to Graeme would be their own plans for the future, only the plans weren't real any longer. She knew now that whatever doubts she might have had about marrying Graeme had crystallised into certainty. Now there wasn't the slightest question in her mind that the lukewarm affair you could scarcely term a romance was over. But how did you tell a man who cared for you that you didn't love him and never would? Mark's clear decisive tones seemed to echo in her mind "A clean cut . . . kindest in the long run." It was almost as if he were dictating the words, not many and as little hurtful as she could make them. "Sorry, I hope this won't come as too much of a shock, but since coming out here I've had time to think things over and it's only fair to let you know I've changed my mind about our plans. It's not that there's anyone else—" She stared at the sentence until the words seemed to intensify on the page. "Isn't it?" The silly teardrop splashed down on the paper and she crumpled it up and threw it aside. She forced herself to write a second note, omitting the part that wasn't true, the part, she thought wryly, that hurt her even more than it would wound him, fool that she was. It was a horrible letter, stilted and unreal, but it was the best she could do. She sealed the flimsy airmail envelope before she could write another which would be no improvement on this.

When she went into the lounge the telephone was ringing. So the line had been repaired! She hurried to pick up the receiver and caught Doris's excited tones. "Is that you, Angela?"

"That's me!" Heart-warming to hear a friendly voice, even over the wire. "How are you, Doris? I hope you've got some news of Kelly's arrival?"

"Oh, I have! I have! This morning! I thought I'd ring you first of all to let you know the good news. The most beautiful baby, with the biggest brown eyes you ever saw in your life. Eve's so thrilled!"

"I can imagine! A wee girl after all those boys! No wonder your daughter's so proud of her—"

"Oh, it's not a her, dear, it's a he and a big nine-pounder at that!"

"Oh dear . . . I hope your daughter isn't disappointed?"

"*Disappointed?* Good lord, no! She's on top of the world! She says she's so used to boys now she doesn't know how she'd cope with a fussy, prissy little girl around the place. She says it would sure to be a boyish type with all those brothers to play with. You know, pack a gun in her belt-holster and play those awful warlike games the boys love. It's really much better this way, Eve says. She's got oodles of clothes for hand-me-downs, not pants, of course, they always go through the knees, but lots of tops!"

Tactfully Angela refrained from any mention of the drawer in the homestead crammed with "think-pinks". Not that she could get a word in had she wished, for Doris, excited and happy, chatted on breathlessly. She enquired about happenings at the station. Had Angela and Mark managed to get back to the homestead on the night of the storm after seeing her off at the airport in town? How was Brian progressing? And John, had Angela heard any more of him? Was Jill still staying at the house? Would it suit Angela if she stayed on for a full month in the south? At last she rang off, and feeling cheered by the friendly tones Angela strolled down the steps.

She decided to take a walk. Of late there had been so many duties to keep her indoors. (Don't kid yourself, it's not the station surroundings you're interested in seeing but Mark—

always Mark). Pushing the thought aside, she moved out into the afternoon sunshine where in the flower plots bedraggled roses and mud-spattered lilies gave evidence of the recent storm. By the pool Rusty was busy with a long bamboo rake scooping up a pink wash of Suva Queen hibiscus blossoms swept by high winds from bushes growing on the bank above. As Angela neared him he glanced up and something in the familiar deep chuckle and crinkled smile touched her. That was what came of being generally disliked, she told herself wryly, it made you pathetically grateful for the slightest sign of affection that came your way.

"Hi, Rusty," she came to stand beside him. "It looks as though the storm has made lots of extra work for you!"

"Keeps me out of mischief!" He chuckled. "Same goes for you, I'd say! Looks like a refugee camp, does Waikare, every time the river floods." He tossed the blossoms on a mounting heap of pink petals. "That Sue, she wouldn't be much help to you . . . all talk, that one. Doris keeps a stock of frozen stuff all ready for times when a crowd appears from nowhere. Took all the credit for looking after them herself, Sue did, I bet?"

Angela's lips curved in a smile. "How did you guess?"

Rusty's small frame shook as he chuckled to himself. "Can't help getting to know folk in isolated places like this. The good and the bad, it sticks out a mile, no matter how folk try to hide it. That Sue, she ain't never seemed to have heard about not counting your chickens before they're hatched," the blue eyes glinted conspiratorially, "know what I mean?"

"I've got an idea."

"So long as you don't let her pull the wool over your eyes." He bent to pick up a blossom and tossed it on the top of the pile. Enigmatically he added, "The boss, he don't say much, but he won't let any woman push him around, no, sir!"

Angela pretended not to understand him, but her spirits rose magically. Rusty was only, what had he termed himself, the "do-anything-man," but come to think of it, wasn't that about the most valuable attribute of all in these remote districts where settlers could be called upon to do all manner of jobs that in the cities would be undertaken by tradesmen or craftsmen? What if Rusty were right? What if the liking, the pushing, the *affection* were all on Susan's side? All at once it seemed to her that sunshine had never seemed so sparkling, air so crystal clear. For once the wind had dropped away and it was very still. Two seabirds soared overhead, white wings outspread against the translucent blue. She heard herself saying in what she hoped was a tone of unconcern, "Where is he working today, the boss?"

Rusty bent to prop up a drooping stem of giant flowering stock. "He's over in the paddock breaking in a new horse. Why don't you take a stroll over there and take a look? He's got his own method when it comes to breaking in his horses and it works like a charm!"

Angela hesitated. She had a swift recollection of a television documentary programme she had once viewed, a mental picture of spurs and whips, of a terrified wild thing roped and thrown to the ground. "It's not too cruel?"

"Cruel? Mark? Girl, you've got the wrong idea about the boss. When it comes to breaking in horses he knows what he's doing. He takes time about it, no hurry, gently does it. It takes plenty of patience believe me but it works in the long run. You have to hand it to the boss, he knows his job!"

Angela was looking puzzled. "But how could he break in a horse gently?"

"Easy if you take your time about it. The boss, he starts right at the beginning, gets the foal used to being handled by him, gets the little chap's confidence, makes the foal feel he's not afraid of him. Mark does that all the time the foal's growing up, and then when the day comes for the young one to have the saddle on his back Mark has no trouble. I've seen him get on a newly-broken mount and ride him around the paddock quiet as can be, no problem." The blue eyes in the weather-roughened face twinkled. "You should go and watch him in action. Know the place I mean? Through the first gate, turn left and follow the sheeptracks to the top of the rise."

"It's an idea, I think I'll do just that!" But in her heart Angela knew it was more than an idea, it was a compulsion, an excuse to see Mark once more. She simply couldn't help herself, why pretend otherwise?

Strolling past garages and implement sheds, she reached the gateway. As usual she had to push aside a cluster of fat woolly sheep contentedly enjoying their dustbath before she could open the gate. The path to the left that Rusty had indicated led down into a bush-filled gully where giant tree-ferns and tall leafy puriri trees met overhead. When she emerged into bright sunlight she climbed the slope and found herself on a grassy plateau where a man was leading a bay mare around a worn dirt track. Angela paused to watch as Mark leaped up into the saddle, but there were no buck jumps or wild sideways leaps in an attempt to unseat the rider. For a moment the mare stood motionless then she continued quietly along the dusty circle in the grass.

She climbed up on the gateway, perching herself on the top rail and swinging tanned legs. As he caught sight of her, Mark waved, "Be with you in a minute!" Soon he was pulling rein beside her. He dropped to the ground and gave the mare an encouraging pat. Angela caught the deep quiet tones. "That's enough for one day, old lady. Take it easy now!" He was slipping away saddle and girth. "Not too bad, was it? Tomorrow we'll try out a trot and canter. You'll catch on in no time at all! We're going to get along fine together, you and I!"

How infinitely soothing were the low masculine tones. So this was the pattern of breaking in the horses bred on the station, a method that produced such unfailingly successful results. Kindness in place of cruelty, patience and understanding rather than ruthlessness or the whip that could break an animal's spirit for all time.

He came to lean on the gate beside her, the bridle jingling from his arm, and she looked down at him, unaware that her eyes were shining. "Is that all there is to breaking in a horse? I guess she won't mind your mounting her next time, or the next?"

"That's the idea, Twenty! Myself, I don't go for that word 'breaking'. There's no need for anything of that sort. Not that I've got any particular magic touch. What you saw just now was the result of months of handling. Ever since that mare was born I've been around with her, won her confidence—"

"I know, I know! Rusty was telling me—"

"Rusty?" His blue eyes squinted against the sun as he grinned up at her. "You don't want to believe all you hear, Twenty! The old boy happens to be prejudiced about some things."

"Including the boss?" Angela's hazel eyes were laughing and provocative.

"Could be."

All at once her expression sobered. Someone else had said those words to her quite recently. Of course, Martha. Now the thought ran through her mind that the advice could work for as well as against her. Like everyone at the station believing that Susan and Mark would be married one of these days—everyone but Rusty, that was. Or was she grasping at straws, clutching at any hope rather than face up to a truth that hurt too much to acknowledge?

Mark gave a friendly pat to the mare standing by the fence. "Away you go, old girl. We'll have another session tomorrow."

How infinitely gentle was his manner with the highly-strung

mare, Angela mused. A tender lover too, she wouldn't wonder. His deep tones cut across her musing. "Ever done any riding, Twenty?"

She shook her head and dropped down beside him on the grass. "I never had the chance."

"Like to?"

"Uh-huh." (I'd like to do anything if you were there with me to show me how, Mark.) The truth hit her like a blow. "Only there isn't much time left now, is there?"

He didn't answer and the next moment she wondered if she had imagined his odd considering look, for he was saying lightly, "Right now I'm going to take you to see the falls. After the rain the other night they should be quite a sight!" Moving towards the Land Rover, he flung saddle and bridle in the back and swung open the passenger door. "Hop in!"

"There are an awful lot of things to see on this station," she murmured. She was conscious of a secret happiness. They were alone together in the stillness and the sunshine and all at once nothing else in the world mattered.

The Land Rover lurched over rough ground as they dropped down into the green gloom of a tree-filled gully, then swept up to the crest of a high hill. Mark brought the vehicle to a stop, pointing out to Angela the southern boundaries where rough bushland was covered in an impenetrable jungle of twisted tea tree. Beyond were the swamplands, choked with mangroves and perilous to all but those familiar with the treacherous depths. They moved on, sweeping down a track cut through thickly-growing native bush and presently Mark braked to a stop over long tree-shadows on the path. "It's a walking track from now on. Not far." Angela's curious gaze took in a twisting track lost to view amongst dense bush. "I'll go ahead," Mark said, "and show you the way!"

She followed him down the overgrown track, stepping carefully over trailing black ropes of supple jack looped from branches high above. Thorny bush lawyer and trailing plants barred their progress, but Mark pushed aside the tangled barriers as Angela made her way forward. In the depths of the bush the air was hot and still, the only sound the buzz of insects. Once from their feet a native pigeon rose with a flutter of iridescent blue-green wings. As they went on Angela could hear the muted roar of a waterfall that gradually became louder. Then at last they emerged from the filtered green light into a grassy clearing and she was conscious of a cloud of spray blowing cool and damp on her face. She stepped back, laughing, then her gaze lifted. A hundred feet up white spray was blowing over the flax and tea-tree growing on the banks as the sun-shot water tumbled in a never-ending white torrent to foam and swirl over rocks far below. "Lovely!" She looked up at him, her face flushed from the heat of the bush-track.

"You haven't seen it all yet! There's something rather special down here. We'll have to wade through the water though—give me your hand!"

At his touch once again the masculine magnetism took over, potent, way beyond her control, so that forgetting everything else Angela stumbled on a slippery rock and would have fallen had it not been for his strong grasp. She realised they were making their way towards a cavern beneath the falls. Inside the damp earth walls were encrusted with small ferns and pools of water lay on the ground. Mark pushed aside long spears of flax and turned towards her with a smile. "Now you can look!"

"A rainbow in the falls," she cried incredulously, "away down here? I just don't believe it!" She was fascinated by the arch of muted colours. Eerie and insubstantial as a dream, the rainbow glistened through the blowing spray.

"There's always a rainbow here," Mark told her, "so long as the sun shines. Thought you'd like it."

"Like it!" Angela thought she had never seen anything as beautiful as the misted colours curving through the blown spray. "It's so funny," she scarcely realised she was speaking her innermost thoughts aloud, "the rainbow, I mean. I used to think that coming out to this country was a bit like looking for—" Her voice faltered into silence as the terrible thought came to her that he'd be bound to put his own interpretation on her particular "pot of gold". A rich Kiwi husband, a wealthy sheep farmer? Stupid, *stupid*! Now she had sent the magic of the moment flying away into nothingness, blown away like the mists swirling around them.

"This, Twenty?" He turned to catch her in his arms and excitement was making her heart beat faster as he drew her close. The next moment very gently his lips brushed her cheek. A breath of wind tossed the flying spray towards them in a misty shower, but neither noticed as at last he found her lips in a kiss that for Angela blotted out the world.

Afterwards she told herself that there must have been some special magic in the misted rainbow, otherwise she would have drawn herself away from him sooner, not let him kiss her when he was already involved with someone else. But she had forgotten Susan, forgotten everything, and it was only with an effort of will that she disengaged herself and drew free. "Pot of gold," she murmured wildly, "that's what I meant."

He said very softly, "That's what I meant too."

Pain twisted her heart. So her fears were justified. He was referring, of course, to Martha and her husband-hunting projects in a new country, what else? He made to take her in his arms once again, but with an unsteady laugh she turned aside, said quickly, "Hadn't we better get back?"

"As you wish!" A muscle twitched at the side of his bronzed cheek. He was silent as they retraced their steps over the water-washed rocks and up the bush track. Glancing towards his set jaw and chilly blue eyes, she wondered if he were already regretting that kiss by the waterfall. But what was a kiss? More likely he had already forgotten the momentary impulse that had impelled him to caress someone whom he usually regarded with a sort of indulgent amusement. Still, she was a girl and he was a man—and Susan was far away.

Hurrying her steps, Angela stumbled on over the overgrown trail. Somehow it didn't bear thinking about, that kiss. To him a mere gesture, to her a moment of ecstasy, of being close at at last to a man who was everything she had ever dreamed of in a lover. How amused he would be, she thought with secret irony, were he to be aware of the truth of her dreams about that pot of gold at the end of the rainbow. For a brief time she had thought she had found it, but evanescent as a dream the moment of fulfilment had slipped from her grasp. You never ever found that pot of gold, not really. Tears stung her eyes and she blinked them away. Imagine Mark, already probably planning a wedding with the daughter of a neighbouring station-owner, becoming seriously interested in Twenty, the shearers' cook! Could anything be more unlikely?

In the days that followed Angela told herself a thousand times that it was crazy, it was hopeless, it just didn't make any sense for her to feel this way about Mark. But love, it seemed, took no account of common sense or resolutions and just to see him was suddenly everything—lighting his pipe, tossing back the thatch of thick black hair, giving the men their orders before riding away for the day's work. Such ordinary things, yet significant because they were a part of him. And underneath it all the pain, the heartache that somehow she must hide from everyone, and especially from him. She was glad now for his casual attitude towards her, and it was only in dreams that he called her by her own name. Let him call her "Twenty", that wey it was easier, for she'd die, she'd just die if he ever guessed the way she felt about him.

So this was love! She knew at last the reason why other affairs of the heart had never really touched her. Only vaguely had she felt that there was a deeper territory of the heart, heights and depths of which she knew nothing. Now she knew for sure. She also knew, she reminded herself bleakly, that loving Mark was a mistake. It was asking for misery. To her he was way out of reach and always would be.

As she prepared meals and performed the usual household chores it seemed incredible to her that no one noticed her inner stress, but apparently the predominantly male household saw nothing different in her and if she had to force herself to eat the meals she prepared at least she succeeded in getting them down.

Jill who might have been the one to notice Angela's quietened spirits said nothing, but then the other girl avoided speaking to her whenever possbile. It was clear that in some mixed-up way she continued to hold Angela responsible for having some part in Brian's accident. It was cruel and unfair, but there was nothing to be done about it. Because she loathed living in an atmosphere of dislike and suspicion Angela made one more attempt to bridge the unhappy gap stretching between them. One morning as she laid the table for breakfast Jill said coldly, "You needn't set a place for Brian. He went out early to help Mark earmark the steers."

"Goodness," Angela paused in surprise, "that seems a tough job for anyone just recovering from an accident."

"It's his decision."

"I suppose so." Angela made a sudden decision on her own account. "Jill," she said appealingly, "there's something—"

The other girl had gone to the door. Now she glanced back over her shoulder. At the hard discouraging expression in the blue eyes Angela's resolution faltered, but she forced herself to go on. "Something I'd like to get straight. I know you think—"

"If it's something to do with your friend Martha, don't bother telling me any more lies! You've done enough damage already between the two of you!" The door slammed angrily behind her and Angela with heightened colour went on with breakfast preparations.

Once or twice she had played with the idea of making another attempt to explain matters to Brian, but there was something about his attitude towards her that stopped her. A certain nervousness often when she appeared. When she tried to talk to him she was aware of unquiet overtones. A worried frown invariably appeared on his tanned face. Was it her imagination or was he asking himself, "How much does she know? Was it true what she said about their not being friends, or are they making a laughing stock of me, she and Martha?"

On another level she was aware of life flowing on around her—Brian's recovery, Mark working long hours, leaving the house at dawn and often returning to a late dinner after darkness had set in. The narrow one-way bridge was now repaired and there were callers once more at the homestead, stock agents, veterinerary surgeons, agricultural experts.

One day a letter arrived from Doris. She was having a wonderful time with her family and the new baby boy was so good he was quite unbelievable. She hated to ask favours, but if Angela could see her way to staying another couple of weeks? She was writing by the same mail to Mark, but she was certain he would be only too pleased for the present arrangement to go on a little longer. *Pleased*, Mark? Mark, who probably never gave her a thought from one day to the next. To whom a kiss was neither here nor there, just part of a day's outing. If only she could think of him in the same way!

She was in the lounge that evening when he came into the room and she saw that he held Doris's letter in his hand. "Hi, Twenty, all alone?"

Hadn't he noticed, for goodness sake, that she was usually alone in the evenings? Jill was somewhere with Brian and Mark invariably worked in his office while she washed up after a late meal.

He flung himself into a low coolie chair. "Heard from Doris today?"

"Yes. I got a letter today too. She seems to be really enjoying herself down south."

He nodded. "She's having a ball. It's about time she took off for a holiday, though I never thought she'd leave a stranger in charge here. Must have taken quite a fancy to you, Twenty!"

Angela gathered her senses together. Ridiculous to feel so stirred up emotionally merely because he was regarding her with a quizzical teasing gleam in his blue eyes. She forced back an impulse to say, "Why shouldn't she like me? Everyone isn't prejudiced against me like you and your brother and Jill." She heard herself saying, "I like her too."

"She's a good sort, Doris." He shot her one of those quick sideways glances. "How do you feel about staying on a bit longer? Letting her have a decent break while she's down there.

It's been the devil of a job to get her away this year and you'd be doing something really worthwhile for her."

As if she needed any persuading, with his blue glance full on her, the strong tanned face she couldn't get out of her mind turned hopefully towards her. His gaze softened. "She'd like you to stay on, and that goes for me too!"

"I'll stay," she said thickly. Heavens, she thought in distress, what if he guesses that staying on here means all the world to me? Even if it's heaven being here it's hell too, but anyway I can't resist the offer. She subdued the excitement running along her nerves, said in what she hoped was an off-hand tone, "If you can stand my cooking."

"Stand it? Twenty, in my book you could get a job as assistant chef around here any old day you choose!"

She tried to laugh naturally. "I'll remember that." Something deep inside her was crying, I'll remember you, every little thing about you and especially your smile . . . your smile.

"If you stay," he was saying, "you'll be able to come along to the rodeo next week."

She nearly betrayed herself by saying quickly, "Will you be riding?"

He grinned. "Always do. It's a sort of tradition at Waikare for the owner to take part in the show. A day or two before I take one of the shepherds with me and we drive the wild horses down from the hills. That way we're sure of getting the real thing for the riders. You'll have a good day there, there's a lot to see. You'll like it."

"Will I?" The thought of watching him ride a bucking wild bronco filled her with horror, yet at the same time she felt such confidence in him that she couldn't really imagine him being thrown or badly hurt in a fall.

"You don't sound too enthusiastic! But wait till you get there! Riders from the States, Canada, Australia, they all come over here to compete and there's always a big crowd watching from the rails. Roping steers, buck-jumping, barrel race, there's a lot to see."

"All right then, I'll give it a go."

He grinned. "Give it a go! You know something, Twenty? You're talking like one of the natives. You'll be one of us before you know it."

"You think so?" She turned away before he could discern the shadow of pain in her eyes. With an effort she brought her mind back to the deep tones.

"I'll send a wire down to Doris, that'll make her day. You're sure about this, Twenty, you've made up your mind?"

She nodded. "I'm sure." Sure, when every nerve in her body was straining to stay here for ever, just as long as he wanted her! "One of us", he had said, but it was only a joke to him. He was the boss again, an employer asking his employee to extend her term of service for a period. Why must she remember at this particular moment that kiss by the waterfall?

Suddenly it was Saturday and the thought that Angela had pushed to the back of her mind could no longer be ignored. Saturday, when Susan was coming to the barbecue at Waikare. Why was it that whenever Susan was at the house Angela allowed herself to be pushed into the background? Mark had told her not to give the matter of preparation for the barbecue a thought, that the men would attend to all that. Angela mused uncharitably that even though everything was arranged regarding the preparation of food for the evening's entertainment Susan would no doubt take it on her own shoulders to organize everyone and everything. Brian had already taken the meat from the huge deep-freeze cabinet in the kitchen and the brick-lined barbecue by the pool was ready laid with fuel.

That evening Angela changed shorts and blue denim blouse for floppy cream-coloured slacks and a gaily printed Mexican peasant blouse. Since coming here to work she had worn her Titian hair tied back from her face, but tonight she brushed out the long strands until they glinted and gleamed, leaving the coppery mass falling free over her shoulders. No need to tell the world how she felt inside. Tonight she was determined to appear gay and carefree.

Already car-lights beamed across the window as vehicles pulled up on the drive. She could hear car-doors slamming, snatches of laughter and through it all, Susan's high clear tones. So the other girl had brought guests with her, probably her visitors from Sydney. When the crowd had moved towards the barbecue Angela closed her door behind her. She had imagined she was the last to leave the house, but as she went down the hall someone was speaking on the telephone and she couldn't help but overhear Brian's tones. He was speaking in a voice quickened with excitement. "Yes, yes, I wouldn't miss it, not now!" Then in a lowered tone, "I've got to go, someone's coming. See you at the rodeo. 'Bye till then!"

She forgot him as she went outside. The sun's setting had left behind a lingering lemon afterglow shading upwards to a pale translucent blue. By the pool leaping flames from the barbecue illuminated long spears of growing flax and tall tea-tree sheltering the brick fireplace. She was crossing the dew-wet grass when someone came hurrying up behind her. "Angela, wait!" She swung around to see Brian, his small-featured face alight with some inner excitement new to him. There was a difference in him tonight, she could sense it. Could it be that the telephone conversation that for some reason he had wished to keep secret so filled his mind that for once he had even forgotten to be uneasy with her? As she glanced up towards his abstracted face it seemed to her that for once he had even forgotten about her being "Martha's friend". At his next words she changed her mind. "Look," his tone was laced with urgency and something else—excitement? curiosity? "Tell me something, will you?"

She paused beside him. Something warned her that the "something" was a matter that mattered a lot to him. She said cautiously, "If I can."

"You can. It's about Martha. You know, your friend, the girl who came out on the ship with you."

"Martha?" She gave an impatient sigh, but Brian deep in his thoughts, didn't notice. What was the use of trying to convince any of them on the subject of Martha?

"You see," he was saying in that quick excited tone so removed from his usual diffident accents, "we were pen friends—well, a bit more than that, actually, at least that's what I thought. And then—" He broke off, looking at her anxiously. "But you know all this. You were her friend. She *must* have told you!"

Angela shook her head. "She didn't!" She was becoming very weary of trying to tell people the truth about Martha. She said on an impatient sigh, "What is it you want to know?"

"I just wanted to ask you about her." Angela made to move on towards the group moving in the shadows of the flickering firelight, but Brian put out a hand to detain her. "Don't go! I want to talk to you. When you first came I'd had it, I didn't care, but now I'm okay again and there are things I'd like to find out, *must* find out, that only you can put me wise to. Tell me, what sort of a girl was she?"

What could she say? Angela stalled for time. "How do you mean?"

"You tell me."

"Well," she said carefully, "she was good company, quick, witty. She always had a ready answer! She dressed beautifully, and of course she had that gorgeous red hair!"

He said very low, "You know I don't mean all that!" He kicked at a loose pebble in the dust of the path. "I guess it comes right down to a few words, really. Could you trust her?"

"Trust her?" There it was, the sixty-four-dollar question, the one she had been dreading. But she pretended not to understand. "She was honest, if that's what you're getting at."

"No, no," he passed a hand over his head in a gesture of frustration. "What I mean is if she told you something that could be right or couldn't be—heck I'm making a mess of this, but you know what I'm getting at. Could you believe her?"

Oh yes, Angela knew very well what he was getting at. The difficulty was in making an answer. She decided to play it straight. "I can only answer for myself. We weren't terribly friendly, you know, on the ship, just part of the same gang who used to knock around together. You know how it is on board ship—"

"No, but I can imagine."

"I—liked her well enough ... until she tricked me into coming here under false pretences. Oh, not that I didn't want to stay in the end," she added quickly, "but—"

Brian was staring at her in surprise. "Tricked you?"

She nodded. "You see, I hadn't seen her since we left the ship in Auckland almost two weeks earlier, until that day we ran into each other on the bus coming north. I told her I happened to be on the lookout for a job, some work on an outback sheep station if I could find it, and she assured me that she had something lined up in that direction, but if I liked I could take the job instead. You mightn't believe this, but I had no idea when she handed me that envelope at the last moment and told me to give it to you what was in it. She never said a word to me on the ship about any other plans. The trouble is," unconsciously she was twisting a long strand of hair round and round her fingers, "no one up here believes me." She sent him a wavering smile. "Unless you do."

In the gloom she couldn't glimpse his expression, but the note of uncertainty was back in his voice. "Damned if I know what to believe." After a moment he added uncertainly, "but you don't know everything. There could have been special circumstances that altered the whole picture. They say there are two sides to every story, don't they?"

Angela was silent.

"You don't go along with that, do you?" His tone quickened. "What if I were to tell you—"

"Brian! I thought you were never coming down here!" Jill came hurrying along the flare-lit path towards them. Except for a quick angry glance she ignored Angela's presence.

"Everyone's here, quite a crowd really. Sue's brought her relations along with her. I was just on my way up to the house to find out what was keeping you." She linked her fingers in his and they strolled away together. As she moved on towards the firelight Angela mused wryly that she was becoming accustomed to being ignored in these threesomes, first Mark and Susan, now Brian and Jill.

As she neared the barbecue area she could see groups moving around, silhouetted against the leaping flames illuminating tall flax and tea-trees. Sea-grass mats were spread on the grass and sausages, chops and steaks sizzled on table-height barbecues. An old carpet square was provided for dancing and music echoed softly from hidden hi-fi speakers. Tables loaded with bottles and glasses sparkled in the firelight. Another table held bowls of various salads and dishes of butter-drenched corncobs. Piles of paper plates and napkins made eating pleasant. You had to hand it to Susan, Angela admitted reluctantly, when it came to helping with an outdoor function, even though the other girl did overdo the organising angle. All the same, she thought hotly, Susan had no right to act as though she were already mistress here, not yet.

"Oh, Twenty, I've been hoping to find you. I want someone to run an errand for me." Susan's schoolmarmish tones sparked a dangerous reaction in Angela. The contemptuous gaze raked Angela's slim figure. "I didn't recognise you in that get-up. Run along to the car, will you, and get me a bag of tomatoes I left on the back seat. Hurry now!"

Angela's eyes sparkled angrily as she faced Susan. Over the turmoil and resentment filling her mind she said quietly and clearly, "*You* get it."

Susan's lips tightened. "Of all the—" She broke off, for Mark, apparently unaware of what had been said, was moving out of the shadows towards them. Susan was smiling now the special smile she seemed to keep just for him. "Hi, Mark! Come and meet some cousins of mine. I've told them so much about you!" They moved away and the awkward moment was forgotten.

Angela was left standing alone.

"It's you! It's really you at last!" She turned to face John's excited smile. He was regarding her with delight, clasping both her hands in his with warm appreciation. "Angie, you look just wonderful!"

She felt a pang of guilt at his obvious pleasure in the meeting when she had all but forgotten him during the last few days. "How did you get here?" she asked.

He grinned, still clasping her hands in his. "Got a lift over with Sue. I'm with the gang shearing on a station a few miles from her home and last night I got a ring on the phone from her letting me in about the barbecue tonight. How lucky can a guy get? Sue said she was bringing an extra car and there was swags of room and I was welcome to come along. Boy, did I jump at the offer!"

"Sue asked you?" Angela was surprised. "That was nice of her, seeing she had so many other friends to bring." Perhaps after all she had misjudged the other girl. Evidently she could show some thought for others.

When it suits her, jeered the dark goblin in her mind. You must have noticed the way she looks at you whenever she can bring herself to speak to you. And Mark . . . she can't bear him to have eyes for any other girl, even when that girl happens to be the shearers' cook! Inviting John to the barbecue tonight and making sure of his arrival there would solve any problems Susan might have in that direction. She pushed the suspicions aside and brought her mind back to John's eager tones. "It seems forever since I've seen you. I've been counting the days. Honestly, I began to think this week would never end!"

"So now you'll be moving on to another shed?"

His face fell. "Don't remind me." He added very low, "I'd give anything to be around now that I've met you. And I've signed that damned contract that keeps me on the move for another month! But after that—say you won't forget me," he pleaded, "even if I can't see you often. That's the only thing that makes it worthwhile all the rush and hard work and heat of the sheds. I mean, the thought that when it's all over I can get back to my own land, my own girl." The young bearded face was all at once anxious and intent.

"Angie, tell me if there's a chance for me, because—"

In an attempt to divert the conversation into less personal channels she said lightly, "But I thought it was the money you were doing all this hard work for, not me."

"It is, it is," gently he carried her fingers to his lips, "but what's a home without the girl I can't get out of my mind?"

"A girl you've only known for a few weeks?" she teased.

"What's time got to do with it? When you meet one girl in a million, get to know her—"

"You don't *really* know me—"

"Angie—"

"It's my being a cook," she said demurely, "it's giving you ideas."

"Ideas, hopes, the lot!" His tone deepened. "Meeting you, knowing you, means everything in the world to me, Angie." He drew her out of the circle of firelight and into the shadows. "Say you're glad to see me."

Laughing, she looked up into the dark-bearded face of this mathematics master-turned-farmer who was growing far too fond of her. Something in the intentness of his look touched her. "Of course I am."

"Don't say it like that," his tone was threaded with urgency, "say it as though you meant it."

"But—" She hesitated. He was nice, sincere, the type of man who would love one woman all his life long. Why couldn't she care for him in a way that mattered? But she had weakly allowed herself to fall in love with the wrong person. "John," she said gently, "if you're thinking—" She broke off, aware of Mark striding purposefully towards her, a wineglass held in his hand. "For you, Twenty!"

"Thank you." There was a look in his eyes she couldn't interpret.

The next moment he was intercepted by one of the shepherds from the station and Angela's dreaming gaze continued to rest on Mark's erect figure.

Why, she wondered, did she so often surprise his gaze on her? Even while he was apparently engrossed in conversation with a group or dancing with Sue. Keeping an eye on her, making certain that the untrustworthy station cook wasn't up to more intrigues? Probably, she thought drearily, in his mind he suspected her of trying to drag John into her matrimonial net, whereas if he only knew . . .

"No use looking at him," John's teasing accents cut across her thoughts, "not with Sue around. From what I hear on the grapevine those two will be making a match of it any day now."

Angela couldn't understand why the words should hurt so much, almost like physical pain tearing through her. It was the truth, wasn't it? The thought made her determined to prove to John, to herself, and most of all to Mark that the boss's love-life was of no particular concern to her. Her opportunity came the next moment as all at once dance music pulsed around them and she was acutely aware of Mark turning towards her. Before he could speak, however, some devil of resentment made her look up at John, surprising him with the brilliance of her smile. "They're dancing," she said quickly. "Shall we—"

For answer he took her hand and they merged into the groups already swaying to the infectious beat of a popular number.

From a corner of her eye she was aware of Mark swinging around on his heel to move in the direction of a group of young farmers gathered at the poolside. Her quick glance went to Susan and she realised that the other girl too was eyeing Mark. Angela wondered if Susan had witnessed the little scene where the boss had found himself turned down as a dance partner by the shearers' cook. As the hours wore on Mark did not again approach her, although she was only too well aware that he and Susan danced often together.

If only the setting wasn't so beautiful, she mused over the ache in her heart, for it was a night made for romance. The soft dark sky blazed with a shower of stars and blowing flares threw into relief great fluffy hibiscus blossoms and thickly-growing flax. Across the firelight would pass a gay tangerine or crimson shirt or a brilliantly patterned patio frock would gleam for a moment before merging into the shadows. Yet to Angela, dancing, laughing, chatting, the scene held the curious unreality of a play she happened to be viewing. Would the sizzling food have had some taste, the picture come alive had she waited for Mark to claim his dance earlier in the evening? He must have seen her deliberate withdrawal and formed his own conclusions. But what else could he expect from her? Never giving her a chance to explain her true position here, deliberately believing the worst of her, and on top of all that *kissing her* when the impulse happened to take him. There was just no understanding him.

It was almost dawn when at last farewells were said and guests began to drift away towards cars, trucks and Land Rovers. John, who had been trying for a long time to get Angela to himself, at last caught her close. "You'll be here for a while at Waikare, won't you?" His voice was low and tender. "I always get this awful thought that you might be just a dream, that you'll slip away somewhere and I'll never find you again." His arm tightened around her. "You'll wait until I come back?"

But Angela was more aware of Mark, who had sauntered towards them, a silent witness to the conversation. Why couldn't he stay with his Sue, who was obviously waiting at the open door of her car to bid him goodnight? Instead of always being around at the most inconvenient moments. Did he appear like this just to annoy her or was he checking up on her once again? She threw him an angry glance, but at something in his face the resentment died away and there was only the awareness of him . . . and the hopeless longing. She forced herself to look up at John. "Don't worry, I'll be around for a few more weeks yet. Doris wrote from the south to ask if I'd help her out by staying a while longer."

"She did?" John's face was alight, his dark eyes shining with relief. "That's the best news I've had for weeks. Why didn't you tell me before?"

Conscious of Mark's nearness, she scarcely knew what she was saying. "You didn't ask me."

"I hate leaving you like this," John muttered in a low tone. "Seems as if I'm never going to get you to myself, but I guess this is it—" He bent to give her a quick kiss, but Angela's lips were unresponsive. She was too aware of Mark and his no doubt mocking expression. Another victim? he'd be thinking. She and Martha must have laid their plans well.

She drew herself away and smiled gaily. "Goodbye. I'll see you some time!"

A man's voice called, "John, are you coming! Where the devil is he?" And John with a last lingering glance towards Angela tore himself away and hurried towards the car where a crowd was already seated.

Only then did Mark saunter towards the cluster of vehicles on the pathway. Why must he watch her all the time? she wondered once again. She was nothing to him, the pain stabbed without warning, she only wished she were.

Pink streaks mingled with the molten gold of sunrise as the men at Waikare went to the house to change into working clothes.

Angela, feeling all at once deflated and weary, changed too, then went into the kitchen where she made fresh coffee and slipped bread into the automatic toaster. The men would be in later for breakfast. Perhaps it was as well she would be kept busy this morning, for she couldn't seem to prevent her thoughts from straying endlessly to Mark. She regretted now not having had that dance with him. To dance with Mark under the stars . . . but at the time she'd been so anxious to prove to him that she much preferred John's company. If only that were true!

CHAPTER NINE

The days flew by, uneventful on the surface yet coloured with the ever-changing pattern of life on a vast station. Very soon now Jill would be leaving to begin nursing training in the city. Angela sensed that the girl's excitement for preparing for a new life was clouded by being forced to leave Brian. Torn both ways as she was, there were times when it seemed Jill all but forgot her hostile attitude towards Angela.

In two weeks Doris would be returning to the homestead to take up her duties here once again, and then . . . At this point Angela's thought invariably came to a dead stop. Was it because a future without even sight of Mark was too painful to contemplate?

But absorbed in her problems as she was she couldn't help but be aware of the subject filling the minds of the men at the station. At dinner that evening the conversation as usual turned in the direction of the annual rodeo to be held in a neighbouring area at the weekend. Mind and heart alerted always to Mark, Angela gathered that he had been a consistently successful competitor in various events for some years. Her heart plunged. What if she were watching him ride and he were injured? The next moment she pulled herself up sharply, reminding herself that Mark was accustomed to taking part in the events, and the dangerous bulldogging and steer-roping held no terrors for him. It was only she who was afraid for him and thank heaven he knew nothing of that!

Unexpectedly Brian, who had up till now taken no part in the conversation, said, "Just for a change I'll give the bulldogging a go this time!"

Mark's penetrating blue stare raked the pale young face. "A bit premature for that sort of thing, aren't you?"

Brian's face was no longer pale as a dark angry flush crept up his cheeks. "How do you mean?"

Mark said evenly, "You know damn well what I mean! You've just collected one knock on the head—"

"So why go looking for another? Is that what you're getting at?" Brian's usual mild tones were tinged with a stubborn determination. "If I can do it why not?"

"Have you had a word with the doc about it?"

"No, and I don't intend to!" All at once Brian's face wore the petulant look of a small boy who was determined to go his own way. Vaguely Angela wondered why the matter of an annual rodeo should be of such importance to him.

Brian muttered beneath his breath, "A man can please himself, can't he?"

Mark's lips twisted in a sardonic grin. "Okay, mate, it's your funeral!"

"But—bulldogging!" Jill was staring aghast towards Brian. "You don't mean it, you can't! Not after—"

"You bet your life I mean it! Why not? Don't you remember last year when I lasted three seconds longer than anyone else and finished up by breaking the record?"

Jill muttered unhappily, "That was last year."

He threw her a dark look. "You're just like all the rest of them around here. You think I can't stick it out, don't you? Well, you're in for a big surprise, the lot of you! I'm well again now and I'm darn well going to prove it!"

Jill gave in with a bad grace. "You're crazy!"

When the meal came to an end Mark took Kevin out with him to look at one of the dogs who had been showing signs of lameness. Angela rose to clear the table and only then did she realise that Jill had waited until the others had left the room before once again raising her objections to Brian taking part in the bulldogging event.

"That rodeo," she groaned, "it *would* come at the weekend when I have to leave and go to town." She eyed him imploringly. "Give it a miss this once, *please*, Brian, just for me?"

He shifted impatiently, his small features set in a stubborn mould. "Why should I? I'm perfectly okay, fighting fit!"

"Fit? For that sort of thing?"

"You don't have to be a muscle man to bring down a bull in the ring!"

Jill said on a long sigh, "If only I could be there!"

"Why? All you want to do is to be on hand to pick up the pieces, isn't that what you're getting at?"

Jill said impatiently, "You're just being difficult! If you get yourself hurt all over again—"

"I won't!"

As if regretting his curtness Brian sent her a wry grin. "And if I do I'll call on you to patch me up again. How about that?"

Jill gave a shaky smile and reached out to clasp his work-calloused hand. "I suppose I'll have to settle for that."

"That's better! I don't know what you're going on about. There's nothing to it. Besides," he hesitated, playing nervously with a fork, "I've got to compete this year."

"Got to?" Jill was eyeing him with a puzzled stare. "What's so special about this year? I've never seen you so determined about anything! It's not as if it matters one way or the other."

He said in a low strained tone, "it does you know."

Jill's voice softened. "If you've got some crazy idea about proving something to yourself—"

"Not to myself, love, someone else—"

Jill said on a bewildered sigh, "If you're thinking of me you don't need to—"

He didn't answer and Angela, feeling embarrassed at witnessing what was fast becoming a lovers' quarrel, rattled the china in the sink. She need not have troubled herself, however, for it was clear that the other two had forgotten she was in the room. She was just Twenty who happened to be around. She was becoming a habit with them all. Unconsciously she sighed. Especially with Mark.

On the morning of the rodeo a general air of excitement pervaded the station. Even Angela, fathoms deep in heartache, and heartache there was no assuaging, couldn't help but be aware of the atmosphere of high spirits flowing around her. For it seemed that everyone, whether in the capacity of onlooker or competitor in the various events, was bound for the rodeo grounds. Angela knew that she too should be looking forward to viewing the novel entertainment, but all she could think of was the fact that the rodeo grounds lay roughly halfway between Waikare and Susan's home and no doubt Susan would be meeting Mark at the rodeo. Why was it she asked herself bleakly that she always spoiled everything by reminding herself of the other girl?

Dragging her thoughts aside, she tried to concentrate on other matters, Jill for instance. Even though Brian might regard the girl with whom he had been brought up in the light of a little sister Angela felt certain that Jill was deeply in love with him. Love took little account of the loved one's responses, didn't she know it! It would be an agonizing experience for Jill to watch Brian taking part in the riding events where a split-second decision could make all the difference between victory or a threat to his already precarious state of health. Funny that she still felt no particular sense of trepidation about Mark, even though he too would be riding the wild horses that he and the shepherds had driven down from the bush-clad hills at the back of the station a few days previously. He was experienced at that type of riding, and if he took a fall he wouldn't be seriously hurt.

Was this mere wishful thinking? Or worse, one more proof of the blind adoration she had for him? She was fast becoming like the other employees at Waikare, trusting to his judgment implicitly, thinking there was no man in all the world like him. It's because of living in this small isolated community, she told herself. There are so few men with whom to compare him. Who was she fooling? For in her heart she knew that all her life she would feel this way about him. Love . . . she fell into a day-dream. At the beginning of their acquaintance, how long ago it seemed, but it was actually only a few weeks earlier, she had hated him. But even then something about him had sparked her into instant awareness of him. Now the spark had caught fire and if she weren't careful the flames would destroy her. She jerked her thoughts aside, forcing herself to dwell on the tasks awaiting her attention.

Yesterday she had prepared a picnic lunch in readiness for the outing and soon she was packing in a woven cane hamper the small savoury pies, club sandwiches and man-sized fruit cake baked in readiness for the outdoor meal. In the chili-bin she stowed away cans of beer for the men and fruit drinks for the children. Presently Mark was placing the bulging island-style hamper in the rear of the Land Rover.

When she came lightly down the steps from the porch, a slim figure in black trouser suit, bright hair caught back with a ribbon, she found that already the drive was crowded with vehicles.

Brian, seated at the wheel of a dust-coated truck, sent her a grin and the thought passed through her mind that today he appeared different from usual. His air of lassitude and boredom had given way to an expression of suppressed excitement. Like everyone else here the general atmosphere of the rodeo must have affected him.

All at once she realised that Mark was striding towards her and as she met his quizzical blue gaze her traitorous heart gave its customary wild leap. "In you get, Twenty!" He was flinging open the door of the Land Rover. As she seated herself inside she realised that young Kevin was in the back of the vehicle.

"Hi, Angela," he leaned forward, "Mark says he has to bring me along to open the gates."

She smiled over her shoulder. "Well, that lets me out!"

Ahead of them a stock truck was moving off, a group of children shouting and waving wildly from the cab. It was followed by a battered truck and as the weatherbeaten face turned smilingly towards them, she realised that the driver was

Rusty. Horns tooted and drivers called to one another, then the cavalcade was taking the curving drive leading out towards the main road.

"You're going to enjoy this outing today, Twenty!" Mark told her, and for no reason at all she was swept by a wave of high sweet happiness. Aloud she admitted, "I've been looking forward to it."

Her heart said, I'm enjoying it already, just being with you. What if she meant no more to him than Kevin in the seat behind? She was with Mark and suddenly everything was exciting. In this sense of newly-heightened perception hills were sharp-cut against the bluest of skies, the morning sunshine burnishing the leaves of the Moreton Bay fig trees was purest gold. She was with him and that was all that mattered. She hadn't realised her gaze was fixed on his strong profile until suddenly he turned his head and at something in his gaze the tell-tale colour crept up her cheek and she quickly averted her gaze. Still the sense of wild happiness, transient and somehow akin to pain, stayed with her. Much too aware of his nearness, she heard herself saying quickly, nervously, "I've never been to anything like this before. I don't suppose," she was unaware of the thread of wistfulness in her voice, "that I ever will again. Tell me, do any of the competitors ride in the rodeo as a living, make it a full-time job?"

They jolted over the cattle-stop and Mark's eyes were on the winding road ahead. "At twenty-five dollars a win and a few shows a year? You've got to be joking! No Twenty, it's not a matter of the cash awards. These guys ride because they'd rather be doing that than anything else in the world. Lots of them are full-time musterers, stockmen, shearers, but others do all sorts of jobs."

She twinkled up at him. "Like managing a sheep station?"

His warm appreciative grin sent her pulses racing. "Among other things. We've had a schoolteacher, an office worker, a couple of insurance salesmen. It's a man's game and we ride because we love it!"

"You know something," Kevin's tones reached her from the back seat, "this is my first rodeo meeting too! You wouldn't believe it, Angela, but the riders come up here from all over the country, right from the foot of the South Island, to compete in the championships!"

Mark threw a teasing glance towards the small overhead mirror. "I can see you've been doing your homework on the subject."

"Have I ever?" Kevin leaned forward eagerly. "There's a rider coming all the way from America and three buckjumpers from Queensland over in Australia. They're here specially to follow the rodeo circuit. You have to stay on the horse until the bell sounds after ten seconds. Ten seconds doesn't seem long, does it, Angela, but I bet when you're up on one of those bucking broncos it would seem like forever! The judge gives twenty-five points to the rider and the horse for each buck! Gee, I can't wait to see you ride today, Mark!" Glancing towards Kevin, Angela saw that the young face was fired with enthusiasm. "I wish I could ride like you! All the shepherds say you've won the Open Steer ride and the Bareback so many times it's just not any fun for them any more!"

Mark laughed. "They were having you on, mate."

Somehow, though, Angela was inclined to believe Kevin's version. She brought her mind back to the wistful tones. "It takes a heck of a lot of saving up for, though, the gear. A saddle sets you back about two hundred and fifty bucks altogether." His tone lightened and he raised a foot encased in a high leather boot. "I've got the boots, though, and the loan of this hat."

"Good for you," Mark encouraged gravely.

Angela turned to regard the boy in surprise. "Are you really competing today?"

"Of course I am," Kevin returned with pride.

"The Youth Steer Ride, isn't that it?" queried Mark.

"That's the one."

Angela laughed. "You know something, Kevin? I always had the idea that you were more at home on the motor-bike." For it was well known on the station that the young farm worker preferred his "mountain goat" for careering over the rough terrain of the hills to the stock horses ridden by Mark and Brian as well as by the shepherds.

"I like the bike," Kevin admitted, "but the rodeo's different. And I can ride you know!" Angela suspected that Kevin's entry in the rodeo event was a matter of not losing face, for to compete with the rest of the staff at the annual event was a tradition of station life. He leaned forward, betraying a hidden anxiety by the tone of his voice. "Anyway, it's the first event, so it will soon be over!"

"You're right, mate," Mark teased. "I'll give you two minutes at the most!" They laughed together.

After a moment Kevin said thoughtfully, "You know what, Angela? I've been talking to the others at the station—you know, about falling and all that, and the fall doesn't count, that's nothing." It was clear that fear lurked behind the brave words. "What you've got to watch for is being kicked by one of the horses or getting your foot caught in a stirrup and being dragged along the ground."

Angela shuddered. As they swept over the Land Rover tracks winding up a sheep-dotted hill she gave voice to her thoughts. "But isn't it cruel?"

It was Mark who answered. "How do you mean? For the horses or riders?"

"Well, both."

He guided the vehicle over a ridge and down towards a gully below. "It's not too bad. Actually the rodeo mounts have a pretty easy life altogether. They're only ridden for a handful of days throughout the year. The rest of the time they're free to do nothing at all. We graze a few of the horses at Waikare; the station who keeps them usually gets the foals in exchange for grazing. Don't worry about cruelty, the SPCA inspectors are there at every meeting, keeping a good watch for any cruelty or infringement of the rules."

Angela looked relieved. "How about the riders?"

"It's not too bad," his tone was careless. "To them accidents are a way of life and a fall is just part of the act."

"I know, I know, but if you happened to be watching someone who was competing and they took a really bad fall—"

His swift sideways glance took in her apprehensive look and the deep tones softened. "You wouldn't be worrying over anyone in particular, would you, Twenty?"

He had caught her unawares, the wide hazel eyes wide with concern. When he looked at her like that . . . "Oh, you know what I mean." she muttered, "you and Kevin and Brian and the shepherds." Somehow she had a suspicion that her heightened colour pinpointed one name in particular.

"The bulldogging always goes over well with the crowd," Mark was saying.

Relieved that the conversation was back on impersonal grounds, Angela said, "it sounds awfully dangerous to me."

Mark smiled his lopsided grin. "Not half as bad as it seems to the onlookers. Stopping a galloping steer in full flight isn't half as difficult as it may look to the audience. Once you get hold of them by their horns they lose their balance and go down fairly easily, even though the animal may weigh a few hundred pounds."

"Goodness!" Angela looked unconvinced. "Are you entering for that event too?"

She had intended the words to sound offhand, disinterested, but to her horror they emerged on a breath of apprehension. Mark would be certain to catch the note of fear in her voice.

He did. "Does it matter so much, Twenty?" he asked softly.

There it was again, the dangerous look, the look against which she had no defence. Now she would have given anything to recall the betraying query. Confused and uncertain, she didn't know what to say.

Kevin came to her rescue, "He's not, you know! This year he's going to give Brian a go, eh, Mark? Girls," he added in a tone of disgust, "are scary about *everything*. My sisters, they used to get het-up over nothing, just because someone was riding a motor-bike."

"Someone?" Mark teased.

"Well, you know what I mean."

They were moving along the road where on either side tall white daisies raised shaggy heads from a tangle of dried grass fern and blackberry. A notice-board nailed to a tree-trunk loomed ahead. "Rodeo" and a painted black arrow. Presently they swept through a small township. The sleepy main street with its timbered corner hotel and handful of old shops put Angela in mind of pictures she had seen of Wild West towns in America. Then they were catching up with other vehicles in the stream of one-way traffic moving towards the sports grounds. Already Angela could hear the lowing of steers. As they swept over a cleared hill crest she found herself looking down on a big tea-tree fenced enclosure far below. Flags unfurled their colours lazily against the blue, and gates enclosed chutes near a corral where horses stood awaiting their turn in the sawdust-covered arena. Ringed around were stock trucks that made excellent grandstands. Family parties were grouped beneath colourful sun-umbrellas blossoming on sun-dried slopes and sheep wandered amongst the picnickers.

As Mark guided the Land Rover through clusters of cars and trucks, stock trailers and jeeps moving over the grassy hill, Angela stared about her. Ambulance men were pitching their tent near a tree-lined enclosure filled with calves and steers. A Maori rider strolled past them, a colourful figure in his wide felt sombrero, high boots and sheepskin-leather chaps. Women wore gay summer frocks with sandals on bare feet, the men, shorts and vividly coloured shirts in tonings of scarlet, tangerine or violet.

The vehicle drew to a stop near the arena and Angela couldn't stop her gaze from roving over the milling crowd in search of an attractive blonde-headed girl.

"There's Susan's car!" Kevin said suddenly, and Angela's spirits plummeted. Who was it who had once said that green cars were unlucky? She had expected to find the other girl here, hadn't she? So why this absurd feeling of let-down?

"That's right." Mark threw a glance towards the late-model car. "She'll be over in the nerve centre of the whole operation today. She'll miss a lot of fun of the show, but she's so darned expert at the job they just can't get along without her in the secretary's tent."

Angela thought waspishly, she would be. Was there anything in this world of country living at which Susan didn't excel? Mark's next words confirmed the unspoken thought.

"She'll be getting someone in to relieve her for a while, though. She's entered for the barrel race—" He broke off at Angela's puzzled expression. "That's something fairly recent in the events, a 'girls only' affair. Susan's been in it for two years running and won both times. Not bad for a local girl."

At the pride in his tone Angela's heart sank a little lower. The thought that she wouldn't now be forced to see Susan hanging on Mark's arm so tenaciously throughout the day was no consolation.

"Gee, she must be good!" The boyish tones underlined Angela's reflections on the other girl's riding prowess. Even to Kevin it seemed Susan was someone special, not to be compared with run-of-the-mill females like his sisters and herself who displayed a certain squeamishness about things like rodeo events and motor-cycles piloted by youthful riders. But Susan was different, she was utterly fearless! Not only had she ridden in the woman's barrel race but she had succedeed in winning it—twice running! Angela realised with a stab of guilt that since coming to Waikare (why not admit the truth? You mean since falling in love with Mark) she had become a totally different person, small-minded, petty-natured and horrible. Else why was she hoping that just for once Susan wouldn't win her event? After all who could blame one for the uncharitable thought? For wasn't Susan about to win the greatest prize of all?

"She'll win her event today too, I shouldn't wonder," enthused Kevin.

Angela wouldn't wonder either. The goblin in her mind who was so fond of pointing out home truths raised his jeering head. Admit it now, she's an ideal partner for Mark. They've got everything in common. She'd step into the life of the homestead as though she'd been there all her life (didn't she act that way already?) And he? On, Mark was adept at hiding his feelings but no doubt the other two had a secret understanding. Her spirits dropped. Wasn't Susan's attitude clearly that of a girl so nearly mistress of the homestead that it made no difference? Don't think of her, don't torture yourself, it never does any good. Already the day, the sparkling sunshiny day, had lost a little of its lustre. She recalled her thoughts to the present, aware that Mark was being hailed on all sides, aware too of the curious and interested glances that followed the tall man and the Titian-haired girl at his side.

Before long other vehicles from Waikare drew alongside the Land Rover and everyone was talking at once. Rugs were laid on clean portions of the dried grass and stools and camp-chairs and picnic baskets brought from trucks and cars, as the party from the outback station prepared to enjoy the buck-jumping and steer riding in the tea-tree enclosed area close by.

Angela dropped down on the rug Mark had spread and found herself seated beside one of the shepherd's wives, a dark pretty girl of about her own age whom Angela had met briefly at various times.

Pamela sent her a shy smile. "Hello, Angela! This is all new to you, I guess. Smoke?" Shc cxtended a packet of cigarettes and the tang of smoke mingled with the strong smell of penny-royal rising from the ground. Angela noticed with surprise that the girl's tanned hand was trembling.

"Shaky, aren't I?" Pamela gave an unsteady laugh. "Silly, but I can't help it! I'm always like this at these shows. Oh well," she exhaled the smoke, "Barry's in the third event, so it's not too long to wait. After that's over I can relax and enjoy myself." Although she was smiling Angela was aware of the look of strain in the grey eyes.

"You know," Angela said wonderingly, "they told me you were a real country girl, brought up on a big station down south. I didn't think you'd mind."

"Don't you believe it!" For a second naked fear glazed the other girl's eyes. "This is one time when Barry and I don't agree," she confided to Angela. "To me rodeo riding may be fine for a single man, but for a married guy who'll be a father next spring I can't see that a sore back or a kick on the head is just part of the fun of trying a quick buck or a twist."

Angela nodded sympathetically. "You've got a point there. I just thought you'd be used to it."

'Watching your husband riding an unbroken horse isn't

exactly the sort of thing you get used to—here he comes now." Pamela broke off as Barry came striding towards them, a tall muscular young man in scarlet shirt and calf-tight jeans, a wide felt hat shading his excited face. "Would you, if he were your husband?"

Pain twisted Angela's heart. If they were husband and wife, Mark and herself. She knew with an ache of longing that if that were so she would never get accustomed to the dangerous sport, never!

A man speaking through a microphone interrupted her thoughts. There was a hush among the crowd as the first event of the day was announced and a call made for youths who had entered their names for the steer riding. "Good luck!" Angela called to Kevin, who was already hurrying towards the chutes where the steers were penned. Her good wishes mingled with the varied comments from the station staff.

Mark came to drop down at her side. "Don't look so worried. They're only riding calves, you know—"

"I know, but—" Angela held her breath as a chute was flung open and a steer rushed out, twisting and turning wildly. She caught a brief glimpse of Kevin's bright green shirt as he kept a precarious hand on a thick rope. Then the boyish figure was tossed down into the dust of the arena. As the steer rushed wildly away in a cloud of dust Kevin, apparently unhurt, snatched up his precious rodeo hat from the ground and hurried away.

One after another, competitors followed the same pattern, each youth keeping aloft for only a few seconds. Angela couldn't understand why the fallen riders weren't trampled to death beneath the flying hooves. More and more steers crowded the enclosure until at last a man in a wide stetson and high boots entered the arena and sent them through a gate and into a paddock. The final competitor, a young Maori lad clad in jeans, scarlet shirt and with flapping sheepskin chaps, miraculously kept his balance until the bell rang and, smiling and waving to the crowd, he dropped to the ground.

As she watched the various events Angela had all but forgotten Pamela's agitation until the open saddle event was announced, a chute was flung open and out shot a bucking, snorting, rearing animal, a rider clinging precariously with his long legs. Angela was aware of Pamela's quick intake of breath as her eyes clung to Barry's set face. He stuck to his mount for a torrid five seconds, then a sudden twist sent him flying ungracefully to the ground. He lay still as the bucking bronco cleared the gate and continued to buck his way amongst the milling steers in the fenced enclosure. Pamela's fingers dug into Angela's bare arm as two ambulance men ran forward, but the next moment Barry was springing to his feet and hurrying out of the ring.

"Thank heaven it's over," Pamela said on a sigh of relief.

Not for me, Angela thought. Deep down she knew that she was as apprehensive at watching Mark ride as Pamela had been about Barry. It made no difference that the circumstances were entirely different, that probably Mark hadn't given her a thought since they had watched Kevin's brief period in the ring. He had left her shortly afterwards. Of course he would be in the secretary's tent with Susan, where else?

At that moment he came striding towards her, but almost at once the open buckjumping event was announced and he turned aside. "Guess that's my call."

She managed a bright smile. "Good luck, number thirty-five!" Good-natured masculine comments flowed around him. "Keep up the good work, boss!" "You can do it again, Mark!" Then he was moving towards the enclosure.

Angela was tense as she watched the chute open and the wild mounts released. Rider after rider came on and without lasting the distance was thrown almost immediately to the ground. Then came the signal for the chute to open for the final competitor. Angela felt her heart plunge as she recognised a familiar lean masculine figure astride a bucking, rearing fury. With his wide sombrero pulled low over his eyes and one hand held aloft Mark stuck to his command. It was clear that his mount was determined to unseat him, but Mark too was determined, even though it appeared a fairly close thing. As the seconds ticked away Angela was holding her breath, barely aware of the encouraging shouts and cries echoing around her. "Stay with it, Mark! Don't forget the glue!" But surely no rider could for long retain his seat on that twisting, bucking mount! Yet still he continued to keep his balance through an interminable ten seconds.

Angela was jumping up and down with excitement, yelling with the rest, then sighing with a terrific sense of relief as the judge's bell shrilled. A cheer went up from the crowd as the rider slipped to the ground and as the horse leaped and bucked its way down the enclosure Mark's glance sought that of the party from the station. No, not the party but—herself! Angela had the ridiculous feeling that he was especially pleased because she had been there to witness his victory. Now he was strolling across the grassy area in the direction of the familiar group, but his gaze was seeking her out. Relief and emotion chased every other thought from her mind and as he reached her she looked up at him, hazel eyes brilliant. "You were marvellous, staying put like that! I couldn't breathe, I was so excited wondering if you'd last the distance! I even forgot to think to myself, what if he falls, gets badly hurt—"

His warm intimate glance belied the lightness of his tone. "And then I lived to ride another day! Anyone would think you cared, Twenty—"

"Oh, I do! I do!" She laughed on her breathless husky note. "I never *knew* ten seconds could be so long! Mark—"

A group of shepherds and their wives surged between them offering congratulations laughing and talking all at once. "Good for you, Mark, you've kept up the record! Why don't you give someone else a chance for a change?"

Angela was scarcely aware of the chattering voices. The heady sense of excitement still possessed her. He'd looked for her, no one else, in the crowd! Those cold blue Hillyer eyes had lighted up at last, and for her! The heady sense of elation lasted even as she watched him leave the party and stroll away in the direction of the secretary's tent.

The picnic lunch was leisurely and enjoyable. There had been no serious accidents to mar the enjoyment of the morning's programme and everyone was in holiday mood. Even when Mark brought Susan with him to join the group on the grass Angela still felt that dizzy sense of happiness. Susan announced to all and sundry that she couldn't afford to stay long, her time was precious, but if they liked she could join them for a quick sandwich and a cuppa. To Angela the other girl's attitude was very like that of a monarch conferring a favour on the rabble. She brought her thoughts up short. There she went again, indulging in a private hate session against Susan, or trying to. Somehow today she was finding it difficult to hate anyone.

It wasn't until a loudspeaker blaring over the crowd called for the entrants for the bulldogging event that Angela realised that so far today she hadn't caught sight of Brian. Perhaps he had met freinds and lunched with them. A masculine voice somewhere near at hand was saying, "Bulldogging, isn't that Brian's speciality?"

"There he is now!" a man's voice answered, "going towards the chutes."

A few minutes later someone said "Wait for it!" and Angela watched fascinated as a bull was released from the chute and galloped down the arena. There was a hush amongst the crowd as a rider galloped alongside the enraged beast, flung himself on the animal's back grasping the horns and endeavouring to slip to the ground. Before he could do that, however, he went flying to the ground, then hurriedly picked himself up and ran out of the ring.

Over and over again the procedure was repeated as various riders were eliminated. One bull that managed to break free of the enclosure was chased by two outriders.

Last of all came Brian, a slight figure mounted on his sturdy stock horse Blazeaway. The next moment he was galloping alongside the beast, flinging himself on the animal's back. Still grasping the horns, he slipped to the ground and digging in his heels as a brake, brought the huge beast down. A roar of applause went up from the watchers and Brian rose to his feet. Angela saw him give a thumbs-up sign to someone at the far end of the enclosure and her gaze went to the chutes. A quick breath escaped her. It couldn't be, not Martha! But it was! There could be no mistaking that cloud of fiery hair. Almost as if she realised Angela had recognised her the other girl moved out of sight amongst the makeshift buildings.

All at once Angela recalled Brian's furtive tones in the telephone conversation on the night of the barbecue, the parting words she couldn't help but overhear. "See you at the rodeo." So—he had had to prove himself to Martha, to demonstrate his manly prowess despite his slight physique and his recent accident. And Martha? How else could she see Brian? How could she visit Waikare knowing that everyone there was aware of the way in which she had let Brian down, and especially herself!

Her thoughts in a wild tumult she realised that Brian was making his way towards the party from the station. A quick glance around her made her aware of the next event as girls wearing jeans, colourful shirts and wide hats moved towards the stands. At that moment Mark strolled into view at the side of a golden-haired girl leading a spirited palomino. All the brittle happiness of the morning died into nothingness, for it was clear that at this moment neither the red-haired stranger nor Twenty, his employee, would interest Mark. He was totally involved with Susan and her barrel race. Surely she *must* have imagined that look in his eyes this morning!

Getting to her feet, she pushed her way through the groups

gathered near the railings and made her way to the back of the chutes and the restless horses penned in the corral. For a moment she feared she was already too late, for Martha was seated at the wheel of a yellow and black rental car.

"Martha! Wait!" Had the other girl heard her frenzied cry? She couldn't tell. Either Martha was avoiding her or the clamour of the crowd had drowned her tones.

Martha had already turned on the ignition key of the car when at last Angela stumbled breathlessly to the window. All the angry accusations that had crowded her mind vanished and instead she demanded "What are you doing here?"

She flinched at the angry, tight look. "What's that to you?" She had forgotten the cruel line of Martha's lips when anyone got in the way of her plans. Already the engine was purring softly and she knew she would have to speak quickly. "You might have told me what you were letting me in for instead of pushing all the blame on to me!" she said hotly.

Martha's cool gaze surveyed her dispassionately. "I don't know what you're complaining about! All I did was to put you in the way of a good thing."

"You were looking for work on a back-country sheep station, you told me so yourself." The icy tones cut deep. "They tell me the boss is single and quite a charmer. Don't tell me you haven't noticed?"

Angela floundered. She had noticed, that was the trouble, but how hide all that from those probing eyes? "That's ridiculous! He's an employer, that's all!" If only Martha hadn't noticed the flags of colour in her cheeks.

The other girl shrugged. "If you want to play it that way, neglect all your opportunities—but then you always were a bit naive and soft as butter when it came to looking after your own interests."

A sick feeling of frustration swept over Angela. Too late she realised she had been successfully diverted from the subject that really mattered. "It's Brian," she said very low, "he's been . . . pretty ill."

With an angry flick of her anger Martha turned off the ignition key and swung around to face Angela. "I suppose you think it's my fault that the idiot turned his car over?"

"It was your fault, in a way."

"Oh, for heaven's sake, Angela! You sound as if you've been pressured into thinking all sorts of wild things about me. If that's what comes of your staying up in the wilds with Brian's folk I'm sorry I sent you there. Just because I didn't jump into his arms the moment the ship docked at the wharf in Auckland—anyway, I've got to go!" Once again the engine purred softly. "I'm not used to these roads and it's a fair mileage back to Whangarei."

"But what about Brian?" Angela was determined to have this out. Martha's cold stare was intimidating, but Angela clung determinedly to the window ledge. "You're not thinking of changing your mind again, going on with things the way you planned them at first?"

"Wedding rings and all that stuff, you mean?" Martha's flashing smile was untinged with humour or gaiety. "Wouldn't you like to know? Why don't you ask Brian yourself if you're so keen to meddle in other folks' affairs?" The car was moving slowly away when Martha flung from the open window, "Not that he's likely to tell you. He's got more sense than I credited him with!"

Angela stood watching the rental car as it bumped and lurched its way over the dried grass to turn into the track winding over the hill towards the main road. Why don't you ask Brian? But what good would that do? Martha was perfectly safe in giving the advice. She was making her way back through the group of picnic parties when someone took her arm and she glanced up into Mark's smiling face. "Come and watch this, Twenty!" He was guiding her towards the railings. "It's something you might be interested in!"

How could she tell him that watching Susan win her barrel event wasn't exactly her idea of riotous enjoyment? Nevertheless she went with him, watching the women riders turn on the barrel where wide cornering loses time yet being too close could upset the barrel and cost the entrant a penalty. When Susan's turn came she made an eyecatching figure in blue jeans, a chased leather belt, pale blue shirt. Her blonde hair was flying behind her as she urged on Coffee, her well trained mount, and of course she won the event. Wouldn't you know that Mark would be there at the railings to watch her ride to victory! When the event was over she came riding towards them and Mark was the first to congratulate her on her win while Angela stood forgotten in the crowd.

When the events were over and Susan had gone they turned away. For a moment Angela was tempted to confess her meeting with Martha a few minutes previously, then she decided against it. It could do no good to mention the other girl's visit here. Oh, come now, be honest with yourself for once! You know very well that to bring up that subject will be to invite even more suspicion and questioning. Why spoil this moment in the sunshine with Mark's bronzed fingers resting on her bare brown arm, his deep voice saying "Come along and we'll take a look at the tug-of-war."

What matter that the only reason he was with her was that his girl-friend was confined with her duties in the tent? That to him she was merely a girl to whom he had given employment, and temporary employment at that! It was no use, nothing seemed to register today but the bittersweet happiness of just—being with him. That was the way he affected her and there seemed nothing she could do about it.

When they reached the long stock truck, muscular men were pulling on either side of the rope. The two sides strained and at last after a hefty tug the rope yielded. Then one party fell in a heap and the victors cheered wildly.

They strolled on together and all at once it seemed to Angela that sunshine blurred and shimmered over green hills and colourful garments. Mark bought pieces of water melon from a small Maori boy and they ate the cool pink wedges, wiping sticky hands on Mark's snowy handkerchief.

The soft lilac dusk was stealing over the hills when the last horse bucked its way down the enclosure and through the gate. Presently Mark, Brian and the shepherds from the station were herding the horses together. Men in high boots and stetsons joined them to move the wild rodeo mounts into paddocks for the night.

It seemed, however, that the day's activities were not yet over for in the grounds wisps of steam rose from the *hangi* prepared earlier in the day by local Maoris.

When the men returned they joined groups gathered around the steam-filled pits. The food was delicious, Ancla thought, succulent pork and tender chicken that had been covered in leaves and steamed for hours in the earth ovens. There was sweetcorn, pumpkin, kumera, all in portions wrapped in a white napkin and served in a native basket woven from freshly-pulled flax.

All at once Angela lost her appetite for the delectable food. Was it because she had just caught sight of Mark standing beside Susan? The two appeared oblivious of the crowd around them as they discussed matters apparently of interest only to themselves. If only it didn't hurt so much. Angela swung blindly away and a male voice said. "Pleased to see me, Angie? I made it!" John's bearded kindly face, dark eyes that were warm and friendly. Perhaps something a bit more than friendly.

"We just knocked off work an hour ago and I had a shower and a change in five minutes flat! One of the gang lent me his old bomb. I told him it was something important, I just had to get here tonight. So it was—important, I mean, to me!" His brown eyes smiled into hers with an expression that was warm and loving. No questions there, no suspicions spoiling everything. She was pleased to see him, of course she was!

Soon the hills around were dark smudges against the golden bars of sunset and as the apricot sky faded a lone star glittered in the clear pale blue. A few of the Maori rodeo riders had brought guitars with them and presently in the star-flecked darkness soft voices took up melodies that ranged from the latest hit tunes to native chants as old as time. To Angela the plaintive Maori songs had an almost unbearable poignancy. Or was it merely that her own feelings were so hopelessly caught up with Mark? As the evening wore on she saw that he had left Susan's side to merge in with various groups of young farmers, his pipe alight. Perhaps he and Sue had quarrelled, perhaps—Oh, why must she think of him all the time? She must stop her gaze from straying endlessly towards the tall lean figure, make a better job of acting out a happiness she was far from feeling, else John might suspect the truth.

It was a relief to her when at last families began folding rugs, gathering up sleepy children and moving towards cars and trucks. All at once she was aware of Mark approaching her. "Time to get cracking, Twenty!" Nothing could be more careless than his tone. She might just as well be Kevin, the way he spoke to her. All at once she was swept by a wave of frustration and anguish. Oh, it was easy for the boss to be nice to her, when it suited him. To share his favours between Susan and herself, never giving himself away. But it was a game at which two could play. She was glad, glad, glad that John had made such a determined effort to be with her tonight. He couldn't have arrived at a more opportune time. "Sorry," she hoped her voice sounded light and disinterested and not sorry at all, "but I promised John I'd go back with him."

The silence seemed to last forever. Angela wished she could discern his face, but the shadows were too deep.

"I get it." At last, he turned away.

"He's mad about that," John observed with some satisfaction, "but I can't be worried. The way things are with me right now I have to grab my chances of being with you when I can!"

"I know." Only a few minutes ago John had pleaded with her to let him drive her back to the station and she had laughed away the suggestion. "You don't really think I'd let you do that? All those hours of driving over rough roads after a day's work in the shearing shed? I wouldn't dream of it!"

Yet now she had changed her mind in the matter. Already, however, she was regretting the childish impulse of revenge. It wasn't fair to John. She suspected he was beginning to care for her much too deeply. Much as she liked him she knew she could never return his feeling. For liking wasn't loving and never would be—unfortunately.

CHAPTER TEN

In the morning Brian did not appear at the breakfast table, but it was not until later that Angela found that his bed had not been slept in. Probably he had decided to spend the night with friends from the rodeo. Yet at the back of her mind the disquieting thoughts niggled. What if his absence from the homestead were connected with Martha's visit to the showgrounds? Nonsense, if he had gone anywhere else it would be more likely to be Auckland where Jill was established among the young trainees at the hospital.

The shrill ringing of the telephone interrupted her musing and she hurried into the hall, hoping the call would be from Brian.

"Oh, it's you Angela?" Jill's voice betrayed the all too familiar note of hostility. "I wanted to have a word with Brian. He promised to ring me last night to let me know how he got on at the rodeo yesterday. I've got to attend classes this afternoon, so I thought I'd better ring him. Is he around at the moment?"

Caught off her guard, Angela hesitated, "No, he's not." Too late she realised that the telephone that seemed to pinpoint any nuance in the voice had betrayed her agitation. For Jill's tone was all at once anxious. "He is there, isn't he?"

"Well, actually—"

"You're keeping something from me!" Jill cried sharply. "He was hurt yesterday, wasn't he? Something's happened! I can tell by your voice!"

There was nothing for it but to tell the truth. "He didn't come back with the rest of us last night. I expect he stayed with one of his mates he ran into at the rodeo. I didn't realise he wasn't here until a while ago."

A silence, then slowly, thoughtfully, "What does Mark say about all this?"

Now indeed Angela had to think quickly. "He hasn't said." Well, that was true enough, seeing he probably didn't yet know of Brian's absence from the house. "Look, why don't you give me your number and I'll ring you back as soon as he shows up—if he shows up."

Instantly suspicious, Jill said, "Why do you say that?"

"No reason at all. I was just thinking aloud."

"I've got to go. I'll ring you back. Goodbye."

So now she had no choice but to tell Mark. She went down

the steps and wandered down to the stockyards. She wouldn't say anything of Martha's appearance at the rodeo. She'd learned all too well that to make any mention of the other girl was to put a thousand miles between herself and her employer, bring the cold hard look back to his eyes. The lowing and calling of the cattle reached her clearly and when she neared the stockyards she saw Mark helped by two shepherds was moving amongst the steers ear-tagging the herd. Catching sight of Angela, he left his task and came to the railings. The blue eyes were decidedly chilly, she saw at once. Because she had returned last night with John? Not a very promising start for what she had to say.

He swept a lock of dark hair back from his eyes. "Hi, Twenty! What brings you down here?"

"I thought I'd like to take a look at the ear-tagging." What would he say if she told him the truth? "Just—looking at you, Mark." She dragged her thoughts back to sanity and tried to concentrate on the deep masculine tones.

"This job was a whole lot more spectacular to watch in the days when we used to throw the cattle and use the branding iron—haven't seen Brian up at the house, have you? He's supposed to be helping down here today, but he seems to be dodging."

"Brian? No, I haven't!" She moistened dry lips. "That's partly why I came down to see you. I don't suppose it's anything to worry about, but his bed wasn't slept in last night."

He sent her a quick surprised look. "That so? Oh well, no need for panic stations. He'll turn up before long."

Angela was unaware that she was twisting long strands of hair nervously around her finger. "There couldn't have been an accident could there?"

"No, you can put that thought right out of your mind, Twenty. We'd have heard by now if he'd run into trouble last night. I guess he's taken off on his own, probably headed down to town to see Jill."

"No, she rang just now. She seemed surprised he hadn't got in touch with her about the rodeo event he won. He was so proud of winning it too!"

Mark shrugged broad shoulders. "It does seem a bit out of character, but," he appeared to put the matter out of his mind, "he'll show up again in his own good time. Maybe there'll be a letter in the next mail. He always was better at putting words on paper than at telling you anything to your face."

"Could be," she agreed.

But the mail next day brought only a letter from Doris, ecstatic over the new baby boy in her family. Gradually as the days went by Angela ceased to expect any word from Brian. Jill, clearly worried and more concerned over his absence from the station than she let on, rang the homstead daily for news. When ten days had slipped by, however, it became obvious that wherever Brian was living he had no intention of letting on his whereabouts to anyone at the station or to the girl who loved him. Angela, writing to Doris in the matter, expressed an opinion that more than likely Brian had gone to find work in one of the larger cities. Always Angela had been conscious of a sense of frustration and restlessness in him and it could well be that once again he had made an effort to strike out on his own. To be a person in his own right doing the work he liked rather than the "kid brother" whom Mark obviously regarded him as. At least, that was what she hoped had happened.

At the back of her mind, however, niggled the uneasy suspicion that Brian's absence was connected with his meeting with Martha at the showgrounds. Could it be that Martha and her business boy-friend had parted? Had he found someone else with whom to place his affections, someone more feminine, more understanding than Martha with her clever dressing and cool wit? Most disquieting of all was the thought that Martha, on finding out the financial standing of the man she had so lightly turned down on arrival in the country, might have had second thoughts in the matter.

Most of the time, though, the matter of her own imminent departure from Waikare chased other thoughts from her mind. So little time left before Doris would return and after that there would be no further excuse to stay on. She told herself she should be glad that she would soon be free once again to continue with her working holiday. But freedom was only a word, and happiness was hearing Mark's step when he returned home at night after a day spent working far from the sheltered homestead. It was glimpsing the changing expressions of his mobile face, the quick interested glance of eyes that could glint with gaiety or amusement or change to icy accusation. Mark . . . he was her world.

She was alone in the kitchen, busy at the sink bench, when someone stole up behind her and strong sinewy arms enfolded her. "Angie!" Laughing and excited, John whirled her around on the polished floor. At last he put her down. "Here, give me that tea-towel," he snatched it from her hand. "It'll be good practice for me later on!" All at once his face sobered. "I've been counting the days," he groaned, "and the way I work things out Doris will be pelting back here at the week-end."

"That's right." She tried for lightness, though her heart sank at his words. "I'll be off again next week." With an effort she forced a note of enthusiasm into her voice. "There are so many places that I've never seen. That was one of the resolutions I made before I left London. While you're in a district be sure to take in all you can while you're there then you won't have to retrace your steps!" Retrace your steps, when every nerve in her body would be straining to return to Waikare! She heard herself running on, "It's such a beautiful country—mountains, lakes, waterfalls." Yet with all these scenic wonders there was only one place she wanted to be and that was right here with Mark. She gave a rueful laugh. "Mark told me once I was like the rare white heron we happened to see one day by the lake. He said the Maoris call it 'the bird of a single flight'."

He swung around abruptly to face her, the fragile china plate he was drying splintering in the towel. He didn't seem to notice.

"Mark said that!" There was an odd stricken look in his brown eyes. He muttered thickly, "It didn't strike you that he could have been meaning something else?"

She stared up at him uncomprehending. "Oh, I know what he meant," she said in a sad little voice. For he had certainly made no secret of his opinion of "Martha's friend". "Anyway, it doesn't make any difference. I'll have to be moving on soon." All the yearning, the ache of longing was in her wistful tones.

He was still regarding her in that strange way. "Where will you go, Angie?" His tones were laced with urgency. "You'll give me an address?"

Absently she wiped down the gleaming stainless steel of the bench. "An address, what's that? I guess it'll be another job . . . somewhere . . ." her voice trailed away. He looked so downcast that she added brightly, "Don't worry, I'll let you have an address when I get one."

"Angie," he said hoarsely, "let's go some place where we can be by ourselves. Why don't we go for a drive, anywhere you say?"

"Okay then, anywhere where there's a road and a view will suit me."

"We'll go over the hill at the back of the house and down to the beach!" A little later he was seeing her into the big old car standing in the driveway His voice was tender. "It's not where you go but who you're with that matters."

Angela laughed, but a stab of pain pierced her. Didn't she know it?

As they bumped and lurched over the uneven ground John said with his warm smile, "I've got to tell you something that's pretty important to me."

She raised a smiling glance. "Tell me now."

"Not now, Angie. Got to keep my mind on driving or I'll slaughter a few sheep." He had dropped to a low gear, moving slowly ahead to avoid the woolly animals scattering away from the wheels on either side. Soon there seemed nothing else in the world but the cleared green hills and the seabirds wheeling and crying overhead. As they cleared a rise she could see a blue sheet of water outspread below then they were running down towards a tidal lagoon. Tern and gulls waded in the shallow waters warmed by the already hot sun and black swans glided along the edge. John ran the car down on the sand and soon they were wading through the warm shallows as they made their way around a rocky point. In the little bay ahead water lapped in a creamy froth on white sand. It was very still with no sound but the soft swish of small waves breaking and receding.

John dropped down on the springy green grass beneath the shade of giant pohutukawa trees clinging to the bank. The tortuous roots snaked down the slope and above, a shower of fluffy blossoms splashed red against a hot blue sky.

Angela sank down beside him and lay back, her strung-up nerves soothed by the soft wash of the waves that were a-glitter with sundazzle.

His kiss took her by surprise and before she could offer any protest she felt his mouth on hers, his voice low and hoarse in her ears. "Angie, Angie, if you only knew how I've longed for this—"

She felt nothing, no response at all and he must have sensed her lack of feeling. Drawing away, he looked down at her with his soft dark gaze that was laced with tenderness and something else—pain? disappointment?

"It doesn't mean a thing to you!" he muttered in a hoarse low tone. "I don't either, do I?" He plucked restlessly at the grass. "I should have waited a bit, given you time to get fond of me, but time's running out and I thought, I hoped . . ." He seemed to struggle with himself. After a moment he said quietly, "It's no use hoping things'll change, is it? I mean, there's someone else—"

"No, no, it's not that. It's just—" she groped in her mind for words to ease the blow. He was in love with her, deeply, hopelessly in love. She should have seen this moment coming. Now it was too late. She said inadequately, "I scarcely know you. Sounds silly, doesn't it, when you think of it, only a few weeks—"

He brushed the words aside. "I think of you night and day, Angie, you're my life now, there's nothing else. I even dared to hope that you might even marry me, stick by me while I broke in that new land of mine." His voice was barely audible, "With you beside me, Angie, I could do miracles. Without you—"

"I'm sorry." Such a trite little thing to say to a man facing bitter disappointment, yet she could think of nothing to say to soften the blow.

He looked at her squarely, the dark eyes shadowed with pain. "There's someone else, isn't there?"

"No." To her distress the hot colour flooded her cheeks. She turned her face aside. "How could there be?" she said in a strangled tone.

He was silent for a moment. When the pink had faded from her face she glanced at him again. He appeared to have himself in hand. "Well, I guess it was worth a try!" The expression of sadness as he looked at her gave the lie to the light words. How easily he had given in. She had expected him to refuse to take "no" for an answer, to insist that they keep in touch despite her decision. Could he have guessed her secret? What if he had? The thought was so dismaying that she sprang to her feet, saying nervously, "Let's explore a bit further on, shall we? Around the next point!"

Slowly he rose, his eyes never leaving her flushed face. "All I want in the world is right here." She pretended not to hear.

When they got back to the house sunshine sparkled in the waters of the pool. "It's so hot! Do you feel like a dip?" Angela indicated the tiled rectangular a short distance away, but John shook his head.

"I may as well get back to the job." A sudden light of hope broke through his heavy expression. "Unless you want me to stay?"

For a moment Angela forgot to keep the bright interested note in her voice. She said listlessly, "If you like."

"No, I'd better get along. There's nothing for me to stay for—now." The note of pain in his low tones made her aware of the anguish he was suffering, but there was nothing she could do about it. She said, "I'll come and see you off."

They strolled back towards the car and stood for a moment in silence. John's troubled gaze held a depth of feeling there was no disguising. "Oh, *Angie*—" suddenly he caught her close, caressing the long bright hair, whispering against her soft cheek, "tell me if there's a chance?"

"Not . . . the way you mean."

"I guess it's goodbye, then." His deep tones broke. He kissed her with tenderness and passion, then swiftly turned away and got into the car.

She stood waving as he drove away. It was the least she could do for him. She would never see him again, for to do so would, she knew, merely prolong his suffering and raise false hopes that could never be realised. Wearily she pushed the hair back from her forehead. Oh, why was everything so wrong? No one was happy, and it was all her own fault for coming here in the first place. Yet somehow, in spite of all the heartache and misery, she wouldn't have it otherwise. She had known Mark and that was all that mattered.

Slowly she made her way back to the house. She knew she ought to be making preparations for departure, organising herself for the future, but somehow she couldn't seem to get herself into gear. Was it because deep in her heart a faint hope still lingered that if she waited just a little longer something would happen that would keep her here for a few more weeks? She sighed. Miracles, however, didn't happen along to order and the weekend loomed ahead just as though it were any ordinary couple of days and not the end of a dream.

Forcing herself to concentrate on the present, she decided to do some baking. She had become quite successful at sponge cakes, and if by chance she had a failure the thick dairy cream whipped to thickness concealed any fallen areas in the finished product. But no matter what she did with her hands the anguish refused to die away. Today there was the added realisation that she had brought pain to John, who really loved her.

She was still in the kitchen when Mark strolled into the room. He was wearing his working gear of drill shorts and light open-throated shirt. "Busy, Twenty?" He sent his wide felt hat spinning to the table and went to help himself to a drink of cool beer from the refrigerator in the corner.

She nodded. "Sort of."

He glanced appreciatively around at the array of small pastry tarts and feather-light sponges. "You know something, Twenty, for a city girl you're learning fast."

She refused to rise to the bait. "I thought I'd better have something ready in the tins for Doris when she gets back."

He stood laconically by the table eyeing her with the glint of amusement that was so confusing. "Anyone would get the idea you were in training—"

Spooning raspberry jam into tiny pastry cases, she said stiffly, "For what?"

"Oh, I don't know, a spot of country living? John could do with a wife to give him a hand when he's breaking in his new property."

"You talk as though he wants a girl to work around the farm," she said crossly. Why did he always spark the worst in her?

He shrugged broad shoulders. "You should know."

"Well, I do! He asked me to marry him and I—" She stopped short. Horrified, she realised she had fallen right into the trap. Why couldn't she have kept quiet, let poor John keep his disappointment to himself without her blabbing it out to all and sundry? He was still waiting. He seemed in no hurry at all today, standing in the kitchen, needling her into saying things she knew she was going to regret terribly when she had time to think about it.

"Go on, Twenty. You were saying . . .?"

There was no help for it. He had left her in a cleft stick. "I refused him," she muttered. At least she'd let him know that someone loved her, wanted her. Funny little unreliable Twenty from whom he appeared to derive so much entertainment, who alternately amused and exasperated him.

"Great!"

She stared at him bewilderedly. "What's good about that?" Her tone said, "And what's it to you anyway?"

"Tell you some time. Right now I've got to get cracking!" He swept a jam tart from beneath her hand and went out, whistling a tune as he strolled outside.

That evening she had finished her chores for the day and was seated in the lounge when the telephone rang. She answered the call to hear Susan's clipped tones. "Is that you, Angela?" Some nuance, a note of triumphant excitement in Susan's voice left Angela with a premonition of disaster. "Is Mark about? There's something I wanted to tell him. It's about Brian."

The thought flashed through Angela's mind that Susan was waiting, hoping Angela would express some curiosity in the matter. Once again the warning signal flashed in her mind and she felt that even though the message might not concern her, the less she said at the moment the better. "I'll get him," she told Susan, and fled.

Mark was in the small room along the passage he called his office. When she knocked lightly on the door and entered the room she found him seated at a desk littered with papers. He glanced up, his abstracted gaze changing to one of interest and pleasure. But of course, she told herself, stifling the momentary surge of happiness, no doubt he was tired of working on his tallies and only too glad of any interruption.

"What's the problem, Twenty?" Their glances locked and with an absurd sensation of sinking in deep waters she dragged her thoughts aside and said quickly, "It's Susan, on the phone. She wants to speak to you . . . something about Brian."

"Brian!" He leaped to his feet and accompanied her along the passage.

As he picked up the telephone receiver she went into the lounge and closing the door behind her fixed her eyes on the newspaper in her hand. But all the time her thoughts were with Mark. She could hear the deep murmur of his voice and it seemed an age until he came into the room where she sat alone.

The moment she glimpsed his face she knew something was very wrong. The icy blue of his eyes struck a chill in her heart, but she made her voice light and friendly. "Did you get some good news? I mean," at his forbidding expression her voice faltered, "he's all right, isn't he?"

"So far as I know there's not a thing wrong with him." Running a hand along the mantel, he felt for his pipe, took a lighter from his pocket.

"Well then, you found out something?"

He flicked the lighter and over the flame his intent gaze met her own. "Why didn't you tell me that Martha was at the rodeo that day? That she met Brian there?" His voice was rapier-sharp. "It was Martha, wasn't it, the red-haired girl he was seen talking to by the chutes that day?"

She dropped her gaze, swallowing unhappily. "Yes, it was her. But—"

"And you didn't let me in on it? *Why*, Twenty? What was the idea of keeping it to yourself?"

She had no answer ready, for how could you say, I thought if I told you you would suspect me of being in on the whole thing, helping the other two to arrange a meeting. I thought you would hate me all over again and I couldn't risk it. She whispered, "I didn't think it was all that important at the time—"

"*Important!*"

"Then afterwards—"

"Afterwards," the inexorable tones prompted.

"I don't know," she said helplessly, "I just didn't, that's all."

She could see suspicion clouding his eyes and small wonder! She was giving an impression of being either an utter dimwit or, worse, someone who had taken pains to keep the meeting a secret. At that moment he had moved a long way from her. She knew that whatever small amount of trust she had managed to engender during her stay here had fled and she was back to sneaky two-faced Angela, Martha's friend, who couldn't tell the truth if she tried. The thought stung her to make some defence and she cried angrily, "Anyway, how did you know?"

His lips twisted sardonically. "Your guilty look right at this moment, for one thing, and for another the local grapevine reports seeing a stranger at the rodeo who was looking for Brian, a girl with flaming red hair who took care to keep herself pretty well out of sight on the grounds. But of course," his tone was soft and deadly, "you know all about this. You were seen talking to her afterwards just before she left in the rental car!"

So he knew about that too. With a sickening feeling of despair she realised that once again he was her enemy. It was there in his accusing stare, his steely tone. He had utterly lost faith in her. And just when he had begun to believe in her a little.

"Truly," she went doggedly on, "I got the shock of my life to see Martha there. I just couldn't believe my eyes, though I should have known after that telephone conversation I overheard the other night—" The moment the words had left her lips she knew she had put herself in a worse position than ever.

He pounced on the words. "So there was something arranged between those two beforehand? Something you knew about?"

"Yes—no! I didn't realise—" All at once she was more angry than she had ever been in her life. The hazel eyes blazed and her husky voice shook with an intensity of feeling. "It was only after I saw them together that it struck me they had arranged to meet at the rodeo! And if you want to know why I didn't tell you that—well I'm telling you now! It was because I knew you wouldn't believe me!"

Something in his disbelieving hard glance sparked her to run wildly on saying the hateful things that bubbled up from somewhere deep inside her. "I suppose it was Susan who let on to you about all this," she flung bitterly towards him. "That ring on the telephone just now—"

He said quietly, "Actually quite by chance she happened to run into one of the rodeo riders this morning and he mentioned having seen them together. The grapevine around here is very efficient. Susan thought she'd better pass the information on to me in case it happened to have some bearing on Brian taking off like he did."

"You believe *her*," she muttered childishly over the pain in her heart, "you always believe *her*."

"Why shouldn't I? Sue isn't in the habit of lying—"

"Or cheating or hiding things?" Frantically she wound a coppery strand of hair round and round her finer. The husky tones were choked with tears. "Is that what you're telling me?" she cried unsteadily.

"I didn't say that, Twenty!"

"But that's what you're thinking, isn't it? Anyway, you're all wrong about me," she cried recklessly, "and I'll prove it to you too!" Even as she spoke a plan was forming in her mind. Why not find Martha herself and make the other girl admit to this hard-eyed man whom she loved so desperately, so hopelessly, that Angela had had nothing to do with Martha's scheming? Yes, that's what she would do. She didn't know how she'd manage it, but somehow . . . She refused to leave here for ever knowing that he still thought the worst of her. "Give me a day off work," she challenged him, "and I'll show you!"

"No problem, Twenty. You're due for some leave, anyway. I was going to put it to you."

She raised eyes bright with unshed tears. "Tomorrow?"

"If you like."

Swiftly she followed up her advantage. "And you'll let me have a driver for the day. I want to go to Whangarei."

He nodded. "Can do. What was it you had in mind?"

But she had had more than enough of his sardonic look, his disbelieving blue stare. "I'll tell you if my plan works out," she returned fiercely.

He didn't press her further. "It's up to you, Twenty. I'll see that you have a car around at the door right after breakfast. Okay?"

"Thanks a lot," she said stiffly, and turned towards the door.

His mocking smile recalled her. "You know something, young Twenty?"

Flushed with anger, she tossed the long bright strands of hair back from her face and threw a backward glance over her shoulder. "What?"

"Just—you look wonderful when you get really het-up! That high flush in your face really does something for you!"

"Thanks very much!" Angela relieved her pent-up feelings by slamming the door behind her with such violence that the noise reverberated throughout the silent rooms.

CHAPTER ELEVEN

That night Angela lay awake hour after hour, tossing, turning, thinking, planning. The blinding anger that had possessed her earlier in the day had died away, leaving only the dull ache of misery and, admit it, the searing jealousy of Susan. It wasn't fair for Mark to be so quick to believe the other girl, almost as quick as he was in condemning her. But she would *make* him believe her! Not love her, that thought had become so far beyond her reach as the blazing triangle of stars forming the Southern Cross she could glimpse through the uncurtained window. All at once it had become the most important thing in the world that Mark should change his opinion of her and time was running out. Maybe in finding Martha she would also succeed in locating Brian. There was always a chance of success. She had a whole day to pursue her enquiries and anything could happen in a day. Anything? Like Mark saying "I was all wrong about you, Twenty. Sorry. Don't go, Twenty, stay here with me. I love you." How ridiculous could you get? In spite of herself the tears came and she dashed them away, forcing herself to think of tomorrow. She'd have to have some plan.

She was awakened from uneasy sleep by the throaty calls of the plump native pigeons perched on a high tree behind the homestead. Recollection arrived with a rush and she leaped out of bed, pulling on a filmy lilac nylon brunch coat and snatching up her toilet bag on her way to the bathroom and a quick shower.

She would leave breakfast ready for Mark and Kevin when they arrived back at the house. But there was no need, she found a little later as she made toast for herself and sipped a mug of coffee, for it was clear that the two had already helped themselves to an early meal. That left her little to do beyond preparing a light lunch of ham and salad. Presently wearing blue denim jacket and brief skirt, blue and white sneakers on her feet, she hurried down the steps. Early as she was, however, the car was already drawn up below and she could see someone seated in the driver's seat.

The next moment a tall lean masculine figure got out to open the passenger door and she halted, staring full into Mark's unreadable face. "Don't look so staggered, Twenty! You did say nine o'clock!"

Darn him, he knew very well what was making her look surprised. "I know I know, but I didn't expect—"

His face was deadpan.

"The driver? Oh, I had to run into town today, some urgent business turned up. I thought it would be a good chance to take you in and pick up the other thing at the same time."

"Oh." Hot with shame, she got into the dust-coated late-model car. How could she have been so crazy as to have imagined even for a moment that he wanted to accompany her to town? It just showed that love could make you blind, lead you into forgetting that merely because you were longing to be with him every minute of the day the feeling wasn't a two-way one.

He slipped the car into gear and they moved past the shepherds' bungalows. Pamela was looking out of a window, smiling and waving, and Angela waved in return. How strange, she found herself thinking, that the other girl was probably envying her this trip to town for the day. If only Pamela knew the unenviable task she had set herself there!

Mark seemed to pick up her thoughts. "You're pretty determined about this idea of yours, aren't you, Twenty?"

"A bit," she admitted in a low voice. No need to let him know that the determination was prompted by his own attitude towards her. She just had to clear herself of everything of which he was silently accusing her before she left here for ever. Pain clutched her heart at the thought of how little time was left.

"Been to Whangarei before?"

"No, I told you I'd just got off the ship a couple of weeks before I came here." "The ship". Now he'd be linking her with Martha once again, unfavourably of course. If only she hadn't worded her answer in that particular way!

"That's good," his even tones wrenched her from her thoughts. "It'll all be new to you. I'll be able to show you around, take you for a run out to a few of the beaches along the coast."

"Thank you, but I'll be . . . busy."

"Shouldn't take you too long," he observed carelessly.

He didn't believe her. It was beginning to become a refrain, her theme song at Waikare. He thought she was only talking, making a gesture, but she would make him change his mind.

"Don't look like that, Twenty." His cool sideways glance took in the shadowed eyes, the droop of the soft lips. "This is your day off, a sort of holiday, remember?"

"Is it?"

"Well it was your idea," he pointed out. "You *must* be enjoying it, Twenty, a day like this! Tell me, did you ever in your life see such a big blue saucer of a sky. And those tree-ferns down in the gully, clear-cut against the blue! What more could you want?"

I want your, trust Mark. I want to mean something to you. You think I'm just Twenty, a silly kid who lets everyone down. But I'm a woman, Mark, a woman who loves you. Aloud she murmured slowly, "it's beautiful, all of it."

"I knew," he observed with satisfaction, "that you'd come around to my way of thinking!"

So it was to be a "be-kind-to-Twenty" day. If he were going to be nice to her, she couldn't bear it, not today. Twenty! Not anyone you could take seriously, just a silly kid who couldn't help telling lies at every opportunity. A kid who had some wild notion in her head about finding her friend Martha. She hadn't a hope in the world, of course. She was a stranger herself in the place, but might as well go along with her. The odd things she did were quite amusing . . . up to a point.

And yet, and yet . . . She stole a glance towards the strong profile at her side. Tough and brown and alive-looking with the look in his eyes of a man accustomed to gazing into far distances. Once again she forgot everything else in the acute consciousness of his nearness.

The winding north road was new territory to Angela. They swept along a windy ridge then dropped down and soon they were climbing once again, running through a clean white country township on the brow of a hill. On either side of the line of modern stores green paddocks fell away. "That was Wellsford," Mark told her. "Nice little country town. They say the place got its name by using the first letter of the names of the early settlers." He skirted a dead possum lying on the road. Presently they were moving between long lines of toa-toas, their feathery banners tossing in the wind, then they approached forestry huts gleaming through thickly-planted pine plantations.

Ahead rose gorse-covered hills, the perfume of the yellow blossoms strong on the air, then they were climbing the steep bush-clad slopes where the winding road swung around endless bends with always a higher hill above. Now the damp pungent smell of thickly growing native bush was all around them. Tall pungas with their lacy umbrella-like fronds brushed against the roof of the car and beside them tiny waterfalls trickled down fern-encrusted banks. Up and up until at length they reached the summit and Mark pulled off the highway at a look-out-point of the mountain. "It's quite a climb up the Brynderwyns." Carelessly he threw an arm around the back of her seat. "From up here you can see for miles!" She struggled to follow his gaze, but she was acutely conscious of his nearness. She fancied he was touching her hair but of course that was ridiculous. Probably he wouldn't touch her for a bet now that he distrusted her more than ever. She tried to concentrate on his voice. "Over there, Twenty, your first glimpse of the Pacific!"

She nodded. "It's got that misty blue look of really deep water."

"Fantastic, isn't it?" He gestured towards the vista spread far beyond the bush-covered hills dropping away below. "See that mountain that looks as though it's rising up out of the sea?" She followed his glance towards a high jagged peak piercing the translucent blue. "That's Old Manaia. From the road when you get close it looks like the profile of a Maori *wahine* carrying a baby in a shawl on her back piccaninny fashion." His gaze roved over the clusters of gay red and green roofs glimmering through greenery, in the distance. "Over there's Whangarei. They call it the "sunshine city" and that's not a bad description." His eyes narrowed. "One of these days I'm going to build me a boat and take off from the boat harbour there, go cruising around the Bay of Islands, laze around in the sun on the beaches. All you need is the craft, the time, and the right companion. How does that strike you, Twenty?" He sent her his teasing grin, the sort, she told herself bitterly, he probably kept for children and herself. The thought brought with it a tide of resentment and she heard her own voice saying, "You should keep it in mind for Susan."

"Why Susan?" She could have sworn the bewilderment in his gaze was genuine. "How do you mean?"

She said very low, "I was thinking of a honeymoon."

"You do get hold of some odd ideas, Twenty."

"There's nothing odd about honeymoons," she muttered, unable now to control the anger and frustration that had taken over.

"That depends."

All at once the humiliating thought struck her that he had no doubt been referring to a male friend to help crew that dream craft of his. And she had betrayed all too clearly her interest in his love life. Oh, why did she say these things? She never used to be so stupidly emotional! Blame it on falling in love with a man who couldn't care less about her. Now she could have bitten out her tongue, for his face had hardened, all the light-hearted friendliness (even if it had been merely surface variety) wiped away. No question whatever that in his book she was right back to being "Martha's friend" with matrimonial dealings on her mind! Once again she had spoiled everything with her thoughtless remarks.

"We'd better get cracking." He thumbed the starter and guided the car down the winding bush-lined highway. Presently they were moving into the suburban areas of New Zealand's most northerly city and in silence she watched as the timber homes with their blazing flower borders, asters, petunias, stocks, went flashing by. Blossoming shrubs studded spreading lawns around modern ranch-style homes. Bougainvillea threw its scintillating cerise mantle over fences and open porches and everywhere along their way jacarandas flung their shower of fragile lilac blossoms high against the blue.

Soon they were moving into the city, pausing at a red light. Then the signal flashed green and they were swinging into a wide street lined with attractively-dressed shop windows. She caught glimpses of summer clothing, fishing gear, underwater needs, picnic and barbecue outfits, all the requirements of life in high summer in a town ringed by flawless sandy beaches.

"Would you put me down here, please, Mark?"

He braked to a stop alongside the kerb. "Right! See you in half an hour?"

She eyed him in consternation. "Oh, I'll need much more time than that!"

"Two hours, then!" He made no mention of Martha or of Angela's purpose in coming here. He didn't wish her luck. He simply consulted the silver watch on his bronzed wrist. "Pick you up here then, okay?"

She hesitated. "I expect I'll be ready then, but I'll meet you here anyway to let you know how I got on."

Watching his face as he guided the car into the traffic of the busy street, she thought bleakly, he still doesn't take me seriously about this. He imagines I'm just talking, pretending. That's the awful part about someone who's never had faith in you, they don't believe anything you say, ever. But if only I can find Martha he'll have to believe me. *I've got to find her!*

The street was crowded with shoppers and no one seemed in a hurry. Sun-tanned women and girls wore gay sleeveless dresses and men were attired in brightly tinted shirts open at the neck, cool shorts and sandals. Sunshine sparked Angela's hair to glinting copper and many interested glances were thrown towards her, but, absorbed in her own problem, she did not notice. She was here in Whangarei. Where to begin her enquiries? A red telephone booth on the street corner gave her an idea. Luckily the booth was empty and inside she thumbed through the directory. If she could locate Harvey she might glean some news of Martha, perhaps even find her address in the city. Unfortunately, she realised the next moment, he would not have been here long enough to have his name in the directory, if indeed he were still here.

She decided to take a long chance and contact one of the supermarkets. If he had planned to go into business someone in the same line might recognise his name. The manager, when she contacted him, proved helpful. Yes, he had met Harvey Brooks in Whangarei a few times and he had his telephone number. Harvey hadn't yet decided whether he was setting up in business in Auckland, Whangarei or Wellington and he travelled a lot between the three places. Still, there was no harm in trying and he wished her luck.

She needed all the luck that was being handed out today, she told herself a few moments later when a telephone call put through to the number elicited the information that yes, Harvey did make his headquarters there while in Whangarei, but at the moment he was away and not expected back for two weeks.

Encouraged by the woman's friendly attitude, Angela took her courage in her hands and explained that it was really a girl-friend of Harvey Brooks whom she was trying to locate. She was a stranger in the country herself and this girl had come out from England on the same ship only a few weeks previously. Martha was the name, Martha Stanaway.

The pleasant voice was helpful. Yes, she told Angela, she knew Martha. The other girl had been to the house on a few occasions. She had written down her address as there was no telephone in the flat and Martha had thought Harvey might wish to contact her. If Angela would wait just a moment . . . Groping in her bag for paper and ballpoint, Angela held her breath. Surely she couldn't be so lucky so soon.

The woman returned in a few minutes. "This is the address, but if I were you I'd get a taxi. It's a bit difficult to explain how to reach there unless you know the town." It was good advice. Angela thanked her unknown helper, then went on down the street with its shady shop awnings until she reached a taxi rank. The driver knew the address and they cruised along various streets until at length he drew up outside a block of newly built brick apartments. She asked him to wait until she returned. "I shouldn't be long."

"Sure." He unfolded his newspaper.

Hurrying in at the entrance, she took the stairs two at a time. Number four was plainly marked over the door and as she rang the bell once, twice, three times, she chould hear the sound echoing in empty rooms. At length the door of number five was opened and a barefooted girl wearing a brief blue nylon negligee thrust a tousled head from the opening. "If you're looking for Martha, she's not there. She left yesterday."

"Left?" Angela's spirits plunged down, down. Still clutching at a ray of hope, she said, "But she'll be back . . . won't she?"

The girl shrugged plump shoulders. "Your guess is as good as mine! All I know is that she paid her rent up to date and took off. For good, if you ask me! She didn't say where she was going, just said something about her plans coming all unstuck and she was moving on—" She broke off, becoming aware of the stricken look of Angela's face, the defeated droop of her shoulders. "Is she a particular friend or something?"

Angela nodded dazedly. "Well, sort of. I was hoping to contact her, that's all."

"Tough luck. Sorry I can't help you. Maybe she'll get in touch with you herself some time. I scarcely knew her really, only spoke to her a couple of times." The plump kindly face expressed surprise that anyone should appear so distressed over not seeing Martha Stanaway. "If she comes back by any chance shall I give her a message? Tell her you called?"

Angela shook her head. "It doesn't matter."

"It's too late, you mean? Oh well, I guess it's just one of those things." Her tone quickened with concern. "You're feeling all right, aren't you? You look so white all of a sudden. If you'd care for some tea it wouldn't take a minute. A drink of water?"

Angela's smile was shaky. "It's kind of you to offer, but no, thanks. I'm quite all right, really."

The plump girl looked unconvinced. "I guess . . . if you say so."

Angela went blindly down the stairs and out to the waiting taxi.

"Where to now, miss?" She stared blankly towards the driver. "Oh, back to the street where you picked me up please."

She thought he looked at her strangely. Did the disappointment show so much?

When she got out at the taxi rank she paid the driver, then started to walk back along the street, not caring or even knowing where she was going. Was there any other way to find Martha? Not that she could think of. One thing was certain, there was nothing to be gained in staying in Whangarei. The slight lead she had had had ended in a blind alley. She could have achieved as much by telephoning directly from the station, saved herself the heartache of being with Mark and knowing all the time . . . He would never believe she had even tried. What a fool she had been to imagine she could solve her problems by a trip to town. Moisture misted her eyes and she saw the sunshiny street through a blur of tears.

When someone hurrying up alongside took her arm, she started violently, then stared up into Mark's face. "You! You waited for me! You've been here in the car all the time!"

Groups of shoppers pressed around them and he guided her towards the edge of the pavement. Angela said in a low tense tone, "You didn't think I'd do anything about finding Martha! You thought I was just talking!"

He stared down at her, "Come on, Twenty, don't take on—"

"Take on?"

"You're all wrong, you know! My bit of business didn't take long to fix up. I simply thought your enquiries might take less time than you expected too." His grip was biting into her bare arm. "Why are you so suspicious?"

She wrenched herself free. "Why are you?" She bit her lip. "I'm sorry I said that! It's just that I was upset about something else."

"You mean, no Martha? That was the big idea in coming here, today I take it?"

She nodded, dropping her lids to hide the shadow in her eyes. "No Martha. But she had been here! I found her flat, but she had left, yesterday."

He said with unexpected gentleness. "Does it matter so much?"

"It seems it does to you," she said in a muffled tone.

"You know something, Twenty?" He studied the downcast lashes on the pale face, "I'm inclined to believe you." His grin was inexpressibly heart-warming to her taut nerves. She stared up at him incredulously. "You do? But I thought—"

"You thought wrong, then." His voice softened. "Did you really imagine that knowing you I'd still think—"

The sense of relief was so great it was making her feel light-headed. "If you want to know what Martha and I talked about that day at the rodeo—" she cried eagerly.

"Forget it, Twenty!" Linking her fingers in his warm grasp, he led her back to the car. When she was seated he swung around to face her. "Now where? What would you like to do now?

Just say the word! How about a look around the town? No? I got the idea that all girls liked to prowl around the stores in a strange city."

"Not this girl," she said very low, "not today."

"Well then," he was leaning back studying her face with the intent blue gaze that was so discomforting. "For someone fresh out from England there's quite a choice. We could have a look around the place, see the boat harbour. Or I could take you for a spin up old Parahaki—" He gestured towards the mountain clad in heavy native bush rising nearby. "Or how about a run out to the ocean beach out at the heads? It's wild and rugged and remote and well worth seeing!"

He was treating her as a visitor to the country, playing the part of a host duty bound to show the English girl the attractions of his own land. All at once it was more than she could bear. She raised her heavy glance. "Let's go home." and saw the relief in his eyes. She had been right, then, he had been merely being polite, pretending. All he really wanted was to get back to his farming duties as quickly as he could.

He swung the car out of the parking lot and soon they were heading out of town, passing through the outlying districts and taking the winding road up the mountain. When they reached the summit with its notice "Pilbrow's Hill", she realised that Mark was guiding the car up a sheer slope towards tea-rooms perched on a crag high above. He tossed her a grin. "May as well stop for something to eat before we take off for home! Especially as I've got the housekeeper with me."

They swept up on to the concrete strip surrounding the hill-top restaurant. As she stepped out of the car Mark was waiting for her. High winds of the mountain-top flung her hair in a veil over her eyes and tossed her into his arms. It was like being on top of the world. Then he caught her hand in his and they hurried up the steps and into a room where a wall of windows brought into view a panorama of bush-clad hills. Beyond were the dark blue shapes of mountains sloping down to the sea.

Presently a waitress brought a tray and Angela nibbled a sandwich and sipped the hot coffee. All the time she was aware of Mark. She could feel his gaze on her face when she wasn't looking, and divined that for some reason she couldn't fathom he appeared to be solicitous about her. She couldn't understand it. A little later, however, moving towards the door, she caught sight of her reflection in a mirror and realised the reason for his expression of concern. Could that really be herself, that ashen-faced girl staring back at her?

Mark opened the door and the force of the gale tore at them. As they went down the steps he threw his arm around her waist, drawing close as they struggled against the high wind. But she knew the gesture didn't mean a thing to him. It was just part of the "be kind-to-Twenty-she's-leaving-soon" kind of day.

The miles fell away and the silence that had fallen between them lasted almost all the way back to the homestead. As they turned in at the main gates and rattled over the cattle-stop, however, Mark veered off into a grassy paddock. To her surprise the car was lurching and bumping in the direction of a tree-shaded stream. She roused herself to ask, "Where are we going?"

"Tell you in a minute!" He was drawing to a stop in a shady spot beneath a towering puriri tree.

She tried to infuse a note of interest in her voice. "Is it something to do with your shopping in Whangarei?"

"How did you guess?" His face was all at once alive with excitement and something else she didn't dare dwell on in case she were mistaken. The boss looking at her like that! He wasn't acting at all in character today. What could be the matter with him? For something to say she asked, "Was it something important?" and had her first inkling of the truth.

"*Was it*?" He swung around to face her. "Like telling you how much I love you, want you!" His tone deepened with emotion and his arms drew her close. A bronzed finger tilted upwards her small rounded chin. "Twenty!" His lips were seeking hers and she was safe in the circle of his arms. All at once the sunshine outside was dazzling. Or was it the look in his eyes, the loving, wanting look that made the whole world a-shimmer?

His hands caressed her bright hair and she caught the low murmur of his voice. "You must have guessed how I felt about you? That I'd never let you go!" Once again she felt the urgent pressure of his lips. "Say you love me," he whispered against her mouth, "say it!"

"I love you," she told him, "*so much!*" And when she could speak once again, "You've no idea how much I was dreading having to leave you. I kept making excuses to myself, putting off the date of going away, hoping for a miracle. And all the time . . ." Her voice died away. The wonder of what was happening at this moment was still a little too much to take in.

"If I hadn't got the idea that you were involved with old John," he told her tenderly, "I'd have told you how I felt about you weeks ago. It wasn't till yesterday I knew I had a chance."

"John?" With tousled hair and flushed cheeks she pulled

herself a little away from him. "But he was nothing to me—at least," a little guiltily she recalled the occasions when she had deliberately fostered that misconception especially for Mark's benefit.

"I know that, now. I had to work fast, Twenty, if I wanted to keep you with me, so I took a chance, went to Whangarei and got you—this." Fishing in his pocket, he drew out a small jeweller's box and the next minute was slipping on her tanned finger a slender gold ring set with a single diamond.

"It's beautiful," she whispered, surprised and delighted and elated all at once. A wonderful ring, although she knew she would have treasured any ring, no matter how insignificant, because he had given it to her as a symbol of their love.

His deep intent gaze was on her tremulous face. "Mrs. Mark Hillyer, how does it sound to you?"

"Just exactly right," she whispered.

"I was hoping you'd say that." He sealed the words with a kiss. Oh, it was heaven to be in his arms, close, close to the whipcord strength of this man she loved.

"And I thought," she murmured wonderingly, "that you and Susan—"

He put a hand on either side of her face, looking into her eyes. "Never in a thousand years, Twenty. Sue and I have known each other all our lives, we've got a heck of a lot in common when it comes to property, horse-riding, all that, but that's all. Thinking of me in a romantic way would be the last thing on Susan's mind. Can you imagine it?"

Yet for all his sureness of tone Angela could imagine it very well, but, wise for once, she kept her thoughts to herself. A fleeting pity for the other girl crossed her mind, but the next minute she reminded herself that Susan's supreme confidence in her own powers of attraction would not for long allow her to feel defeated. She would meet someone else.

His exultant tones broke into her musing. "Twenty, we're going to be the happiest couple in the country!"

She twinkled up at him. "Even though I made such a mess of things with Brian and Martha?" For a second her radiant face sobered. "It was true what I told you that first day. If I could have found Martha in Whangarei she would have said the same—"

"I know all that, my darling—"

"Tell me," she raised a hand with its glittering diamond to caress his bronzed cheek, "just when did you change your mind about my part in it all?"

His lopsided smile was tender. "If you could have seen yourself coming along that street in Whangarei today. Your face, Twenty! Your sad funny little face. You looked for all the world as though you'd got to the end of the road, played your last card and lost!"

"That's just about how I was feeling. But you still haven't told me when," she persisted.

"That's easy—just as soon as I got to know you a bit better—"

"I'd have told you everything at the beginning, but you wouldn't let me."

His lips brushed her soft cheek. "Tell me now."

It all came out in a rush of words. The friendship with Martha that had been no friendship at all, the other girl's self-centred plans that were to bring such humiliation and misery to Brian. Her own unexpected meeting with Martha at the rodeo. "And that's all I know," she finished. "I've no idea what she and Brian arranged between them that day, if they did arrange anything."

"Forget them!" he told her happily. "This is our day!" Easy advice to follow as his lips sought hers and once again the heady rapture took over.

Afterwards, a long time afterwards, he turned the car back towards the driveway. Angela glancing down at the scintillating diamond on her finger marvelled at the perfect fit of the ring, but then, she mused out of a deep sense of utter happiness, today everything was perfect. As her gaze moved to Mark's bronzed profile she felt as though somewhere during the day she had missed a turning and strayed into heaven by mistake.

His arm was thrown around her shoulders as they took the curving pathway. All at once there were endless exciting matters to discuss, for weren't they about to share a whole new life together?

"Just wait," exulted Mark with that new look of pride in his eyes, "until Doris hears the news!"

"Doris?" A shadow fell over Angela's shining happiness. "My being here," she asked anxiously, "it won't mean her having to leave Waikare, will it?"

"Leave, Doris? Lord, no! Not unless she wants to. She's a sort of fixture around the place. She can always make her home here for as long as she likes, she knows that!"

For answer she gave his arm a quick squeeze. Even when she was married to Mark—*married to Mark*—delight surged over her anew at the thought, there would be work a-plenty to keep both her and Doris occupied on the station where each passing season brought its own duties to the men and women who worked there. Besides, the fugitive thought sneaked in from nowhere, there was that drawer up at the house filled with mini-garments in varying tonings of pink. Who knows, Doris might yet attain her wish to make use of them, and right here at Waikare too!

"That's odd!" Mark's deep tones jerked her back to the present, "A strange car in the drive! Let's hope it's someone we know. I can't wait to tell the world our big news!"

The moment they entered the lounge a man and a girl sprang to their feet, hands linked and faces brimming with excitement. It was Jill who greeted them. "At last! We thought you two were never coming back!"

Mark's tone as he faced his younger brother was scarcely welcoming. "Where the devil have you been all this time?"

"That's what I'm here to tell you about—"

"Tell him the other news first," Jill broke in excitedly, "the important bit!"

The thought passed through Angela's mind that Jill without the customary resentful, sulky expression she had always worn at the homestead, was really awfully pretty.

"No, I'll tell them myself! We're engaged!" she cried happily.

"Look, Angela—" There was no hesitation now in the way she said the name. She was thrusting forward a small brown paw where a sapphire gleamed on a third finger. "Brian said it had to be a blue stone to match the colour of my eyes!"

"Congratulations, Jill! I'm so glad for you!" Angela's happy tone rang with good wishes.

Mark was silent.

"Don't be like that," Brian pleaded in his light diffident tones. "Maybe you'll feel differently about things when I tell you what happened. That day at the rodeo—"

Mark's voice was relentless. "When you met up with Martha?"

"That's right. And boy, did I learn a few things that day! She had to meet me there. She knew it would be no use coming to see me at the house, not after the way she'd let me down before, and especially after the mean trick she'd played on you, Angela. Would you believe it? She actually boasted about sending you here after the job you wanted, letting Mark pick you up as arranged and thinking you were Martha! When she let on how she'd let you in for all the blame, that really did it! I thought before that things went wrong when Martha arrived here from the *Ocean Monarch*."

"Now I know it was the best thing that ever happened to

me," he went on. "For years I'd idealized that girl. I needed shock treatment to make me wake up and see the things that were right under my nose all along. She didn't care a thing for me. She was looking for a husband, any husband, so long as he had property or cash. Sounds rugged, doesn't it, but that's the truth! Oh, she put it over very well, but what it amounted to was that her boy-friend in Whangarei, the food-chain guy she met on the voyage out from England, had let her down, taken up with someone else and she'd come running back to me as second choice. She actually put it to me that we could pick up where we'd left off, start making arrangements for getting married. Just like that! That's when it hit me out of the blue. I had a girl already, someone I was in love with and hadn't realised because I'd known her all my life, and I had a fair idea that she was pretty fond of me.

"I got wise to something else that day too. I took a good long look at myself and I said, 'See here, man, if you're ever going to make anything of your life now is the time to start, today.' So instead of going back to Waikare with the others after the rodeo I headed south for Wellington—"

"You might have let me into your plans," Mark's voice was grim.

"I know, I know, but I had to be *sure*. If I had to come crawling back home like last time—well, that would be it, but at least I'd have given it a go! And then it happened! The first day I arrived in the city I landed a job, not just any old job but the type of work I've always wanted, a reporter on the daily paper there. The only snag was I had to agree to a trial period. I told myself that if I made the grade the first thing I'd do would be to look up Jill and ask her to be my wife, and the next thing I'd do would be to come back here and explain, right? The prospects are terrific and that's what matters. Meanwhile Jill wants to see her nursing training through to the finish and I'm going to work like mad to get ahead. We plan to marry in a year's time. You know something Mark," he turned towards his brother, "I never was interested in sheep-farming, but I kept trying. I told myself that with a family history like mine and a brother who's dead keen on the game I must take to it too." There was an unfamilar purposeful ring in his tones and for the first time she saw Brian standing straight and confident, looking Mark squarely in the eye. "Now I know it's not for me!"

Mark nodded, a quizzical gleam in his blue eyes. "I get it. Looks like I'll have to start looking around for a new farm hand. Is that right?"

"That's the story. Say," all at once Brian appeared to become aware of Angela's shining eyes and Mark's expression of barely suppressed excitement, "we weren't interrupting anything, were we?" He glanced enquiringly from Mark to Angela. "There's something about you two today—"

"We may as well put you and Jill in the picture." Although Mark spoke laconically he was unable to conceal his air of pride and elation. "We've got marriage plans too, but we don't believe in waiting, do we, Twenty?" His eyes sought her smiling face and he read the answer in her warm glance. Somehow she didn't mind his calling her "Twenty" any more, not when he said the name in a way that made the word a caress. To be with Mark each day, every day . . . nights too . . . Her heart seemed to skip a beat with pure joy.

The next moment everyone was talking at once, offering congratulations, smiling and laughing, asking questions. Mark was moving towards a cocktail cabinet in a corner of the room. "This calls for a toast!"

Angela, scarcely aware of the voices echoing around her, gazed out of the window where a helicopter hovered low over a hillside. Through a cloud of drifting spray let loose by the pilot to kill patches of thistle on the sun-dried slopes, shimmered the muted colours of a rainbow, the tremulous arch lost in the depths of a punga-filled gully below.

Mark, handing her a goblet of red wine, paused to follow her gaze. "Just a rainbow, Twenty. We often get them when the choppers are spraying. Quite a sight."

She nodded, something plucking at the back of her mind. She had found her rainbow at last, even if it were on a lonely sheep station away in the never-never. Only it wasn't lonely at all, it was heaven, it was home, it was Mark!